THE SHEIKH
AND THE DUSTBIN

by the same author

The Flashman Papers
FLASHMAN
ROYAL FLASH
FLASH FOR FREEDOM!
FLASHMAN AT THE CHARGE
FLASHMAN IN THE GREAT GAME
FLASHMAN'S LADY
FLASHMAN AND THE REDSKINS
FLASHMAN AND THE DRAGON

*

MR AMERICAN
THE PYRATES

*

Short stories
THE GENERAL DANCED AT DAWN
McAUSLAN IN THE ROUGH

*

THE STEEL BONNETS
The Story of the Anglo-Scottish
Border Reivers

George MacDonald Fraser

THE SHEIKH
AND THE DUSTBIN

AND OTHER McAUSLAN STORIES

COLLINS HARVILL
8 Grafton Street, London W1
1988

William Collins Sons & Co. Ltd
London · Glasgow · Sydney · Auckland
Toronto · Johannesburg

BRITISH LIBRARY CATALOGUING IN PUBLICATION DATA

Fraser, George MacDonald, *1925–*
The sheikh and the dustbin.
I. Title
823′.914[F]

ISBN 0–00–222707–X

First published in Great Britain
by Collins Harvill 1988

Photoset in Linotron Times by
Wyvern Typesetting Limited
Printed and bound in Great Britain by
Butler & Tanner Ltd, Frome and London

Author's Note

The General Danced at Dawn, in which Private McAuslan shambled on parade in hard covers eighteen years ago, contained no glossary. This was a foolish oversight on my part which was quickly pointed out by readers, especially in America, who wrote demanding translation of Scottish, Hindustani, Arabic (and sometimes even English) expressions used in the book. Accordingly, when a sequel was published, I took care not only to provide a brief McAuslan dictionary, with a note on Glasgow pronunciation and vocal peculiarities, but to see to it that it went at the beginning, so that people could prepare themselves for what lay ahead. It seems only sensible to do the same thing again.

Military slang, and for that matter everyday English, changes a lot in forty years, and that is the time which has elapsed since the period dealt with in these stories. Some expressions vanish as though they had never been; others imbed themselves in the language. So I make no apology for including some words which may seem universally familiar (somebody, somewhere, is sure to clamour for enlightenment if I don't), along with such dialectical mysteries as "flype", which I haven't heard for decades and is almost certainly unknown outside Scotland.

It remains only to say that where phonetic spelling of a word is necessary, I have used my own discretion, that in Glasgow the letter "j" is frequently pronounced "jie", and that most of the book is, I hope, written in English.

G.M.F.

Glossary

aighe-va	goodbye (Gaelic)
alakeefik	casual, indifferent (f. Arabic)
away for ile	sick, out of action (lit. away for [castor] oil)
banjo	to beat up
Bantams	In World War One, battalions of the Highland Light Infantry made up of men below regulation height
Barlinnie	a prison in Glasgow
bauchle	(v.) to shamble, to make a mess of; (n.) an awkward person
ben	in the back room, behind
buddoo	a desert Arab (f. *bedouin, bedawi*, Arabic)
bus	stop, finished, enough (Hind.)
chawed	resentful, sulky
chiel	child, but frequently used of an adult
chota hazri	early morning tea (lit. little breakfast, Hind.)
chubbarao!	be quiet! (Hind.)
claim	to accost for the purpose of assault
clype	to tell tales
colloguing	conspiring
coronach	Highland lament, death song
corrie	mountain hollow
creature, the	Scotch whisky
dhobi	laundryman (Hind.)
doolaly	mad (from Deolali, India, a transit camp notorious for sunstroke)
douce	respectable, genteel
drookit	drenched, drowned
flype	to turn inside out, esp. of socks
Gartnavel	a Glasgow asylum of the time
Gestapo	regimental police, provost staff
ghillie	Highland attendant on hunter or fisherman
give it lalldy	punish, perform with force
glaikit	awkward, foolish-looking
gommeril	blockhead
greeting, grat	weeping, wept

Gregora, the	Clan Gregor, the MacGregors
grieve	farm foreman
gunfire	early morning tea (Eric Partridge suggests a connection with the morning gun signal)
imshi!	go away! (Arabic)
jankers	defaulters' parade
joco	cheerful (lit. jocose)
keelie	a native Glaswegian
lathi	long baton used by Indian police
Lizars	a well-known Glasgow opticians
manky	dirty
master-gyppo	cook–sergeant (gyppo = stew)
melt	to beat up
mennodge	a curious Glasgow expression, from the French *ménage*, meaning a common account into which money is paid (usually at the "steamie" or communal wash-house), something on the lines of a Christmas club. Cf. "not fit to run a raffle".
midden	dunghill, refuse dump
nyaff	an insignificant person, a pipsqueak
on the burroo	drawing unemployment pay (lit. on the bureau)
pialla	drinking mug (Hind.)
pit the heid on	butt with the head
pit the hems on	finish off, render helpless, contain (lit. stitch up)
Redcap	military policeman
rerr terr	celebration, happy incident, joke (lit. "rare tear")
R.T.O.	Railway Transport Officer
scarper	to flee, make off (rhyming slang, Scapa Flow = go)
selling the dummy	deceiving by a feint (esp. in Rugby football, feigning a pass)
sgian dubh	small dirk carried in hose-top (Gaelic, black knife)
shabash!	bravo! (Hind.)
stoor	dust
tattie-bogle	scarecrow
teuchter	Highlander (derogatory, as yokel)
wog	native, esp. an Egyptian (now a taboo word, of unknown origin. Suggested derivations include f. golliwog, and from Worker on Government Service armband said to have been issued to Nile boat-pullers)

at her bookshelves where Cruden's *Concordance* and Bunyan's *Holy War* lay beside long outdated fashion magazines from Paris, pushing in my chair to the exact inch when I received the almost imperceptible nod of dismissal from the stately, white-haired figure at the end of the table, straight and stiff as her own ebony walking-cane; dreading the cold eye and sharp, quiet voice, even when they were addressed to her maids and not to me. How they endured her, I'll never know; perhaps they knew what I sensed as an infant: like her or not, you could be *sure* of her, and that is a quality that can count far beyond mere kindness.

Anyway, with that background I ought to have mastered the servant problem, but I never have, not from either side. On the occasions when I have had to serve, I have been a disaster, whether shirking my fagging duties at school, or burning toast, dropping plates, and letting the cookhouse boiler go out as a mess orderly and assistant scullion at Bellahouston Camp, Glasgow. Nor am I one of nature's aristocrats, born to be ministered to and accepting it as my due; anything but. I hate being waited on; servants rattle me. I find their attentions embarrassing, and they know it, damn them. There was a butler once, about seven feet tall, with a bald head and frock coat, who received me at a front door; he looked me up and down and said: "Good morning, sir. Would you care to wash . . . at all?" I can't describe what he put into that pause before the two final words, but it implied that I was filthy beyond his powers of description. Nor am I deceived by the wine-waiter unctuously proffering his bottle for my inspection: this bum wouldn't know it from turpentine, is what he's thinking.

Such an advanced state of doulophobia is bad enough in civilian life; for an army officer it is serious, since he has to have a body-servant, or orderly, or batman, call it what you will, whether he likes it or not. This did not trouble me when I first encountered it as a cadet in India; we had native bearers who brought our morning tea, cleaned our kit and rooms, laid out our uniforms, dressed us on ceremonial occasions, and generally nannied us through a fourteen-hour day of such intensive activity that we couldn't have survived without them; there was even a *nappy-wallah* who shaved you as you sat bleary-eyed on the edge of your cot – and never have I had a chin so smooth. It

13

seemed perfectly natural forty years ago; it would not have seemed natural from a white servant – and before anyone from the race relations industry leaps in triumphantly with his labels, I should remark that the Indian cadets were of the same opinion (as often as not, so-called race prejudice is mere class distinction) and were, on the whole, less considerate masters than we were. My own bearer was called Timbooswami, son and grandson and great-grandson of bearers – and proud father of an Indian Army officer. So much for the wicked old British Raj.

My troubles began when I joined my Highland battalion in North Africa and had to have a batman from the ranks of my own platoon. No doubt I had been spoiled in India, but the contrast was dramatic. Where I had been accustomed to waking to the soft murmur of "*Chota hazri*, sahib", and having a *pialla* of perfectly-brewed tea and a sliced mango on my bedside table, there was now a crash of hob-nailed boots and a raucous cry of "Erzi tea! Some o' it's spillt, an' there's nae sugar. Aye, an' the rain's oan again." Not the same, somehow. And where once there had been a fresh-laundered shirt on a hanger, there was now a freckled Glaswegian holding up last night's garment in distaste and exclaiming: "Whit in Goad's name ye been daein' in this? Look at the state o' it. Were ye fu', or whit? Aye, weel, it'll hiv tae dae – yer ither yins arenae back frae the *dhobi*. Unless he's refused them. Aye. Weel, ye gettin' up, or are ye gaunae lie there a' day . . . sur?"

That was Coulter. I got rid of him inside three days, and appealed to Telfer, my platoon sergeant, for a replacement. And I hate to record it, for I like to think well of Telfer, who was a splendid soldier, but he then did one of the most diabolic things any sergeant could do to his new, green, and trusting platoon commander. Without batting an eye, and with full knowledge of what he was doing, this veteran of Alamein and Anzio glanced at his platoon roll, frowned, and said: "What about McAuslan?"

Innocent that I was, those doom-laden words meant nothing to me. I didn't know, then, that McAuslan was the dirtiest soldier in the world, a byword from Maryhill Barracks to the bazaars of Port Said for his foulness, stupidity, incompetence, illiteracy, and general unfitness for the service, an ill-made disaster whom Falstaff wouldn't have looked at, much less marched with through Coventry. This was the Tartan Caliban who had to be forcibly washed by his fellows and locked in cupboards during inspections, whom Telfer was wishing on me as batman. In fairness I can see that a sergeant might go to desperate lengths to keep McAuslan off parade and out of public view, but it was still a terrible thing to do to a subaltern not yet come of age.

I had seen McAuslan, of course – at least I had been aware of a sort of uniformed yeti that lurked at the far end of the barrack-room or vanished round corners like a startled sloth at the approach of authority, which he dreaded; I had even heard his cry, a raucous snarl of complaint and justification, for beneath his unkempt exterior there was a proud and independent spirit, sensitive of abuse. He had fought in North Africa, mostly against the Germans, but with the Military Police on occasion; his crime-sheet was rich in offences of neglect and omission, but rarely of intentional mischief, for McAuslan had this virtue: he tried. In a way he was something of a platoon mascot; the other Jocks took a perverse pride in his awfulness, and wouldn't have parted with him.

Of all this I was happily ignorant at the time, and it gave me quite a start when I got my first view of him, crouched to attention in my doorway, eyeing me like a wary gargoyle preparing to wrestle; he always stood to attention like that, I was to discover; it was a gift, like his habit of swinging left arm and left leg in unison when marching. He appeared to be short in stature, but since he was never fully erect one couldn't be sure; his face was primitive and pimpled, partly obscured by hair hanging over an unwashed brow, his denims would have disgraced an Alexandrine beggar (and possibly had), but the crowning touch was the filthy napkin draped carelessly over one forearm – I believe now that he was trying to convince me that he had once been a waiter, and knew his business.

"14687347Pr'iteMcAuslansah!" he announced. "Ah'm yer new batman, Sarn't Telfer sez. Whit'll Ah clean first?"

The smart answer to that would have been "Yourself, and do it somewhere else", but I was a very new second-lieutenant.

"Ah brung ma cleanin' kit," he went on, fishing a repulsive hold-all from inside his shirt. "Oh, aye, it's a' here," and he shook out on to the table a collection of noisome rags and old iron in which I recognised a battered Brasso tin, several bits of wire gauze and dried-up blanco, a toothbrush without bristles, and a stump of candle. (That last item shook me; was it possible, I wondered, that he performed his toilet by this illumination alone? It would have explained a lot.) It all looked as though it had been dredged from the Sweetwater Canal.

He made a sudden shambling pounce and snatched two rusted objects from the mess with a glad cry. "Aw, there th'are! Goad, an' me lookin' a' ower the shop! Ah thought Ah'd loast them!" He beamed, wiping them vigorously on his shirt, adding a touch of colour.

"What are they?" I asked, not really wanting to know.

"Ma fork an' spoon! They musta got in there that time I wis givin' ma mess-tins a wee polish – ye hiv tae scoor them, sur, ye see, or ye get gingivitis an' a' yer teeth fa' oot, the M.O. sez." He peered fondly at the rusting horrors, like an archaeologist with burial fragments. "Here, that's great! It's been a dam' nuisance bein' wi'oot them at meal-times," he added, conjuring up a picture so frightful that I closed my eyes. When I opened them again he was still there, frowning at my service dress, which was hanging outside the wardrobe.

"That's yer good kit," he said, in the grim reflective tone in which Sir Henry Morgan might have said: "That's Panama." He took a purposeful shuffle towards it, and I sprang to bar his way.

"It's all right, McAuslan – it's fine, it's all clean and ready. I shan't need it until five-thirty, for Retreat." I sought for some task that should keep him at a safe distance from my belongings. "Look, why don't you sweep the floor – out in the passage? The sand keeps blowing in . . . and the windows haven't been washed for weeks; you could do them – from the outside," I added hastily. "And let's see . . . what else?" But he was shaking his matted head, all insanitary reproach.

"Ah'm tae clean yer kit," he insisted. "Sarn't Telfer sez. Ah've tae polish yer buttons an' yer buits an' yer Sam Broon an' yer stag's heid badge, an' brush yer tunic, an' press the pleats o' yer kilt, an' bell yer flashes wi' rolled-up newspaper, an' wash an' dry yer sporran, and see the *dhobi* starches an' irons yer shirts, an' melt the bastard if he disnae dae it right, an' mak' yer bed . . ." He had assumed the aspect of a dishevelled Priest of the Ape People chanting a prehistoric ritual, eyes shut and swaying slightly, ". . . an' lay oot yer gear, an' blanco yer webbin', an' bring yer gunfire in ra mornin', and collect yer fag ration, an' fetch ye tea an' wee cakes frae the Naafi for yer elevenses unless ye fancy a doughnut, an' take ma turn as mess waiter oan guest nights, an' . . ."

"Stop!" I cried, and he gargled to a halt and stood lowering and expectant. It was that last bit about being a mess waiter that had hit home – I had a nightmare vision of him, in his unspeakable denims, sidling up to the Brigadier's wife with a tray of canapés and inquiring hoarsely, "Hey, missus, ye want a sangwidge? Ach, go on, pit anither in yer bag fur efter . . ."

"We can discuss it tomorrow," I said firmly. "My kit's all ready for Retreat, and I'm on the range until five, so you can fall out until then. Right?"

It isn't easy to read expressions on a face that looks like an artist's impression of Early Man, but I seemed to detect disappointment in the way he blinked and drew his forearm audibly across his nose. "Can Ah no' help ye oan wi' yer gear?" he suggested, and I snatched my bonnet from beneath his descending paw in the nick of time and hastily buckled on my belt and holster. "Thanks all the same, McAuslan," I said, withdrawing before he decided my collar needed adjustment – and he looked so deprived, somehow, that like a soft-hearted fool I added: "You can comb the sporran if you like . . . you better wash your hands first, perhaps, and be sure to hang it straight. Right, carry on."

They say no good deed ever goes unpunished, but I could not foresee that in combing the big white horse-hair sporran he would drop it on the floor, tramp on it, decide that it needed rewashing, and then try to dry it over the cookhouse stove while the master-gyppo's back was turned. They got the blaze under control, and probably only the gourmets noticed that the evening meal tasted of burned horse-hair. Meanwhile McAuslan, escaping undetected through the smoke, galloped back to my billet and tried to repair the charred remnant of my sporran by scraping it with my *sgian dubh*, snapping the blade in the process; he next tried daubing the stubble with white blanco, and dripped it on my best black shoes, which he then rendered permanently two-tone by scrubbing the spots with his sleeve. Warming to his work, he attempted to steal a sporran from

17

Second-Lieutenant Keith next door, was detected and pursued by Keith's batman, and defended his plunder by breaking my ashplant over the other's head. After which they called the provost staff, and the Jeeves of 12 Platoon was removed struggling to the cells, protesting blasphemously that they couldnae dae this tae him, he hadnae finished gettin' Mr MacNeill ready fur tae go on Retreat.

All this I learned when I got back from the range. I didn't attend Retreat – well, you look conspicuous in mottled grey brogues and a bald, smoking sporran – and was awarded two days' orderly officer in consequence; it was small comfort that McAuslan got seven days' jankers for brawling and conduct prejudicial. I summoned him straight after his sentence, intending to announce his dismissal from my personal service in blistering terms; he lurched into my office (even in his best tunic and tartan he looked like a fugitive from Culloden who had been hiding in a peat-bog) and before I could vent my rage on him he cleared his throat thunderously and asked:

"Can Ah say a word, sur?"

Expecting apology and contrition, I invited him to go ahead, and having closed his eyes, swayed, and gulped – symptoms, I was to learn, of embarrassment – he regarded me with a sort of nervous compassion.

"Ah'm sorry, sur, but Ah'm givin' notice. Ah mean, Ah'm resignin' frae bein' yer batman. Ah'm packin' it in, sur, if ye don't mind." He blinked, wondering how I would receive this bombshell, and my face must have been a study, for he added hastily: "Ah'm sorry, like, but ma mind's made up."

"Is it, by God?" I said. "Well, get this straight, McAuslan! You're not *resigning*, my son, not by a dam' sight, because—"

"Oh, but Ah am, sur. Beggin' yer pardon. Ah want ye tae understand," he continued earnestly, "that it's nuthin' personal. Ye're a gentleman, sur. But the fact is, if Ah'm lookin' efter you, Ah hivnae time tae look efter mysel' – an' Ah've got a lot o' bother, I can tell ye. Look at the day, frinstance – Ah wis rushed, an' here Ah'm oan jankers – och, it's no' your fault, it's that wee nyaff o' a batman that works fur Mr Keith. Nae co-operation—"

"McAuslan," I said, breathing hard. "Go away. Go quickly, before I forget myself. Get your infernal carcase on jankers, and

18

tell the Provost Sergeant he can kill you, and I'll cover up for him—'

"Awright! Awright, sur! Ah'm gaun!" He beat a shambling retreat, looking puzzled and slightly hurt. 'Keep the heid, sur." He saluted with crestfallen dignity. "Ah wis just gaun tae say, ye'll be needin' anither batman, an' ye could dae worse than Chick McGilvray; he's Celtic-daft an' a bit casual, but – awright, sur, Ah'm gaun! Ah'm gaun!'

You know, when our sister regiment, the Black Watch, was first raised centuries ago, it was unique in that every *private soldier* had his own batman – and in next to no time that great fighting regiment had mutinied. It was now clear to me why: several hundred batmen in the McAuslan mould had simply proved too great a strain.

On the principle that any recommendation of his must be accursed, I did not approach McGilvray. Instead I spoke sternly to Sergeant Telfer – who had the grace to admit that eagerness to get shot of McAuslan had warped his judgment – and told him I would engage replacements on a trial basis. There was no shortage of volunteers, for a batman's life is a cushy billet, with perks and time off, but none of them was any real improvement on Coulter, although all were grace itself compared to the Dark Destroyer who had succeeded him.

There was Fletcher, Glasgow spiv, dead shot, and platoon dandy, who kept my kit immaculate – and wore it himself in his sorties after female talent. Next there was Forbes, nicknamed Heinie after Himmler; he was small, dark, and evil, a superb footballer who performed his duties with ruthless efficiency, but whose explosive temper bred friction with the other batmen. After him came Brown, alias Daft Bob, an amiable dreamer who supported Partick Thistle (that's a tautology, really) and was always five minutes late; he was also given to taking afternoon naps on my bed with his boots on. And there was Riach, who came from Uist and belonged to that strict religious sect, the Wee Frees; he had a prejudice against working on the Sabbath, and only did it under protest. (I once asked him how, during active service in the Far East, he had brought himself to kill Japanese on Sunday, and he ground his teeth in a grim, distant way and said that was all right, it was a work of necessity and mercy.)

19

I parted from each trialist in turn, without rancour. Perhaps I was hard to please – no, I was impossible to please, partly because I disliked being waited on and feeling my privacy invaded, but also because it was dawning on me that Scots (as I should have learned from my grandmother) are not natural servants; they have too much inborn conceit of themselves for the job, and either tyrannise their employers, like my grand-mother and Coulter (although I'm sure her technique was that of the rapier, where his was the bludgeon), or regard them as victims to be plundered in a patronising way. Of course there are exceptions; Hudson of *Upstairs, Downstairs* does exist, but you have to be exceptional yourself to employ him (I never thought the Bellamy family were *quite* up to him, and I doubt if he did either).

Anyway, there were no Hudsons in 12 Platoon, and I wondered how it was that the other young officers got by – MacKenzie, heir to a baronetcy, had an easy, owner–serf rela-tionship with his orderly, and the rest of the subalterns seemed to take personal attendance for granted, without noticing it. That is the secret, of course: you have to be of the fine clay that isn't even aware of servants, but regards them as robots or talking animals who just happen to be around, lubricating you unobtrusively through life. The moment you become sensitive to their mere presence, never mind their thoughts, you stamp your-self as a neurotic peasant, like me, unfit to be looked after. So I concluded – and it never occurred to me that I was someone's grandson, and possibly seeking an unobtainable ideal.

Finally, in despair, I offered the job to McAuslan's nominee, McGilvray, a grinning, tow-headed Glaswegian who confessed that he hadn't volunteered because he didn't think he was cut out for it – that was a change, anyway. Mind you, he was right, but he wasn't alone in that, and he was a cheery, willing vandal who, beyond a tendency to knock the furniture about and gossip non-stop, had only one serious defect: I had to darn his socks. This after I had noticed him limping slightly, made him take off his plimsolls, and discovered two gaping holes repaired by whipping the edges together into fearsome ridges.

"No wonder you get blisters, you Parkhead disaster," I rebuked him. "Did no one ever teach you to darn? Right, get me some wool and a needle and pay attention . . ."

Darning socks was a vital art in those days; if you couldn't darn you couldn't march – unless you were one of those eccentrics who dispensed with socks and filled their boots with tallow, and I wasn't having him doing that, not within fifty yards of my perfumed bower. But my tuition was wasted; he just couldn't darn, and before you knew it I was inspecting his socks regularly and mending them myself, while he beavered away on my brass and webbing and explained why Celtic weren't winning these days. From time to time I would wonder resentfully why the hell I was doing this, but I knew that if I didn't it wouldn't get done at all, and you know how it is: line of least resistance, etc., and I couldn't be bothered finding yet another batman – which was an utterly trivial matter anyway, alongside the important things that were happening to me at that time. Such as getting to know and work well with my platoon, discovering that mutual reliance which is a gift (and an honour) beyond price, enjoying the acceptance that comes in a Highland battalion when the Jocks stop calling you "MacNeill" among themselves and give you a nickname ("Darkie", I discovered), getting my second pip, feeling at home in one of the world's most famous regiments, preparing to go home on leave after three years . . .

The self-imposed task of darning McGilvray's socks was a small price to pay for all of that. Mind you, I could have done without it; it was a piece of nonsense, really . . . perhaps when I came back off leave I'd find another batman. Yes, definitely.

It was a whole month's leave, what they called L.I.A.P., meaning leave in advance of Python, which was the codeword for demobilisation. I qualified because, having been in the ranks in India, I'd been overseas longer than most of the subalterns; consequently I found myself barraged with requests to go and see their families. This was a phenomenon of the time which may be hard to understand in these days of instant world travel – anyone going home was expected to visit his comrades' parents, just so that they could hear about their boy from someone who'd actually been with him. Letters weren't the same as being able to talk to and touch someone who'd been with Jack or Billy; it was a great reassurance in those days.

So, apart from a commission to buy the Colonel half a dozen of his favourite Lovat pipes ("and don't let them fob you off with any damned Bulldogs or patent puffers, d'you hear?") I had four or five addresses to call at in and around Glasgow and Edinburgh. That was after I had undergone the extraordinary experience of "coming home from the war", which must differ from person to person, I suppose, but is like nothing else in life. For this young soldier, unmarried and unattached, it was a going home to parents, a wonderful elated reunion full of laughter and babbling and maternal tears, and aunts exclaiming, and father shaking his head and grinning with satisfaction before going through to his surgery, bursting quietly with the news for his patients, and my MacNeill grandmother, ninety-three years old, bright-eyed and laughing softly in Gaelic as she preened herself in the Arab shawl I had brought her. (I wonder if she remembered my MacDonald grandmother's remark to her as they listened together to Chamberlain's declaration of war in 1939: "Well, Mrs MacNeill, the men will be going away again." Only a Highland matriarch would put it quite like that. If my MacNeill grandmother did remember, she was probably reflecting that now the last of the men was home; the first ones she had seen returning, as a little girl, had been from the Crimea.)

It was very happy, but it was strange. They looked the same to me, of course, but now and then I realised that they were recognising the boy of 18 whom they remembered, in this much bigger, sunburned young man of 21. That's an odd feeling. So is standing alone in the quiet of your room, just as you remember it but a little smaller, staring at each familiar thing of childhood and thinking: that day of the Sittang ambush . . . that terrible slow-motion moment at Kinde Wood when the section went down around you in the cross-fire . . . that night when the Japs came up the Yindaw road, the little ungainly figures in the light of the burning trucks, passing by only a few yards away . . . that hectic slashing mêlée at the bunkers under the little gold pagoda where L— bought his lot and J— had his hat shot off and the ground was dark and wet with blood – while all *that* was happening, a world and a lifetime away, *this* was here: the quiet room, just as it had always been, just as it is now. The porcupine-quill inkstand that the old man brought home from East Africa, the copy of *Just William* with its torn spine, the bail you broke with your fast ball against Transitus (it must have been cheap wood), the ink-stain low down on the wallpaper that you made (quite deliberately) when you were eight . . . Nothing changed, except you. Never call yourself unlucky again.

I couldn't sleep in bed that night. I did something I hadn't done since Burma, except on a few night exercises: I went out into the garden with a blanket and rolled up under a bush. God knows why. It wasn't affectation – I took good care that no one knew – nor was it sheer necessity, nor mere silliness in the exuberance of homecoming. At the time I felt it was a sort of gesture of thanksgiving, and only much later did I realise it was probably a reluctance to "come home" to a life that I knew there could be no return to, now. Anyway, I didn't sleep a bloody wink.

After just a few days at home (which was in Northern England) I took off for Scotland. My excuse was that I had to make the visits I had promised, but the truth was I was restless and impatient. Three years of adventure – because there's no other word for that kaleidoscope of travel and warfare and excitement and change in strange lands among weird exotic peoples – had done its work, and once the elation of just being home, so long dreamed of, had passed, there was the anti-climax, the desire to be off and doing again. It was no big psychological deal of the kind you see in movies; I wasn't battle-happy, or "mentally scarred", or hung up with guilt, nor did patrols of miniature Japanese brew up under my bed (as happened to one of my section whenever we came out of the line: we used to tell him to take his kukhri to them, and when he had done so to his satisfaction, swearing and carving the air, we all went back to sleep again, him included). It was just that my life was now outside that home of boyhood, and I would never settle there again. Of course no word of this was said, but I'm sure my parents knew. Parents usually do.

I was nearly two weeks in Scotland, staying at small hotels and making my afternoon calls on families who had been forewarned of my coming; it was a succession of front-rooms and drawing-rooms, with the best tea-service and sandwiches and such extravagance of scones and home-made cakes as rationing allowed (I had to remind myself to go easy on the sugar, or I would have cleaned them out), while I was cross-examined about Drew or Angus or Gordon, and photographs of the poor perishers were trotted out which would have curled their toes under, and quiet aunts listened rapt in the background, and younger brothers and sisters regarded me with giggling awe. They were such nice folk, kind, proper, hanging on every word about their sons, tired after the war, touchingly glad that I had come to see them. It was fascinating, too, to compare the parents with the young men I knew, to discover that the dashing and ribald Lieutenant Grant was the son of a family so douce that they said grace even before afternoon tea; that the parents of the urbane Captain D—, who had put him through Merchiston and Oxford, lived in a tiny top-floor flat in Colinton; and that Second Lieutenant Hunter, a pimply youth with protruding teeth, had a sister who was a dead ringer for Linda Darnell (and whose R.A.F. fiancé stuck to her like glue all through tea).

But the most interesting calls were the last two. The first was to a blackened tenement in Glasgow's East End, where McGilvray's widowed mother lived with his invalid great-uncle, on the third floor above a mouldering close with peeling walls, urchins screaming on the stairs, and the green tramcars clanging by. Inside, the flat was bright and neat and cosy, with gleaming brass, a kettle singing on the open black-leaded grate, an old-fashioned alcove bed, and such a tea on the table as I had not seen yet, with gingerbread and Lyle's golden syrup. Mrs McGilvray was a quick, anxious wee Glasgow body, scurrying with the tea-pot while Uncle chuckled and made sly jokes at her; he was a small wheezy comedian with a waxed moustache and a merry eye, dressed in his best blue serge with a flower in his buttonhole and a gold watch-chain across his portly middle; he half-rose to greet me, leaning on a stick and gasping cheerfully, called me "l'tenant", informed me that he had been in the H.L.I. in the first war, and wha' shot the cheese, hey? (This is a famous joke against my regiment.) When he had subsided, wiping his eye and chuckling "Ma Goad, ma Goad", Mrs McGilvray questioned me nervously across the tea-cups: was Charlie well? Was Charlie behaving himself? Was Charlie giving me any bother? Was Charlie saving his pay or squandering it on drink, cards, and loose women? (This was actually a series of questions artfully disguised, but that was their purport.) Was Charlie attending Church? Was he taking care? Were his pals nice boys?

"In Goad's name, wumman," cried Uncle, "let the man get his tea! Yattety-yattety-yattety! Cherlie's fine! Thur naethin' wrang wi' him. Sure that's right, L'tenant?"

"He's fine," I said, "he's a great lad."

"There y'are! Whit am Ah aye tellin' ye? The boy's fine!"

"Aye, well," said Mrs McGilvray, looking down at her cup. "I aye worry aboot him."

"Ach, women!" cried Uncle, winking at me. "Aye on aboot their weans. See yersel' anither potato scone, L'tenant. Ma Goad, ma Goad."

"Does he . . ." Mrs McGilvray hesitated, "does he . . . do his work well? I mean . . . looking after you, Mr MacNeill?"

"Oh, indeed he does. I think I'm very lucky."

"Ah'd sooner hae a cairter lookin' efter me!" wheezed Uncle. "Heh-heh! Aye, or a caur conductor! Ma Goad, ma Goad.'

"Wheesht, Uncle! Whit'll Mr MacNeill think?"

"He'll think yer an auld blether, gaun on aboot Cherlie! The boy's no' a bairn ony langer, sure'n he's no'. He's a grown man." He glinted at me. "Sure that's right? Here . . . will ye tak' a wee dram, L'tenant? Ach, wheesht, wumman – can Ah no' gie the man a right drink, then? His tongue'll be hingin' oot!" At his insistence she produced a decanter, shaking her head, apologising, while he cried to gie the man a decent dram, no' just dirty his gless. He beamed on me.

"Here's tae us! Ninety-Twa, no' deid yet!"

"Whisky at tea-time – whit'll Mr MacNeill think o' ye?" wondered his niece, half-smiling.

"He'll no' think the worse o' me for gie'n him a wee dram tae the Ninety-Twa," said Uncle comfortably. He raised his glass again. "An' tae the Bantam's, hey, L'tenant? Aye, them's the wee boys! Ma Goad, ma Goad . . ."

Mrs McGilvray saw me to the door when I left, Uncle crying after me no' tae shoot ony cheeses gaun doon the stair. When I had thanked her she said:

"I wonder . . . Charlie doesnae write very often. D'you think . . .?"

"He'll write every week," I assured her. "He's a great lad, Mrs McGilvray. You're very lucky."

"Well," she said, clasping her hands, "he's always been right enough. I'm sure you'll look after him." We shook hands and she pecked me quickly on the cheek. "Take care, laddie."

Uncle's hoarse chuckle sounded from the inner room. "Come

ben, wumman! Whit'll the neebors say, you hingin' aboot the stairheid wi' sojers!'

She gave me a despairing look and retreated, and I went down the stairs, stepping over the children and reflecting that I was certainly not going to be able to change my batman now.

The final visit was to MacKenzie's people, who lived in a fifteenth-century castle-cum-mansion in Perthshire, a striking piece of Gothic luxury in beautiful parkland with a drive a mile long through banks of cultivated heather; it contained its own salmon river, a fortune in standing timber, and a battalion of retainers who exercised dogs, strolled about with shotguns, and manicured the rhododendrons. Sir Gavin MacKenzie was his son thirty years on, tall, commanding, and with a handshake like a mangle; the red had apparently seeped from his hair into his cheeks, but that was the only difference. In manner he was cordial and abrupt, a genuine John Buchan Scottish aristo – which is to say that he was more English than any Englishman could ever hope to be. If you doubt that, just consider such typical "Englishmen" as Harold Macmillan, David Niven, Alec Douglas-Home, Jack Buchanan, Stewart Granger, and Charles II.

This was the only visit on which I actually stayed on the premises overnight. We dined at a long candle-lit table in a large and clammy hall with age-blackened panelling covered with crossed broadswords, targes, and flintlocks, with silent servitors emerging occasionally from the gloom to refuel us. At one end sat Sir Gavin in a dinner jacket and appalling MacKenzie tartan trews cut on the diagonal; at the other, Lady MacKenzie, an intense woman with a staccato delivery who chain-smoked throughout the meal. From time to time she and her husband addressed each other in the manner of people who have met only recently; it was hard to believe that they knew each other well enough to be have begotten not only their son but a daughter, seated opposite me, a plain, lumpy sixteen-year-old with the magnificent MacKenzie hair, flaming red and hanging to her waist. The only other diner was a pale, elderly man with an eye-glass whose name I didn't catch – in fact, looking back, I'm not sure he was there at all, since he never spoke and no one addressed him. He drank most of a bottle of Laphroaig during the meal, and took it with him when the ladies withdrew, leaving old man MacKenzie and me to riot over the port.

Coming on the evening of the day I had spent with the McGilvrays, it was an odd contrast. Lady MacKenzie had chattered non-stop about her son, but without asking any questions, and his sister had not, I think, referred to him at all, but since she had the finishing-school habit of talking very quickly to her armpit it was difficult to be sure. Sir Gavin had spoken only of the Labour Government. Now, when we were alone, he demanded to know why, in my opinion, Kenny had not joined the Scots Guards, in which he, Sir Gavin, had held an exalted position. Why had he chosen a Highland regiment? It was extraordinary, when he could have been in the Brigade; Sir Gavin couldn't understand it.

I said, trying not to smile, that it was possible some people might prefer a Highland regiment, and Sir Gavin said, yes, he knew *that*, but it wasn't the point. Why young Kenneth? It seemed very odd to him, when the family had always been in the Brigade, and he could have kept an eye on the boy – "I mean, I don't know your Colonel – what's his name? No, don't know him. Good man, is he?"

"They don't come any better," I said. It seemed fairly obvious to me why young Kenneth, a firebrand and a maverick, had chosen not to be in father's regiment, but that could not be said. Sir Gavin looked glum, and said he didn't know anything *about* Highland regiments – fine reputation, of course, but he didn't know how they *were*, d'you see what I mean? With the Guards, you knew where you were. Life for a young officer was cut and dried . . . Highland regiment, he wasn't so sure. Suddenly he asked:

"Is he a *good* officer?"

"Kenny? Yes. His Jocks like him."

"His what?"

"His Jocks – his men."

"Oh." He frowned. "What about your Colonel?"

"I'm sure he thinks Kenny's a good officer." Indeed, Sir Gavin didn't know about Highland regiments, where the opinion of the men is the ultimate test, and every colonel knows it. Sir Gavin chewed his cigar and then said:

"You were a ranker, weren't you? Very well – in Burma, would you have . . . accepted Kenneth as your platoon commander?"

27

I mentally compared Kenny with the brisk young man who'd once challenged me to a spelling bee and caught me out over "inadmissible", and who'd died in a bunker entrance the next day. A good subaltern, but no better than MacKenzie.

"Yes," I said. "Kenny would have done."

"You think so?" he said, and suddenly I realised he was worried about his son. In the Guards, he could have served *with* him in spirit, so to speak – but he didn't know how Highland regiments *were*, he'd said. Did the boy fit into that almost alien background? Was he a good officer? Like Mrs McGilvray, he aye worried about him, if for a different reason. So it seemed sensible to start talking about Kenny, describing how he got on in the regiment, how he and his platoon sergeant, McCaw, the Communist Clydesider, formed a disciplinary alliance that was a battalion byword, recalling incidents in which Kenny had figured, our own companionship, things like that, no doubt babbling a bit, while Sir Gavin listened, and kept the decanter going, now and then asking a question, finally sitting in silence for a while, and then saying:

"Well, I'm glad he's all right. Thank you."

It was two in the morning when we finally rose, port-bloated and drowsy – he must have been partially kettled, for he insisted on a frame of snooker with accompanying brandies before we parted for the night. "John'll look after you," he said, hiccoughing courteously, and I was aware of a dim sober figure at the foot of the massive staircase, waiting to conduct me to my room -- which brings me back, after this digression of homecoming, to where I was in the first place.

John was a footman, the only one I have ever encountered outside the pages of Georgette Heyer and Wodehouse, and he would have fitted into them perfectly, along with the rest of the MacKenzie ménage. No doubt I was a trifle woozy with tiredness and Croft's Old Original, but I have no impression that I had to stir so much as a finger in order to get into bed. His shadow flitted about me, my clothes vanished, towel and soap and warm water swam into my ken, followed by pyjamas and a cup of some bland liquid, and then I was between the sheets and all was dark contentment. When I woke two hours later there was a tray at the bedside with various mineral waters, biscuits, and a glass of milk, all under a dim night-light. I think the milk had been spiked, for the first two hours after waking next morning passed in a beatific haze; I seem to remember curtains being drawn and a cup of tea appearing, and then I was borne up gently into a sitting position and presently subsided, shaven, while a voice murmured that my bath had been drawn – not filled or running, you understand, but drawn. At that point he vanished, and when I emerged from the bathroom, more or less awake, there was a breakfast tray on the window table, with porridge and Arbroath smokies and ham and eggs and such morning rolls as God's Own Prophet eats only in Glasgow bakeries; the *Scotsman* and the *Bulletin* lay beside it (not that I was fit for more than the Scottykin comic strip), my clothes were laid out, pressed, brushed, and beautiful, my shoes a-gleam, and even my cap badge and sporran chains had been polished.

This, it slowly dawned on me, was living, and it took an immense effort to decline the MacKenzies' invitation to stay on, but I suspected that after a few days of John's attention I would have forgotten how to tie my shoe-laces and wave bye-bye. As I travelled south again, and later on the flight to Cairo, I had day-dreams in which the press-gang had been reintroduced, and John had been crimped into my personal service; it would give me a new outlook on life, and I would rise effortlessly to general rank and a knighthood, possibly even C.I.G.S., for nothing less was conceivable with that mysterious retainer sorting me out; I would have to live up to the ambience he created. At that point the dreaming stopped, as I realised that I simply wasn't made for that kind of destiny, or for the ministrations of people like John.

This was driven home with a vengeance in Benghazi, of all unlikely places, where I had to spend three days between flights on the way back to the battalion. I had just entered the room allotted me in the transit camp when there was a clump of martial feet on the verandah, and into the doorway wheeled a gigantic German prisoner-of-war. From the crown of his blond shaving-brush skull to his massive ammunition boots and rolled socks must have been a cool six and a half feet; in between he wore only tiny khaki shorts and a shirt which appeared to have been starched with concrete. He crashed to attention, stared at the wall, and shouted:

"Saar, Ai em yewer betmen. Mai nem is Hans. Pliz permit thet Ai unpeck yewer kit."

My immediate reaction was: how the hell did we ever beat this lot? For what I was looking at was one of Frederick William's Prussian giants, the picture of a Panzer Grenadier, the perfect military automaton. He was, I learned later, captured Afrika Korps, waiting to be repatriated and meanwhile employed to attend transients like myself. When I had recovered and told him to carry on, he stamped again, ducked his head sharply, and went at my valise like a great clockwork doll, unpacking and stowing with a precision that was not quite human; it was a relief to see that there wasn't a knob on the side of his neck.

It was my first encounter with the German military, and I didn't mind if it was the last. In his heel-clicking way he was as perfect a servant as John had been, for while John had worked his miracles without actually being there, apparently, and never obtruding his personality, Hans succeeded by having no personality at all. It was like having a machine about the place, bringing tea by numbers; you could almost hear the whirr and click with every action. In fact, he was a robot-genie, with the gift of sudden shattering appearance; he would be out on the verandah, standing at ease, and if I so much as coughed he would be quivering in the doorway shouting "Saar!", ready to fetch me a box of matches or march on Moscow. I began to understand Frederick the Great and Hitler; given a couple of million Hanses at your beck and call, the temptation to say "Occupy Europe at once!" must be overpowering.

I say he had no personality, but I'm not so sure. In three days he never betrayed emotion, or even moved a facial muscle except to speak; if he had a thought beyond the next duty to be performed, you would never have known it. But on the last night, I had gone up to the mess in khaki drill, having left my kilt hanging by its waist-loops on the cupboard door. Coming back, I glanced in at my window, and there was Hans standing looking at the kilt with an expression I hadn't seen before. It was a thoughtful, intense stare, with a lot of memory behind it; he moved forward and felt the material, traced his thumb-nail along one of the yellow threads, and then stepped back, contemplating it with his cropped head on one side. I may be wrong, but I believe that if ever a man was thinking, "Next time, you sons-of-bitches", he was. I made a noise approaching the doorway, and when I went in he was turning down the bed, impassive as ever.

But whatever secret thoughts he may have had in his Teutonic depths, Hans, as a servant, was too much for me – just as the disembodied John had been. As I observed earlier, you have to be a Junker, or its social equivalent (with all that that implies) to be able to bear having the Johns and Hanses dance attendance on you; if you are just a gentleman for the working day, you must stick to your own kind.

I reached the battalion the following evening, asked the jeep driver to drop off my kit at my billet, and walked over to 12 Platoon barrack-room. They were there, loafing about, lying on their cots, exchanging the patter, some cleaning their kit, others preparing to go out on the town: the dapper Fletcher was combing his hair at a mirror, fox-trotting on the spot; Forbes, in singlet and shorts, was juggling a tennis ball on his instep; Riach was writing a letter (to the Wee Frees' Grand Inquisitor, probably); Daft Bob Brown was sitting on his bed singing "Ah've got spurs that jingle-jangle-jingle, so they doo-oo!" and at the far end Private McAuslan, clad à la mode in balmoral bonnet and a towel with which he had evidently been sweeping a chimney, was balanced precariously on his bed-end, swiping furiously at moths with his rifle-sling; from his hoarse vituperations I gather he blamed their intrusion on Sergeant Telfer, the Army Council, and the Labour Government of Mr Attlee. He and Sir Gavin MacKenzie should have got together.

One of the corporals saw me in the doorway and started to call the room to attention, but I flagged him down, and the platoon registered my appearance after their fashion.

"Aw-haw-hey, Wullie! The man's back!"

"See, Ah told ye he hadnae gone absent."

"Hiv a good leave, sur?"

"Way-ull! Back tae the Airmy again!"

"Whit did ye bring us frae Rothesay, sur?"

"Aye, it'll be hell in the trenches the morn!"

and so on with their keelie grins and weird slogans, and very reassuring it was. I responded in kind by bidding them a courteous good evening, looked forward to meeting them on rifle parade at eight and kit inspection at ten, and acknowledged their cries of protest and lamentation. McGilvray came forward with my Sam Browne in one hand and a polishing rag in the other.

"Yer leave a'right, sur? Aw, smashin'. Ah'm jist givin' yer belt a wee buff – Captain McAlpine asked tae borrow it while ye were away, an' ye know whit he's like – Ah think he's been hingin' oot a windae in it; a' scuffed tae hellangone! But the rest o' yer service dress is a' ready; Ah bulled it up when Ah heard ye wis back the night."

Well, I thought to myself, you're not John or Hans, thank God, but you'll do. They can keep the professionals – and they can certainly keep McAuslan, and the farther away the better – and we'll get by very nicely.

He was looking at me inquiringly, and I realised I had been letting my thoughts stray.

"Oh . . . thanks, McGilvray. I saw your mother and great-uncle; they're fine. Come and finish the belt in my room and I'll tell you about them." I was turning away when a thought struck me, and I paused, hesitating: I could sense that stern shade with her black ebony cane frowning down in disapproval from some immaculate, dusted paradise, but I couldn't help that. "Oh, yes, and you'd better bring your socks with you."

Sorry, Granny MacDonald, I thought, but a man's got to do what a man's got to do.

Captain Errol

Whenever I see television newsreels of police or troops facing mobs of rioting demonstrators, standing fast under a hail of rocks, bottles, and petrol bombs, my mind goes back forty years to India, when I was understudying John Gielgud and first heard the pregnant phrase "Aid to the civil power". And from that my thoughts inevitably travel on to Captain Errol, and the Brigadier's pet hawks, and the great rabble of chanting Arab rioters advancing down the Kantara causeway towards the thin khaki line of 12 Platoon, and my own voice sounding unnaturally loud and hoarse: "Right, Sarn't Telfer – fix bayonets."

Aid to the civil power, you see, is what the British Army used to give when called on to deal with disorder, tumult, and breach of the peace which the police could no longer control. The native constabulary of our former Italian colony being what they were – prone to panic if a drunken *bazaar-wallah* broke a window – aid to the civil power often amounted to no more than sending Wee Wullie out with a pick handle to shout "Imshi!"; on the other hand, when real political mayhem broke loose, and a raging horde of fellaheen several thousand strong appeared bent on setting the town ablaze and massacring the European population, sterner measures were called for, and unhappy subalterns found themselves faced with the kind of decision which Home Secretaries and Cabinets agonise over for hours, the difference being that the subaltern had thirty seconds, with luck, in which to consider the safety of his men, the defenceless town at his back, and the likelihood that if he gave the order to fire and some agitator caught a bullet, he, the subaltern, would go down in history as the Butcher of Puggle Bazaar, or wherever it happened to be.

That, as I say, was in the imperial twilight of forty years ago, long before the days of walkie-talkies, C.S. gas, riot shields,

water cannon, and similar modern defences of the public weal –
not that they seem to make riot control any easier nowadays,
especially when the cameras are present. We didn't have to
worry about television, and our options for dealing with infuri-
ated rioters were limited: do nothing and get murdered, fire over
their heads, or let fly in earnest. There are easier decisions,
believe me, for a youth not old enough to vote.

The Army recognised this, and was at pains to instruct its
fledgling officers in the techniques of containing civil commo-
tion, so far as it knew how, which wasn't far, even in India, with
three centuries of experience to draw on. Those were the post-
war months before independence, when demonstrators were
chanting: "Jai Hind!" and "Pakistan zindabad!", and the
Indian police were laying about them with *lathis* (you really
don't know what police brutality is until you've seen a *lathi*
charge going in), while the troops stood by and their officers
hoped to God they wouldn't have to intervene. Quetta and
Amritsar were ugly memories of what happened when someone
opened fire at the wrong time.

Bangalore, where I was completing my officers' training
course, was one of the quiet spots, which may have been why the
authorities took the eccentric view that instruction in riot control
could be imparted through the medium of the theatre. If that
sounds unlikely, well, that's the Army for you. Some genius
(and it wasn't Richard Brinsley Sheridan) had written a play
about aid to the civil power, showing the right and wrong ways of
coping with unrest; it was to be enacted at the garrison theatre,
and I found myself dragooned into taking part.

That's what comes of understudying Gielgud, which is what I
like to think I had been doing, although he didn't know it. In the
last relaxed weeks of our officers' training, a few of us cadets had
been taking part in a production of *The Harbour Called
Mulberry* for India Radio, with Cadet MacNeill as the Prussian
general riveting the audience with his impersonation of Conrad
Veidt; it was natural that when Gielgud's touring company
arrived in town with a double bill of *Hamlet* and *Blithe Spirit*, and
some of his cast went down with Bangalore Belly, our amatuer
group should be asked to provide replacements in case they
needed a couple of extra spear-carriers. I was fool enough to
volunteer, and while we were never required even to change into

costume, let alone go on stage, we convinced ourselves that we were, technically, understudying the lead players – I mean to say, Bangalore Belly can go through unacclimatised systems like wildfire, and in our backstage dreams we could imagine being out there tearing the Soliloquy to shreds while Gielgud was carted off to the sick-bay. He wasn't, as it happened, but no doubt he would have been reassured if he'd known that we were ready to step in.

That by the way; the upshot was that, having drawn attention to ourselves, my associates and I were prime targets when it came to choosing the cast for the aid-to-the-civil-power play, a knavish piece of work entitled *Nowall and Chancit*. I played Colonel Nowall, an elderly and incompetent garrison commander, which meant that I had to wear a white wig and whiskers and make like a doddering Aubrey Smith in front of a military audience whose behaviour would have disgraced the Circus Maximus. The script was abysmal, my moustache kept coming loose, the prop telephone didn't ring on cue, one of the cast who took acting seriously dried up and fainted, and in the last act I had to order my troops to open fire on a rioting crowd played by a platoon of Indian sepoys in loin-cloths who giggled throughout and went right over the top when shot with blank cartridges. The entire theatre was dense with cordite smoke, there seemed to be about seven hundred people on stage, and when I stood knee-deep in hysterical corpses and spoke my deathless closing line: "Well, that's that!" it stopped the show. I have not trod the boards since, and it can stay that way.

My excuse for that reminiscence is that it describes the only instruction we ever got in dealing with civil disorder. Considering that we were destined, as young second-lieutenants, to lead troops in various parts of the Far and Middle East when empires were breaking up and independence movements were in full spate, with accompanying bloodshed, it was barely adequate. Not that any amount of training, including my months as an infantry section leader in Burma, could have prepared me for the Palestine troubles of '46, when Arab and Jew were at each other's throats with the British caught in the middle, as usual; the Irgun and Stern Gang were waging their campaign of terror (or freedom-fighting, depending on your point of view), raid, ambush, murder, and explosion were commonplace, the Argyll and Sutherlands had barbed wire strung across the *inside* corridors of their Jerusalem barracks, and you took your revolver into the shower. It was a nerve-racked, bloody business which you learned as you went along; commanding the Cairo–Jerusalem night train and conducting a security stake-out at the Armistice Day service on the Mount of Olives added years to my education in a matter of days, and by the time I was posted back to my Highland battalion far away along the North African coast I felt I knew something about lending aid to the civil power. Of course, I didn't know the half of it – but then, I hadn't met Captain Errol.

That wasn't his real name, but it was what the Jocks called him because of his resemblance to Flynn, the well-known actor and bon viveur. And it wasn't just that he was six feet two, lightly moustached, and strikingly handsome; he had the same casual, self-assured swagger of the man who is well content with himself and doesn't give a dam whether anyone knows it or not; when you have two strings of ribbons, starting with the M.C. and M.M. and including the Croix de Guerre and a couple of exotic Balkan gongs at the end, you don't need to put on side. Which was just as well, for Errol had evidently been born with a double helping of self-esteem, advertised in the amused half-smile and lifted eyebrow with which he surveyed the world in general – and me in particular on the day he joined the battalion.

I was bringing my platoon in from a ten-mile route march, which they had done in the cracking time of two and a half hours, and was calling them to march to attention for the last fifty yards to the main gate, exhorting McAuslan for the umpteenth time to get his pack off his backside and up to his shoulders, and pretending not to hear Private Fletcher's sotto voce explanation that McAuslan couldn't march upright because he was expecting, and might, indeed, go into labour shortly. Sergeant Telfer barked them to silence and quickened the step, and I turned aside to watch them swing past – it was a moment I took care never to miss, for the pride of it warms me still: my platoon going by, forty hard young Jocks in battle order, rifles sloped and bonnets pulled down, slightly dusty but hardly even breaking sweat as Telfer wheeled them under the archway with its faded golden standard. Eat your heart out, Bonaparte.

It was as I was turning to follow that I became aware of an

elegant figure seated in a horse-ghari which had just drawn up at the gate. He was a Highlander, but his red tartan and white cockade were not of our regiment; then I noticed the three pips and threw him a salute, which he acknowledged with a nonchalant forefinger and a remarkable request spoken in the airy affected drawl which in Glasgow is called "Kelvinsaid".

"Hullo, laddie," said he. "Your platoon? You might get a couple of them to give me a hand with my kit, will you?"

It was said so affably that the effrontery of it didn't dawn for a second – you don't ask a perfect stranger to detach two of his marching men to be your porters, not without preamble or introduction. I stared at the man, taking in the splendid bearing, the medal ribbons, and the pleasant expectant smile while he put a fresh cigarette in his holder.

"Eh? I beg your pardon," I said stiffly, "but they're on parade at the moment." For some reason I didn't add "sir".

It didn't faze him a bit. "Oh, that's a shame. Still, not to panic. We ought to be able to manage between us. All right, Abdul," he addressed the Arab coachman, "let's get the cargo on the dock."

He swung lightly down from the ghari – not the easiest thing to do, with decorum, in a kilt – and it was typical of the man that I found myself with a valise in one hand and a set of golf-clubs in the other before I realised that he was evidently expecting me to tote his damned dunnage for him. My platoon had vanished from sight, fortunately, but Sergeant Telfer had stopped and was staring back, goggle-eyed. Before I could speak the newcomer was addressing me again:

"Got fifty lire, old man? 'Fraid all I have is Egyptian ackers, and the Fairy Coachman won't look at them. See him right, will you, and we'll settle up anon. Okay?"

That, as they say, did it. "Laddie" I could just about absorb (since he must have been all of twenty-seven and therefore practically senile), and even his outrageous assumption that my private and personal platoon were his to flunkify, and that I would caddy for him and pay his blasted transport bills – but not that careless "Okay?" and the easy, patronising air which was all the worse for being so infernally amiable. Captain or no captain, I put his clubs and valise carefully back in the ghari and spoke, with masterly restraint:

"I'm afraid I haven't fifty lire on me, sir, but if you care to climb back in, the ghari can take you to the Paymaster's Office in HQ Company; they'll change your ackers and see to your kit." And just to round off the civilities I added: "My name's MacNeill, by the way, and I'm a platoon commander, not a bloody dragoman."

Which was insubordination, but if you'd seen that sardonic eyebrow and God-like profile you'd have said it too. Again, it didn't faze him; he actually chuckled.

"I stand rebuked. MacNeill, eh?" He glanced at my campaign ribbon. "What were you in Burma?"

"Other rank."

"Well, obviously, since you're only a second-lieutenant now. What kind of other rank?"

"Well . . . sniper-scout, Black Cat Division. Later on I was a section leader. Why . . . sir?"

"Black Cats, eh? God Almighty's Own. Were you at Imphal?"

"Not in the Boxes. Irrawaddy Crossing, Meiktila, Sittang Bend—"

"And you haven't got a measly fifty lire for a poor broken-down old soldier? Well, the hell with you, young MacNeill," said this astonishing fellow, and seated himself in the ghari again. "I'd heap coals of fire on you by offering you a lift, but your platoon are probably waiting for you to stop their motor. Bash on, MacNeill, before they seize up! Officers' mess, Abdul!" And he drove off with an airy wave.

"Hadn't you better report to H.Q.?" I called after him, but he was through the gate by then, leaving me nonplussed but not a little relieved; giving lip to captains wasn't my usual line, but he hadn't turned regimental, fortunately.

"Whit the hell was yon?" demanded Sergeant Telfer, who had been an entranced spectator.

"You tell me," I said. "Ballater Bertie, by the look of him." For he had, indeed, the air of those who command the guard at Ballater Station, conducting Royalty with drawn broadsword and white spats. And yet he'd been wearing an M.M. ribbon, which signified service in the ranks. I remarked on this to Telfer, who sniffed as only a Glaswegian can, and observed that whoever the newcomer might be, he was a heid-case – which means an eccentric.

That was the battalion's opinion, formed before Captain Errol had been with us twenty-four hours. He had driven straight to the mess, which was empty of customers at that time of day, smooth-talked the mess sergeant into paying the ghari out of bar receipts, made free with the Tallisker unofficially reserved for the Medical Officer, parked himself unerringly in the second-in-command's favourite chair, and whiled away the golden afternoon with the *Scottish Field*. Discovered and gently rebuked by the Adjutant for not reporting his arrival in the proper form, he had laughed apologetically and asked what time dinner was, and before the Adjutant, an earnest young Englishman, could wax properly indignant he had found himself, by some inexplicable process, buying Errol a gin and tonic.

"I can't fathom it," he told me, with the pained expression he usually reserved for descriptions of his putting. "One minute I was tearing small strips off the chap, and the next you know I was saying 'What's yours?' and filling him in on the social scene. Extraordinary."

Having found myself within an ace of bell-hopping for Captain Errol by the same mysterious magic, I sympathised. Who was he, anyway, I asked, and the Adjutant frowned.

"Dunno, exactly. Nor why we've got him. He's been up in Palestine lately, and just from something the Colonel said I have the impression he's been in some sort of turmoil – Errol, I mean. That type always is," said the Adjutant, like a dowager discussing a fallen woman. "Wouldn't be surprised if he was an I-man."

"I" is Intelligence, and the general feeling in line regiments is that you can keep it; I-men are disturbing influences best confined to the higher echelons, where they can pursue their clandestine careers and leave honest soldiers in peace. Attached to a battalion, they can be unsettling.

And Captain Errol was all of that. As he had begun, with the Adjutant and me, so he went on, causing ripples on our placid regimental surface which eventually turned into larger waves. One of the former, for example, occurred on his first night in the mess when, within half an hour of their first acquaintance, he addressed the Colonel as "skipper". It caused a brief silence which Errol himself didn't seem to notice; officially, you see, there are no ranks in the mess, but junior officers (of whom captains are only the most senior) normally call the head man "sir", especially when he is such a redoubtable bald eagle as our Colonel was. "Skipper" was close to the edge of impertinence – but it was said so easily and naturally that he got away with it. In fact, I think the Colonel rather liked it.

That, it soon became plain, was Errol's secret. Like his notorious namesake, he had great charm and immense style; partly it was his appearance, which was commanding, and his war record – the family of Highland regiments is a tight little news network, and many of the older men had heard of him as a fighting soldier – but most of it was just personality. He was casual, cocky, even insolent, but with a gift of disarmament, and even those who found his conceit and familiarity irritating (as the older men did) seemed almost flattered when he gave them his attention – I've seen the Senior Major, a grizzled veteran with the disposition of a liverish rhino, grinning sourly as Errol teased him. When he was snubbed, he didn't seem to notice; the eyebrow would give an amused flicker, no more.

The youngest subalterns thought him a hell of a fellow, of course, not least because he had no side with them; rank meant nothing to Errol, up or down. The Jocks, being canny judges, were rather wary of him, while taking advantage of his informality so far as they thought it safe; their word for him was "gallus", that curious Scots adjective which means a mixture of reckless, extrovert, and indifferent. On balance, he was not over-popular with Jocks or officers, especially among the elders, but even they held him in a certain grudging respect. None of which seemed to matter to Errol in the least.

I heard various verdicts on him in the first couple of weeks.

"I think he's a Bad News Type," said the Adjutant judicially, "but there's no doubt he's a character."

"Insufferable young pup," was the Senior Major's verdict. "Why the devil must he use that blasted cigarette holder, like a damned actor?" When it was pointed out that most of us used them, to keep the sweat off our cigarettes, the Major remarked unreasonably: "Not the way he does. Damned affectation."

"I like him," said plump and genial Major Bakie. "He can be dashed funny when he wants. Breath of fresh air. My wife likes him, too."

40

"Captain Errol," observed the Padre, who was the most charitable of men, "is a very interesting chentleman. What d'ye say, Lachlan?"

"Like enough," said the M.O. "I wouldnae let him near my malt, my money, or my maidservant."

"See him, he's sand-happy. No' a' there," I heard Private McAuslan informing his comrades. "See when he wis Captain o' the Week, an' had tae inspect ma rifle on guard? He looks doon the barrel, and says: 'I seem to see through a glass darkly.' Whit kind o' patter's that, Fletcher? Mind you, he didnae pit me on a charge, an' me wi' a live round up the spout. Darkie woulda nailed me tae the wall." (So I would, McAuslan.)

"Errol? A chanty-wrastler," said Fletcher – which, from that crafty young soldier, was interesting. A chanty-wrastler is a poseur, and unreliable.

"Too dam' sure of himself by half," was the judgment of the second-in-command. "We can do without his sort."

The Colonel rubbed tobacco between his palms in his thoughtful way, and said nothing.

Personally, I'd met plenty I liked better, but it seemed to me there was a deeper prejudice against Errol than he deserved, bouncy tigger though he was. Some of it might be explained by his service record which, it emerged, was sensational, and not all on the credit side. According to the Adjutant's researches, he had been commissioned in the Territorials in '39, and had escaped mysteriously from St Valéry, where the rest of his unit had gone into the P.O.W. bag ("there were a few heads wagged about that, apparently"). Later he had fought with distinction in the Far East, acquiring a Military Cross ("a real one, not one of your up-with-the-rations jobs") with the Chindits.

"And then," said the Adjutant impressively, "he got himself cashiered. Yes, busted – all the way down. It seems he was in charge of a train-load of wounded, somewhere in Bengal, and there was some foul-up and they were shunted into a siding. Some of the chaps were in a bad way, and Errol raised hell with the local R.T.O., who got stroppy with him, and Errol hauled out his revolver and shot the inkpot off the R.T.O.'s desk, and threatened to put the next one between his eyes. Well, you can't do that, can you? So it was a court-martial, and march out Private Errol."

"But he's a captain now," I said. "How on earth—?"

"*Chubbarao*, and listen to this," said the Adjutant. "He finished up late in the war with those special service johnnies who were turned loose in the Balkans – you know, helping the partisans, blowing up bridges and things and slaughtering Huns with cheese-wire by night. Big cloak-and-dagger stuff, and he did hell of a well at it, and Tito kissed him on both cheeks and said he'd never seen the like—"

"So that's where he got the M.M."

"And the Balkan gongs, and the upshot of it was that he was re-commissioned. It happens, now and then. And of late he's been undercover in Palestine." The Adjutant scratched his fair head. "Something odd there – rumours about terrorist suspects being knocked about pretty badly, and one hanging himself in his cell. Nasty business. Anyway, friend Errol was shipped out, p.d.q., and now we're landed with him. Oh, and another thing – he's to be Intelligence Officer, as if we needed one. Didn't I say he was the type?" The Adjutant sniffed. "Well, at least it should keep him out of everyone's hair."

The disclosures of Errol's irregular past were not altogether surprising, and they helped to explain his *alakeefik* attitude and brass neck. Plainly he was capable of anything, and having hit both the heights and the depths was not to be judged as ordinary mortals are.

His duties as I-man were vague, and kept him out of the main stream of battalion life, which may have been as well, for as a soldier he was a contradictory mixture. In some things he was expert: a splendid shot, superb athlete, and organised to the hilt in the field. On parade, saving his immaculate turn-out, he was a disaster: when he was Captain of the Week and had to mount the guard, I suffered agonies at his elbow in my capacity as orderly officer, whispering commands and telling him what to do next while he turned the ceremony into a shambles. Admittedly, since McAuslan was in the guard, we were handicapped from the start, but I believe Errol could have reduced the Household Cavalry to chaos – and been utterly indifferent about it. Doing well or doing badly, it was all one to him; he walked off that guard-mounting humming and swinging his walking-stick, debonair as be-damned, and advising the outraged Regimental Sergeant-Major that the drill needed tightening up a bit. (He actually addressed him as "Major", which is one of the things that are never done. An R.S.M. is "Mr So-and-so".)

Being casual in all things, he was naturally accident-prone, but even that did nothing to deflate him, since the victim was invariably someone else. He wrecked the Hudson Terraplane belonging to Lieutenant Grant, and walked away without a scratch; Grant escaped with a broken wrist, but there was no restoring the car which had been its owner's pride.

He was equally lethal on blue water. Our garrison town boasted a magnificent Mediterranean bay, strewn with wrecks from the war, and sailing small boats was a popular pastime among the local smart set; Errol took to it in a big way, and from all accounts it was like having a demented Blackbeard loose about the waterfront. I gather there is a sailing etiquette about giving way and not getting athwart other people's hawses, of which he was entirely oblivious; the result was a series of bumps, scrapes, collisions, and furious protests from outraged voyagers, culminating in a regatta event in which he dismasted one competitor, caused another to capsize, and added insult to injury by winning handsomely. That he was promptly disqualified did not lower the angle of his jaunty cigarette-holder by a degree when he turned up at the prize-giving, bronzed and dashing, to applaud the garrison beauty, Ellen Ramsay, when she received the Ladies' Cup. She it was who christened him the Sea Hog – and was his dinner companion for many nights thereafter, to the chagrin of Lieutenant MacKenzie who, until Errol's arrival, had been the fair Ellen's favoured beau.

None of which did much for Errol's popularity. Nor, strangely enough, did an odd episode which I thought was rather to his credit. The command boxing tournament took place, and as sports officer I had to organise our regimental gladiators – which meant calling for volunteers, telling them to knock off booze and smoking, letting them attend to their own sparring and training in the M.T. shed, and seeing that they were sober and (initially) upright on opening night. If that seems perfunctory, I was not a boxer myself, and had no illusions about being Yussel Jacobs when it came to management. Let them get into the ring and lay about them, while I crouched behind their corner, crying encouragement and restraining the seconds from joining in.

The tournament lasted three nights, and in winning his semifinal our heavyweight star, Private McGuigan, the Gorbals Goliath, broke a finger. Personally I think he did it on purpose to avoid meeting the other finalist, one Captain Stock, a terrible creature of blood and iron who had flattened all his opponents with unimagined ferocity; he was a relic of the Stone Age who had found his way into the Army Physical Training Corps, this Stock, and I wouldn't have gone near him with a whip, a gun, and a chair. Primitive wasn't the word; he made McAuslan and Wee Wullie look like Romantic poets.

Left to find a substitute willing to offer himself for sacrifice at the hands of this Behemoth, I got no takers at all, and then someone said he had heard that Errol used to box a bit, and must be about the right weight. There was enthusiastic support for this suggestion, especially from the older officers, so I sought the man out in his room, where he was reclining with a cool drink at his elbow, shooting moths with an air pistol – and hitting them, too.

"What makes you think I could take Stock, if you'll pardon the expression?" he wondered, when I put it to him. "Or doesn't that matter, as long as we're represented?"

"Someone in the mess said you used to be pretty useful . . ."

"Did they now? That's handsome of them." He grinned at me sardonically. "Who proposed me – Cattenach?" This was the second-in-command, Errol's principal critic. "Never mind. It's not on, Dand, thanks all the same. I haven't boxed for ages. Too much like work."

"There's no one else in the battalion," I said subtly.

"Stop waving the regimental colours at me." He picked off a large moth on the wing, bringing down a shower of plaster. "Anyway, I'm an interloper. Let Cattenach take him on if he's so damned keen; God knows he's big enough. No, you'll just have to tell 'em I've retired."

So I reported failure, and there was disappointment, although no one was daft enough to suggest that Errol was scared. The Adjutant, who was a romantic, speculated that he had probably killed a man in the ring – his fiancée's brother, for choice – and vowed never to box again; he would have joined the Foreign Legion, insisted the Adjutant, if it hadn't been for the war. Others joined in these fine flights, and no one noticed the Colonel sauntering out of the mess, but later that evening he told me casually that I could pencil in Errol for the final; he had been persuaded, said the Colonel, filling his pipe in a contented way. Knowing his fanaticism where the battalion's credit was concerned, I wondered what pressure he had applied, and concluded that he probably hadn't needed any, just his gentle, fatherly insistence which I knew of old. He could have talked a salmon out of its pool, the same Colonel – and of course the possibility that his man might get half-killed wouldn't even cross his mind.

It crossed mine when I saw Errol and Stock face to muzzle in the ring; so might Adonis have looked in the presence of a silverback gorilla. Stock stood half a head taller, two stone heavier, and about a foot thicker, especially round the brow. He came out at the bell like a Panzer tank – and Errol moved round him as though on rollers, weaving and feinting until he'd sized him up, and then began systematically left-handing him to death. It was Carpentier to the town drunk; Stock clubbed and rushed and never got near him until the second round, when he had the ill-judgment to land a kidney-punch. Errol came out of the clinch looking white and wicked, and thereafter took Stock apart with clinical savagery. The referee stopped it in the third, with Stock bloodied and out on his feet; Errol hadn't a hair out of place, and I doubt if he'd been touched more than half a dozen times.

But as I said, he got no credit from that fight. It had been so one-sided that all the sympathy was for the battered Stock, and there was even a feeling that Errol had been over-brutal to a man who wasn't in his class as a boxer. Which was unfair, since he had been reluctant to fight in the first place – my guess is that he knew exactly how good he was, and that Stock would be no contest. But if he compared the polite clapping as he left the ring with the thunder of applause for his groggy but gamely smiling opponent, it didn't seem to worry him; he strolled back to the changing-room cool and unruffled as ever.

It was immediately after this that he finally fell from grace altogether, and the mixed feelings of the mess hardened into positive dislike. Two things happened to show him at his worst; neither was earth-shattering in itself, but in each case he displayed such a cynical indifference that even his friends could find no excuses.

In the first instance, he stole another man's girl – and it wasn't a case of cutting out someone like MacKenzie, the battalion Lothario, with Ellen Ramsay, whose admirers were legion (including even the unlikely Private McAuslan, whose wooing I have described elsewhere). Boy met, dated, and parted from girl with bewildering speed in post-war garrisons, and no harm done; Errol himself must have been involved with half the nurses, A.T.S., Wrens, and civilian females, and no one thought twice, except to note jealously that while the rest of us had to pursue, he seemed to draw them like a magnet.

But the case of Sister Jean was different. She was a flashing-eyed Irish redhead, decorative even by the high standard of the hospital staff, and her attachment to a U.S. pilot at the bomber base was the real thing, what the Adjutant called Poignant Passion, engagement ring, wedding date fixed, and all – until Errol moved in on the lady. I was on detachment at Fort Yarhuna during the crisis, but according to MacKenzie it had started with casual cheek-to-cheek stuff on the dance-floor at the Uaddan Club, progressing to dates, picnics, and sailing-trips on Errol's dinghy while the American was absent on his country's service, dropping sandbags on the desert (I quote MacKenzie). In brief, Jean had been beglamoured, her fiancé had objected, a lovers' quarrel had ensued with high words flying in Irish and American, the ring had been returned, the pilot had got himself posted to Italy in dudgeon, and the hapless patients in Sister Jean's ward were learning what life was like under the Empress Theodora.

"Talk about hell hath no fury," said MacKenzie. "She's lobbing out enemas like a mad thing. You see, not only is her romance with Tex kaput, *bus*, washed up; on top of that, the unspeakable Errol has given her the gate and is pushing around the new Ensa bint – who is a piece of all right, I have to admit. What women see in him," he added irritably, "I'm shot if I know. The man's a tick, a suede-shoe artist, a Semiramis Hotel creeper of the lowest type."

"Didn't anyone try to steer him away from Jean?" I asked, thinking of the Colonel, who when it came to intervening in his junior officers' love lives could have given Lady Bracknell a head start. "Why didn't you tackle him yourself?"

"Come off it. Remember what happened to Stock? Actually,

Ellen Ramsay did get stuck into him at one stage . . . gosh, she's a honey, that girl," said MacKenzie, smiling dreamily. "I think I'll take her grouse-shooting when we go home. You know, dazzle her with Perthshire . . . Eh? Oh, well, she tore strips off Errol, and he just laughed and said: 'Why, darling, I didn't know you cared,' and swanned off, cool as be-damned, to take Jean swimming. And now, having wrecked her future, and Tex's, he goes around blithe as a bird, as though nothing had happened. Yes – a total tick, slice him where you will."

A fair assessment, on the face of it, and the temperature dropped noticeably in the mess when Errol was present, not that he seemed aware of it. Otherwise the incident was closed; for one thing, there were far more urgent matters to think about just then. Political trouble was beginning to brew in our former Italian colony, with noisy nationalist demonstrations, stoning of police posts by Arab gangs, and the prospect that we would be called out to support the civil administration. If there's going to be active service, the last thing you need is discord in the mess.

Even so, Errol's next gaffe came close to blowing the lid off with his bête noire, Cattenach, the second-in-command; it was the nearest thing I ever saw to a brawl between brother-officers, and all because of Errol's bloody-minded disregard for other people's feelings. He had set off early one morning to shoot on the salt flats outside the town, and came breezing in just as we were finishing breakfast, calling for black coffee and telling Bennet-Bruce that his shotgun (which Errol had borrowed, typically) was throwing left. Bennet-Bruce asked if he'd had any luck.

"Nothing to write to the *Field* about," said Errol, buttering toast. "In fact, sweet dam'-all, except for a couple of kites near the Armoury. Weird-looking things."

Cattenach lowered his paper. "Did you say near the Armoury? Where are these birds?"

"Where I left them, of course; somewhere around the Armoury wall. They weren't worth keeping."

Cattenach looked thoughtful, but went back to his paper, and it wasn't until lunchtime that he returned to the subject. He brought his drink across from the bar and stopped in front of Errol's chair, waiting until he had finished telling his latest story and had become aware that Cattenach was regarding him stonily. The second-in-command was a lean, craggy, normally taciturn man with a rat-trap mouth that made him look like one of the less amiable Norman barons.

"You may be interested to know," he said curtly, "that the 'kites' you shot this morning were the Brigadier's pet hawks."

There was a startled silence, in which the Padre said: "Oh, cracky good gracious!", and Errol cocked an incredulous eyebrow. "What are you talking about – hawks? Since when do hawks stooge around loose, like crows!"

"They were tame hawks – something unique, I believe," said Cattenach, enjoying himself in his own grim fashion. "A gift to the Brigadier from King Idris, after the desert campaign. Quite irreplaceable, of course, as well as being priceless. And you shot them. Congratulations."

Well, you and I or any normal person would at this point have lowered the head in the hands, giving little whimpering cries punctuated by stricken oaths and appeals for advice. Not Errol, though; he just downed his drink and observed lightly:

"Well, why didn't he keep them on a leash? I thought it was usual to put hoods over their heads."

We stared at the man, and someone protested: "Oh, come off it, Errol!", while Cattenach went crimson and began to inflate.

"Is that all you've got to say?" he demanded, and Errol regarded him with maddening calm.

"What d'you expect me to say? I'm sorry, of course." If he was he certainly didn't sound it. "I'll send the old boy a note of apology." He gave Cattenach a nod that was almost dismissive. "Okay?"

"Just . . . that?" growled Cattenach, ready to burst.

"I can't very well do anything else," said Errol, and picked up a magazine. "Unless you expect me to rend my garments." To do him justice, I believe that if anyone else had brought him the glad news, he'd have shown more concern, but he wasn't giving Cattenach that satisfaction – just his cool half-smile, and the second-in-command had to struggle to keep a grip on himself in the face of that dumb insolence. He took a breath, and then said with deliberation:

"The trouble with you, and what makes you such an unpleasant regimental liability, is that while most of us couldn't care more, you just couldn't care less."

No one had ever heard Cattenach, who was normally a quiet soul, talk with such controlled contempt – and in the mess, of all places. A little flush appeared on Errol's cheek, and he rose from his chair, but only to look Cattenach in the eye and say:

"You know, that's extremely well put. I think I'll enter it in the mess book."

That was when I thought Cattenach was going to hit him – or try to, because Errol, for all his composure, was balanced like a cat. Suddenly it was very ugly, the Padre was making anxious noises, and the Adjutant was starting forward, and then Cattenach turned abruptly on his heel and stalked out. There was a toe-curling silence – and of course I had to open my big mouth, heaven knows why, unless I thought it was time to raise the conversation to a higher plane.

"Why can't you bloody well wrap up, just for once?" I demanded, and was told by the Adjutant to shut up. "I think you've said enough, too," he told Errol. "Right – who's for lunch?"

"I am, for one," said Errol, unabashed. "Drama always gives me an appetite," and he sauntered off to the dining-room, leaving us looking at each other, the Padre muttering about the pride of Lucifer, and the M.O., after a final inhalation of the Tallisker, voicing the general thought.

"Yon's a bad man," he said. "Mercy is not in him."

That was a fact, I thought. Not only had he shown a callous disregard for the feelings of the Brigadier, bereaved of his precious pets, he had strained the egalitarian conventions of the mess to the limit in his behaviour to Cattenach – who, mind you, had been making a meal of his own dislike for Errol. It was all enough to make one say "Tach!", as my grandmother used to exclaim in irritation, and lunch was taken in general ill-temper – except for Errol, who ate a tranquil salad and lingered over his coffee.

And then such trivia ceased to matter, for at 2.15 came the sudden alarm call from the Police Commissioner to say that the unrest which had been simmering in the native quarter had suddenly burst into violence: a mob of Arab malcontents and *bazaar-wallahs* were rioting in the Suk, pillaging shops and fire-raising; one of the leading nationalist agitators, Marbruk es-Salah, was haranguing a huge gathering near the Yassid Market, and it looked only a matter of time before they would be spilling out of the Old City and rampaging towards the European suburbs. Aid to the civil power was a matter of urgency – which meant that at 2.45 the two three-ton trucks bearing the armed might of 12 Platoon pulled up on the great dusty square east of the Kantara Bridge, and I reviewed the force with which I was expected to plug that particular outlet from the native quarter.

In theory, the plan for containing unrest was simple. The Old City, an impossible warren of tall crumbling buildings and hundreds of crooked streets and narrow alleys, spread out like a huge fan from the waterfront; beyond the semi-circular edge of the fan lay the European suburbs of the Italian colonial era, girdling the squalid Old City from sea to sea in a luxurious crescent of apartment buildings, bungalows, shops, restaurants, and broad streets – a looter's paradise for the teeming thousands of the Old City's inhabitants, if they ever invaded in force. To make sure they didn't, the 24 infantry platoons of our battalion and the Fusiliers were supposed to block every outlet from the Old City to the New Town, and since these were innumerable, careful disposition of forces was vital.

Kantara was an easy one, since here there was an enormous ditch hemming the native town like a moat, and the only way across was the ancient bridge (which is what Kantara means) which we were guarding. It was a structure of massive stones which had been there before the Caesars, twenty feet broad between low parapets, and perhaps twice as long. From where I stood on the open ground at its eastern end, I could look across the bridge at a peaceful enough scene: a wide market-place in which interesting Orientals were going about their business of loafing, wailing, squatting in the dust, or snoozing in the shadows of the great rickety tenements and ruined walls of the Old City. Behind me were the broad, palm-lined boulevards of the modern resort area, with dazzling white apartments and pleasant gardens, a couple of hotels and restaurants, and beyond them the hospital and the beach club. It looked like something out of a travel brochure, with a faint drift of Glenn Miller on the afternoon air – and then you turned back to face the ancient stronghold of the Barbary Corsairs, a huge festering slum crouched like a malignant genie above the peaceful European suburb, and felt thankful for the separating moat-ditch with only that single dusty causeway across it.

"Nae bother," said Sergeant Telfer. Like me, he was thinking that thirty Jocks with fifty rounds apiece could have held that bridge against ten times the native population – provided they were empowered to shoot, that is. Which, if it came to the point, would be up to me. But we both knew that was highly unlikely; by all accounts the trouble was at the western end of the Old City, where most of our troops were concentrated. Kantara was very much the soft option, which was presumably why one platoon had been deemed enough. They hadn't thought it worth while giving us a radio, even.

Since it was all quiet, I didn't form the platoon up, but showed them where, in the event of trouble, they would take up extended line, facing the bridge and about fifty yards from it, out of range of any possible missiles from beyond the ditch. Then they sat in the shade of the trucks, smoking and gossiping, while I prowled about, watching the market for any signs of disturbance, vaguely aware of the discussion on current affairs taking place behind me.

"Hi, Corporal Mackie, whit are the wogs gettin' het up aboot, then?"

"Independence." Mackie had been a civil servant, and was the platoon intellectual. "Self-government by their own political leaders. They don't like being under Allied occupation."

"Fair enough, me neither. Whit's stoppin' them?"

"You are, McAuslan. You're the heir to the pre-war Italian government. So do your shirt up and try to look like it."

"Me? Fat chance! The wogs can hiv it for me, sure'n they can, Fletcher? It's no' my parish. Hi, corporal, whit wey does the government no' let the wogs have it?"

"Because they'd make a bluidy mess o' it, dozy." This was Fletcher, who was a sort of Churchillian Communist. "They're no' fit tae run a mennodge. Look behind ye – that's civilisation. Then look ower there at that midden o' a toon; that's whit the wogs would make o' it. See?"

So much for Ibn Khaldun and the architects of the Alhambra. Some similar thought must have stirred McAuslan's strange mental processes, for he came out with a nugget which, frankly, I wouldn't have thought he knew.

51

"Haud on a minnit, Fletcher – it was wogs built the Pyramids, wisn't it? That's whit the Padre says. Aye, weel, there ye are. They cannae be that dumb."

"Those werenae wogs, ya mug! Those were Ancient Egyptians."

"An Egyptian's a wog! Sure'n he is. So don't gi' me the acid, Fletcher. Anyway, if Ah wis a wog, Ah wid dam' soon get things sortit oot aboot indamapendence. If Ah wis a wog—"

"That's a helluva insult tae wogs, right enough. Ah can just see ye! Hey, fellas, meet Abu ben McAuslan, the Red Shadow. Ye fancy havin' a harem, McAuslan? Aboot twenty belly-dancers like Big Aggie frae the Blue Heaven?" And Fletcher began to hum snake-charmer music, while his comrades speculated coarsely on McAuslan, Caliph of the Faithful, and I looked through the heat haze at the Old City, and thought about cool pints in the dim quiet of the mess ante-room.

It came, as it so often does, with daunting speed. There was a distant muttering from the direction of the Old City, like a wind getting up, and the market-place beyond the bridge was suddenly empty and still in the late afternoon sun. Then the muttering changed to a rising rumble of hurrying feet and harsh voices growing louder. I shouted to Telfer to fall in, and from the mouth of a street beyond the market-place a native police jeep came racing over the bridge. It didn't stop; I had a glimpse of a brown face, scared and staring, under a peaked cap, and then the jeep was gone in a cloud of dust, heading up into the New Town. So much for the civil power. The platoon were fanning out in open order, each man with his rifle and a canvas bandolier at his waist; they stood easy, and Telfer turned to me for orders. I was gazing across the bridge, watching Crisis arrive in a frightsome form, and realising with sudden dread that there was no one on God's green earth to deal with it, except me.

It's quite a moment. You're taking it easy, on a sunny afternoon, listening to the Jocks chaffing – and then out of the alleys two hundred yards away figures are hurrying, hundreds of them, converging into a great milling mob, yelling in unison, waving their fists, starting to move towards you. A menace beats off them that you can feel, dark glaring faces, sticks brandished, robes waving and feet churning up the dust in clouds before them, the rhythmic chanting sounding like a barbaric war-song –

and you fight down the panic and turn to look at the khaki line strung out either side of you, the young faces set under the slanted bonnets, the rifles at their sides, standing at ease – waiting for you. If you say the word, they'll shoot that advancing mob flat, and go on shooting, because that's what they're trained to do, for thirty bob a week – and if that doesn't stop the opposition, they'll stand and fight it out on the spot as long as they can, because that's part of the conscript's bargain, too. But it's entirely up to you – and there's no colonel or company commander to instruct or advise. And it doesn't matter if you've led a section in warfare, where there is no rule save survival; this is different, for these are not the enemy – by God, I thought, you could have fooled me; I may know it, but I'll bet they don't – they are civilians, and you must not shoot unless you have to, and only you can decide that, so make up your mind, Dand, and don't dawdle: you're getting nine quid a week, after all, so the least you can do is show some initiative.

"Charge magazines, Sar'nt Telfer! Corporals, watch those cut-offs! Mackie – if McAuslan gets one up the spout I'll blitz you! Here – I'll do it!" I grabbed McAuslan's rifle, jammed down the top round, closed the cut-off, rammed home the bolt, clicked the trigger, and thumbed on the safety-catch while he squawked indignantly that he could dae it, he wisnae stupid, him. I shoved his rifle into his hand and looked across the bridge again.

The rattle of the charging magazines had checked them for barely an instant; now they were coming on again, a solid mass of humanity choking the square, half-hidden by the dust they were raising. Out front there was a big thug in a white burnous and red tarboosh who turned to face the mob, chanting some slogan, before turning to lead them on, punching his arms into the air. There were banners waving in the front rank – and I knew this was no random gang of looters, but an organised horde bent on striking where they knew the forces of order were weakest – I had thirty Jocks between them and that peaceful suburb with its hotels and pleasant homes and hospital. Over their heads I could see smoke on the far side of the market . . .

"Fix bayonets, Sarn't Telfer!" I shouted, and on his command the long sword-blades zeeped out of the scabbards, the locking-rings clicked, and the hands cut away to the sides.

"Present!" and the thirty rifles with their glittering points went forward.

That stopped them, dead. The big thug threw up his arms, and they halted, yelling louder than ever and shaking fists and clubs, but they were still fifty yards from the bridge. They eddied to and fro, milling about, while the big burnous exhorted them, waving his arms – and I moved along the line, forcing myself to talk as quietly as the book says you must, saying the proper things in the proper order.

"Easy does it, children. Wait for it. If they start to come on, you stand fast, understand? Nobody moves – except Fletcher, Macrae, Duncan, and Souness. You four, when I say "Load!", will put one round up the spout – but don't fire! Not till I tell you." They had rehearsed it all before, the quartet of marksmen had been designated, but it all had to be repeated. "If I say 'Over their heads, fire!', you all take aim, but only those four will fire on the word. Got it? Right, wait for it . . . easy does it . . . take Blackie's name, Sarn't Telfer, his bayonet's filthy . . . wait for it . . ."

It's amazing how you can reassure yourself, by reassuring other people. I felt suddenly elated, and fought down the evil hope that we might have to fire in earnest – oh, that's an emotion that comes all too easily – and walked along the front of the line, looking at the faces – young and tight-lipped, all staring past me at the crowd, one or two sweating, a few Adam's apples moving, but not much. The chanting suddenly rose to a great yell, and the crowd was advancing again, but slowly this time, a few feet at a time, stopping, then coming on, the big burnous gesticulating to his followers, and then turning to stare in my direction. You bastard, I thought – you know what it's all about! We can fire over your head till we're blue in the face, but it won't stop you – you'll keep coming, calling our bluff, daring us to let fly. Right, son, if anyone gets it, you will . . .

They were coming steadily now, but still slowly; I judged their distance from the bridge and shouted: "Four men – load! Remainder, stand fast! Wait for it . . ."

A stone came flying from the crowd, falling well short, but followed by a shower of missiles kicking up the dust ahead of us. I walked five slow paces out in front of the platoon – believe it or not, that can make a mob hesitate – and waited; when the first stone reached me, I would give the order to fire over their heads. If they still kept coming, I would take a rifle and shoot the big burnous, personally, wounding if possible – and if that didn't do it, I would order the four marksmen to take out four rioters. Then, if they charged us, I would order rapid fire into the crowd . . .

By today's standards, you may think that atrocious. Well, think away. My job was to save that helpless suburb from the certain death and destruction that mob would wreak if they broke through. So retreat was impossible on that head, never mind that soldiers cannot run from a riot and if I ordered them to retire I'd never be able to look in a mirror again. But above all these good reasons was the fact that if I let that horde of yelling maniacs reach us, some of my Jocks would die – knifed or clubbed or trampled lifeless, and I hadn't been entrusted with thirty young Scottish lives in order to throw them away. That was the real clincher, and why I would loose up to three hundred rounds rapid into our attackers if I had to. It gets terribly simple when you're looking it in the face.

The shouting rose to a mad crescendo, they were a bare thirty yards from the bridge, the burnous was leaping like a dervish, you could sense the rush coming, and without looking round I shouted:

"Four men – over their heads . . . fire!"

It crashed out like one report. One of the flag-poles jerked crazily – Fletcher playing Davy Crockett – and the crowd reared back like a horse at a hedge. For a splendid moment I thought they were going to scatter, but they didn't: the big burnous was playing a stormer, grabbing those nearest, rallying them, urging them forward with voice and gesture. My heart sank as I took Telfer's rifle, for I was going to have to nail that one, unarmed civilian that he was, and I found myself remembering my awful closing line: "Well, that's that" from that ghastly play in Bangalore . . .

"Having fun, Dand?" said a voice at my elbow, and there was Errol beside me, cupping his hands as he lit a cigarette. Thank God, reinforcements at the last minute – and then I saw the solitary jeep parked by the trucks. Nobody else. He drew on his cigarette, surveying the crowd.

"What'll you do?" he asked conversationally – no suggestion of assuming command, you notice; what would *I* do.

55

"Shoot that big beggar in the leg!"

"You might miss," he said, "and sure as fate we'd find a dead nun on the ground afterwards. Or a four-year-old orphan." He gave me his lazy grin. "I think we can do better than that."

"What the hell are you on, Errol?" I demanded, in some agitation. "Look, they're going to—"

"Not to panic. I'd say we've got about thirty seconds." He swung round. "You, you, and you – run to my jeep! Get the drum of signal wire, the cutters, the mortar box, and double back here – now! Move!"

"Are you taking command?"

"God, you're regimental. I'll bet you were a pig of a lance-jack. Here, have a fag – go on, you clot, the wogs are watching, wondering what the hell we're up to."

The lean brown face with its trim Colman moustache was smiling calmly under the cocked bonnet; his hand was rock-steady as he held out the cigarette-case – it was one of those hammered silver jobs you got in Indian bazaars, engraved with a map and erratic spelling. And he was right: the yelling had died down, and they were watching us and wondering . . .

Three Jocks came running, two with the heavy drum of wire between them on its axle, the third (McAuslan, who else?) labouring with the big metal mortar box, roaring to them tae haud on, he couldnae manage the bluidy thing, damn it tae hell . . .

"Listen, Dand," said Errol. "Run like hell to the bridge, unrolling the wire. When you get there, cut it. Open the mortar box – it's empty – stick the end of the wire inside, close the lid. Got it? Then scatter like billy-be-damned. Move!"

Frankly, I didn't get it. He must be doolaly. But if the Army teaches you anything, it's to act on the word, no questions asked – which is how great victories are won (and great disasters caused).

"Come on!" I yelled, and went for the bridge like a stung whippet, followed by the burdened trio, McAuslan galloping in the rear demanding to know whit the hell was gaun on. Well, I didn't know, for one – all I had room for was the appalling knowledge that I was running straight towards several hundred angry *bazaar-wallahs* who were bent on pillage and slaughter. Fortunately, there isn't time to think in fifty yards, or to notice anything except that the ragged ranks ahead seemed to be stricken immobile, if not silent: the big burnous, out in front, was stock-still and staring, while his followers raged behind him, presumably echoing McAuslan's plea for enlightenment. I had a picture of yelling, hostile black faces as I skidded to a standstill at the mouth of the bridge; the two Jocks with the wire were about ten yards behind, closing fast as they unreeled the long shining thread behind them; staggering with them, his contorted face mouthing horribly over the mortar box clasped in his arms, was Old Insanitary himself. He won by a short head, sprawling headlong and depositing the box at my feet.

"The cutters!" I snapped, as he grovelled, blaspheming, in the dust. "The cutters, McAuslan!"

"Whit cutters?" he cried, crouching like Quasimodo in the pillory, and then his eyes fell on the menacing but still irresolute mob a scant thirty yards away. "Mither o' Goad! Wull ye look at yon? The cutters – Ah've goat them! Here th'are, sur – Ah've goat them!" He pawed at his waist – and the big wire cutters, which he had thrust into the top of his shorts for convenient carriage, slid out of view. And it is stark truth: one handle emerged from one leg of his shorts, the second handle from the other.

I'm not sure what I said, but I'll bet only dogs could hear it. Fortunately MacLeod, one of the wire-carriers, was a lad of resource and rare self-sacrifice; he hurled himself at McAuslan, thrust his hand down the back of his shorts, and yanked viciously. There was an anguished wail and a fearsome rending of khaki, the cutters were dragged free, and as I grabbed them in one hand and the wire in the other, McAuslan's recriminations seemed to fill the afternoon. He was, it appeared, near ruined, an' see his bluidy troosers; there wis nae need for it, MacLood, an' ye'll pey for them an' chance it, handless teuchter that ye are . . .

For some reason that I'll never understand, it steadied me. I clipped the wire, and as I unsnapped the mortar box catches it dawned on me what Errol was up to, the lunatic – and it seemed only sensible to lift the lid slowly, push in the wire, fumble artistically in the interior before closing the lid as though it were made of porcelain, and spare two seconds for a calculating look at the bewildered mob beyond the bridge. To my horror, they were advancing – I looked back at the platoon, fifty yards off, and sure enough Errol was kneeling at the other end of the wire, which was attached to a metal container – a petrol jerry-can, as it turned out. He had one hand poised as though to work a plunger; with the other he waved an urgent signal.

"Get out of it!" I yelled, and as MacLeod and his mate scattered and ran I seized McAuslan by the nape of his unwashed neck, running him protesting from the bridge before throwing him and myself headlong.

It worked. You had only to put yourself in the shoes of Burnous and Co. to see that it was bound to. We weren't wiring things up for the good of their health, they must have reasoned: that sinister mortar box lying on the bridge must be packed with death and destruction. When I had rolled over and got the sand out of my eyes they were in full retreat across the market square, a great disordered rabble intent on getting as far as possible from that unkown menace. In a few seconds an army of rioters had been turned into a rout – and the man responsible was sitting at his ease on the jerry-can, giving me an airy wave of his cigarette-holder as I trudged back to the platoon.

"You mad son-of-a-bitch!" I said, with deep respect, and he touched his bonnet in acknowledgement.

"Psychology, laddie. Not nearly as messy as shooting poor wee wogs, you bloodthirsty subaltern, you. That would never have done – not on top of the Brigadier's hawks. Not all in one day. Cattenach would have had kittenachs." He chuckled and stood up, smoothing his immaculate khaki drill, and shaded his eyes to look at the distant remnant of the riot milling disconsolately on the far side of the market-place.

"Aye, weel, they'll no' be back the day," he said, imitating a Glasgow wifey. "So. Where will they go next, eh? Tell me that, MacNeill of Barra – or of Great Western Road, W.2. Where . . . will . . . they . . . go?"

"Home?" I suggested.

"Don't you believe it, cock. Marbruk wasn't with 'em – he'll still be holding forth to the main body down at Yassid. Oh, if we'd lost the bridge he'd have been over sharp enough, with about twenty thousand angry wogs at his back. But now . . . I wonder."

I was still digesting the outrageous bluff he'd pulled. I indicated the jerry-can and the string of wire running to the bridge. "Do you usually carry that kind of junk in your jeep?" I asked, and he patted me on the shoulder, as with a half-wit.

"I'm the Intelligence Officer, remember? All-wise, all-knowing, all full of bull. Oh, look – soldiers!" Half a dozen Fusilier trucks were speeding down the New Town boulevard towards us, and Errol shook his head in admiration as he climbed into his jeep.

"Locking the stable door," said he, and winked at me. "I'd better go and see which one they've left open. Buy you a drink at Renucci's, nine o'clock, okay?" He waved and revved off with a horrific grinding of metal, changing gears with his foot, which takes lots of practice.

When I showed the Fusilier Company Commander the mortar box with its fake wire he didn't believe it at first, and then congratulated me warmly; when I told him it had been Errol's idea he grunted and said, "Oh, him", which I thought both ungrammatical and ungrateful, and told me I was to withdraw my platoon to the hospital. So I passed the remainder of that fateful day chatting up the nursing staff, drinking tea, and listening with interest to Private McAuslan telling Fletcher that it was a bluidy good job that bomb hadnae gone off on the bridge, because me an' Darkie an' MacLood an' Dysart would hiv' got blew up, sure'n we would.

"It wisnae a bomb, ye bap-heid! He wis kiddin' the wogs. There wis nothin' tae it."

"Are you tellin' me, Fletcher? Ah wis there! Ah cairrit the bluidy thing! Help ma Goad, if Ah'd known! That man Errol's a menace, so he is; he coulda goat us a' killed, me 'an Darkie an' MacLood an' Dysart . . ." You can fool some of the people all of the time.

It was only when the alert was over, and I had sent the platoon back to barracks with Telfer and foregathered at Renucci's for the promised drink with Errol, that I learned what had been happening elsewhere. It had been high drama, and the clientele of Renucci's bar and grill were full of it. After our episode at the bridge, things had fallen out as Errol had foreseen: Marbruk es-Salah, after whipping up his followers at Yassid Market, had launched them at dusk through the old Suk slave-market in an attempt to invade the business area of the New Town, two miles away from Kantara. Part of the Suk had been burned and the rest pillaged, and the enormous crowd would undoubtedly have broken out with a vengeance if they had not suddenly lost their leader.

"Nobody seems to know exactly what happened," a stout civilian was telling the bar, "except that Marbruk was obviously making for the weakest point in the security cordon – you won't credit it, but there wasn't even a constable guarding the Suk Gate. God knows what would have happened if they'd got beyond it; sheer devastation and half the New Town up in smoke, I expect. Anyway, that's when Marbruk got shot—"

"But you said there were no troops there," someone protested.

"Nor were there. It seems he was shot *inside* the Suk. What with the uproar and the fact that it was dark, even his immediate henchmen didn't realise it at first, and when they did – sheer pandemonium. But they'd lost all sense of direction, thank God – otherwise we wouldn't be standing here, I daresay."

"Who on earth did it? Did the police get him?"

"You're joking, old boy! In the Suk, during a riot, at night? I should think our gallant native constabulary are too busy drinking the assassin's health."

"I heard they got Marbruk's body out . . ."

I lost the rest of it in the noise, and at that moment Errol slipped on to the stool next to me and asked what I was drinking.

"Antiquary – hang on, I want to hear this."

"Evening, Carlo." Errol rapped the bar. "Antiquary and Glenfiddich and two waters, at your good pleasure." He seemed in fine fettle, glancing bright-eyed over the crowd. "What's to do?"

"Marbruk's dead."

"You don't say? That's a turn-up." He whistled softly, fitting a cigarette into his holder. "How'd it happen?"

I indicated the stout civilian, who was continuing.

". . . probably one of his political rivals. You know what they're like – pack of jackals. With Marbruk gone, there'll be a fine scramble among his lieutenants."

"It wasn't one of the gang with him," said a police captain. "Burgess saw the body and talked to informers. Shot twice, head and heart, almost certainly with a rifle, from a roof-top."

"Good God! A sniper? Doesn't sound like a *bazaar-wallah*!"

"Whoever it was, here's to him," said the stout civilian. "He probably saved the town in the nick of time."

Our whisky arrived and Errol studied the pale liquid with satisfaction. "First today. *Slàinte mhath.*" He sipped contentedly. "Yes, that's the good material. Had dinner?"

"Too late for me, thanks. I'll have a sandwich in the mess. I've got a report to write."

"How Horatius kept the bridge?" He grinned sardonically.

"You can leave me out of it."

"Don't be soft! It was your idea that did it!"

"They won't like it any better for that. Oh, well, please yourself."

"Look, if it wasn't a rival wog, who was it?" someone was exclaiming. "It can't have been police or military, without authority – I mean to say, it's simple murder."

"And just Marbruk – the king-pin. A political rival would have tried to knock out that right-hand man of his, Gamal Whatsit, wouldn't he?"

"Well, perhaps . . . or it may just have been a personal feud . . ."

Errol was lounging back on his stool, studying the menu on the bar, but I had the impression he was listening, not reading. I noticed that like me he was still in K.D., belt, and revolver, and less spruce than usual: there was a smudge of oil on his shirt and one sleeve was dirty. He looked tired but otherwise at peace with the world.

"When you've finished inspecting me, MacNeill," he said, still scanning the menu, "how about getting them in again?"

"Sorry. Two more, Carlo."

"Anyway, it was a damned fine shot," said the police captain. "Two damned fine shots – and as you say, just in time, from our point of view."

"You won't break a leg looking for the murderer, eh?"

"Oh, there'll have to be an inquiry, of course . . ."

"I'll bet there will," Errol murmured, and laughed softly – and something in the sound chilled my spine as I put my glass to my lips. Sometimes a sudden, impossible thought hits you, and in the moment it takes to swallow a sip of whisky you know, beyond doubt, that it's not only possible, but true. It fitted all too

61

well . . . "killing Huns with cheese-wire by night" . . . the expertise with small arms . . . the rumours of anti-terrorist brutalities in Palestine . . . the scientific destruction of a boxing opponent . . . the cold-blooded nerve of his bluff at Kantara Bridge . . . all that I knew of the man's character . . .

"Steak, I think," said Errol, closing the menu. "About a ton of Châteaubriand garni – that's parsley on top, to you – preceded by delicious tomato soup. Sure I can't tempt you? What's up laddie, you look ruptured?" The whimsical glance, the raised eyebrow, and just for an instant the smile froze on the handsome face. He glanced past me at the debating group, and then the smile was back, the half-mocking regard that was almost a challenge. "The cop's right, don't you agree? A damned good shot. You used to be a sniper – what d'you think?"

"Someone knew his business."

He studied me, and nodded. "Just as well, wasn't it? So . . . as our stout friend would say – here's to him." He raised his glass. "Okay?"

"*Slàinte*", I said, automatically. There was no point in saying anything else.

We drank, and Errol turned on his stool to the dining-room arch immediately behind him. A little Italian head-waiter, full of consequence, was bowing to a couple in evening dress and checking his booking-board.

"Table for one, please," said Errol, and the little man bared his teeth in a professional smile.

"Certainly, sir, this way—" His face suddenly fell, and he straightened up. "I regret, sir – for dinner we have to insist on the neck-tie."

"You don't mean it? What, after a day like this? Oh, come off it!"

"I am sorry, sir." The head-waiter was taking in Errol's informal, not to say untidy, appearance. "It is our rule."

"All right, lend me a tie, then," said Errol cheerfully.

"I am sorry, sir." The waiter was on his dignity. "We have no ties."

Errol sat slowly upright on his stool, giving him a long, thoughtful look, and then to my horror laid a hand on his revolver-butt. The head-waiter squeaked and jumped, I had a vision of inkpots being shot off desks – and then Errol's hand

62

moved from the butt up the thin pistol lanyard looped round his neck, and smoothly tightened its slip-knot into a tie.

"Table for one?" he asked sweetly, and the head-waiter hesitated, swallowed, muttered: "This way, sir," and scurried into the dining-room. Errol slid off his stool, glass in hand, and gave me a wink.

"Blind 'em with flannel, laddie. It works every time." He finished his drink without haste, and set his glass on the bar. "Well . . . almost every time." He gave his casual nod and sauntered into the dining-room.

The investigation of Marbruk es-Salah's murder came to nothing. There was no more nationalist unrest until long after our departure, when a republic was established which turned into a troublesome dictatorship – so troublesome that forty years later the American air force raided it in reprisal for terrorist attacks, bombing our old barracks. This saddened me, because I had been happy there, and it seemed wasteful, somehow, after all the trouble we'd had just preserving that pleasant city from riot and arson and pillage. I'm not blaming the Americans; they were doing what they thought best – just as we had done. Just as Errol had done.

I lost sight of him when I was demobilised; he was still with the battalion then, going his careless way, raising hackles and causing trouble. Many years later, a wire-photo landed on my newspaper desk, and there he was among a group of Congo mercenaries; the moustache had gone and the hairline had receded, but there was no mistaking the cigarette-holder and the relaxed, confident carriage; even with middle-aged spread beneath his flak-jacket, he still had style. Yes, I thought, that's where you would end up. You see, there's no place for people like Errol in a normal, peace-time world; they just don't belong. Their time lay between the years 1939 and 1945 – and even then they sometimes didn't fit in too comfortably. But I wonder if we'd have won the war without them.

The Constipation of O'Brien

Apart from the three afternoons devoted to games (which in our battalion meant football, no matter what the time of year) the most popular event of 12 Platoon's working week was undoubtedly the Education Period. Not that they were especially thirsty for academic improvement, but the period came last on Friday afternoon, at the end of the week's soldiering, and following immediately after a bathing parade which consisted of lolling on the warm sand of a gloriously golden North African beach, idly watching the creamy little waves washing in from the blue Mediterranean – the kind of thing millionaires would have paid through the nose for, but which in those balmy post-war years the British Army provided free. And there was no Hotel Ptomaine just over the skyline in those days, crammed with reddened tourists, bad drains, and abominable canned music; just a thousand miles of nothing stretching literally to Timbuctoo on the one hand, and Homer's sunlit sea on the other, apparently unsailed since Ulysses went down over the horizon to distant Djerba.

It was, consequently, a fairly torpid audience that I used to find awaiting me in the platoon lecture room afterwards, all 36 of them jammed into the two back rows, snoozing gently against the whitewashed walls, whence Sergeant Telfer would summon them to git tae the front and wake yer bluidy selves up. When they had obeyed, blinking and reluctant, I would announce:

"Right. Education Period. Pay attention, smoke if you want to. Now, what we're going on with this afternoon is . . ."

The formula never varied; it was as settled and comforting as a prayer. Whether the subject was British Way and Purpose (whatever that was, something to do with why we'd fought the war, as if anybody cared), or Care of the Feet, or How-to-get-civilian-employment-when-you-are-demobilised (a particularly useful lecture that, since it was delivered by a subaltern who'd never held a steady job in his life to a platoon who'd spent most of their time on the dole), or any of the numerous subjects prescribed by the Army Bureau of Current Affairs, it was invariably introduced as "what we are going on with". Why, I don't know; it probably dated from Marlborough's time, and it has been the signal for successive legions of young British soldiers to settle themselves contentedly on their benches and sleep with their eyes open, dreaming about Rita Hayworth (or Florrie Ford or Nell Gwynn, depending on the era) while their platoon commander gasses earnestly at them.

There is a whole generation of elderly men in these islands today who, if you whisper "what we are going on with" in their ears, will immediately relax, with an expression of feigned interest in their glassy eyes, gently munching their lips as a prelude to dropping off. That's what army education does for you. The only way I ever discovered of reclaiming my platoon's attention during a lecture was to drop in a reference to football or women; once, to settle a bet with the Adjutant, I read them a very long passage from Hobbes' *Leviathan*, and when they were drowsing nicely I suddenly began a sentence with the words "Gypsy Rose Lee" – the effect was electric: 36 nodding heads snapped up as though jerked by wires, quivering like ardent gun-dogs, and 72 eyes gleamed with animation. From a lecturing point of view it posed me a difficult problem of smooth continuity, but it won me my bet.

Two subjects only were barred at education periods – religion and politics. In fact, they could be mentioned provided they weren't, in the Army's mysterious phrase, discussed "as such" – a distinction which went for nothing when Lieutenant MacKenzie, product of Fettes and the grouse-moors, and politically somewhere to the right of Louis XIV, got embroiled during a lecture (on Useful Hobbies, of all things) with his platoon sergeant, one McCaw, who in civilian life was a Communist Party official on Clydeside. Exchanges like: "If ye'll pardon me for sayin' so, comrade – Ah mean, sir" and "I'll pardon nothing of the sort, my good man – I mean, sergeant – the General Strikers should have been put up against a wall and shot, and don't dam' well argue", are not conducive to good order and military discipline. Especially when the platoon sit egging on their betters with cries of: "Kenny's the wee boy! Kenny's tellin' 'im!" and "Get tore in, McCaw! Go on yersel'!"

So politics we avoided, gratefully; for one thing, the Jocks knew far more about it than we did. Religion was even trickier, with that fundamentalist–atheist, Catholic–Protestant mixture – I recall one ill-advised debate on "Does God Exist?" which would have had the Council of Trent thumbing feverishly through their references, and ended with a broken window. And of course religion in the Scottish mind – or the Glasgow mind, anyway – is inextricably bound up with sport, to such an extent that I have seen an amiable dispute on the offside rule progress, by easy stages, through Rangers and Celtic, to a stand-up fight over the fate of some ancient martyr called the Blessèd John Ogilvie, in which Private Forbes butted a Catholic comrade under the chin. I wouldn't have thought either of them cared that much, but there you are.

Thereafter I confined the education periods to personal monologues on Interesting Superstitions, How Local Government Works, and What Should We Do with Germany Now? That last elicited some interesting suggestions, until they discovered that I wasn't advocating mass bombing or deportation, but social and political restructuring, as laid down in the Army pamphlet. After that they just dozed off again in the warm North African afternoon, salty and soporific from their swimming, until the cook-house call sounded for tea.

And then one day the Colonel, finding mischief as colonels will, discovered that his clerk at company headquarters couldn't orient a map. This is a simple technical matter of laying a map out so that its north corresponds with magnetic north; normally you do it with an army compass. Apparently the clerk couldn't use a compass, which didn't surprise me – I knew there was at least one member of my platoon who didn't know north from south, and God help the man who tried to teach him. But the Colonel was shocked; he sent out word that every man in the battalion must become a proficient map-reader henceforth, so on the next education period my lecture-room had 18 maps and compasses laid out on the big table, one to every two men, working together. This is a very sound idea; it halves the chance of total ignorance, theoretically anyway.

Looking over my platoon, I wasn't so sure. Most of them were bright boys, but there in the front rank stood the legendary Private McAuslan, the dirtiest soldier in the world, illiteracy and uncleanliness incarnate, glaring with keen displeasure at the compass in his grimy hand.

"Whit the hell's this, then? Darkie no' gaun tae give us a speech the day? Ah thought we were jist meant tae *listen* tae edu-macation. Sure that's right, Fletcher?"

"Sharrup," said Private Fletcher. "Yer gaun tae learn tae read a map."

"But Ah cannae read. Darkie knows Ah cannae read. Sure he knows Ah've been tae the Edu-macation Sergeant for a course, an' the daft bugger couldnae learn me anythin'. He's a clueless nyaff, yon," added McAuslan, in disgust at the Education Sergeant's shortcomings. "Couldnae teach ye the right time, him."

"Readin' a map's no' like readin' a book, dozy. It's jist a matter o' lookin' at the map an' seein' where ye are."

McAuslan digested this, slowly, strange expressions following each other across his primitive features. Finally:

"Ah know where Ah am. Ah'm here." He dismissed the map with a sniff that sounded like a sink unblocking. "An' Ah don't need this bluidy thing tae tell me, either."

At this point, fortunately, Sergeant Telfer called them to attention, and I got off to a smooth start by telling them that what we were going on with this afternoon was map-reading and, more specifically, map-orientation.

"It's quite easy," I said, with lunatic optimism, aware of McAuslan's fixed stare; it was rather like being watched by a small puzzled gorilla with pimples. "We just have to turn the map round so that it points north. Right?" I decided, in an unwise moment, to conduct a simple test, just to make sure that everyone knew what the points of the compass were – McAuslan, I was pretty certain, didn't know them from Adam, but there might be others in the platoon who shared his ignorance.

"Suppose that's north," I said, indicating the wall behind me, "where is south-west?"

Indulgently, the platoon pointed as one man to the correct far corner of the room – with the usual single exception. McAuslan was pointing to the ceiling. By heaven, I thought, ex McAuslano semper aliquid novi. How had he worked that one out?

"Haud on, sur," he said, and I realised that his raised hand had been designed simply to catch my attention. "Ah mean, 'scuse me." He breathed heavily. "Wid ye mind repeatin' that?"

"It's all right, McAuslan," I said hurriedly. "I'm just establishing that if that's north, then that's south, and that's east, over there, and that's west. See?"

"But you said—"

"Now, the points of the compass are divided into 360 degrees, which means that between each of the four main points there are—"

My frantic burst to escape from him didn't work; his hand was up again, and he was frowning like a judge who has just heard a witness use an obscenity.

"Degrees?" he said suspiciously.

"That's right, McAuslan," I beamed. "Degrees; 360 of them—"

"Like onna thermometer?"

I fought back a vision of myself lying in a fever, with McAuslan kneeling by my bed in a nurse's wimple, trying to take my temperature with an army compass. "Not exactly," I said, and strove to think of a simple explanation. By God, it would have to be simple. "Let's see," I said, improvising madly, "the degrees on a thermometer go up and down, but the degrees on a compass go round in a circle."

Well, I know I'm a rotten teacher, but with McAuslan it was hard to know where to begin, honestly. And there were 35 other men in the platoon to think of, who knew what I was talking about, badly and all as I might be doing it. While McAuslan was reflecting on degrees which rotated, as against those which leaped perversely up and down, I hastened on to a practical demonstration of the army compass, showing how it must be applied to the eye so that one could see the reflected numbers moving past. Within two minutes the platoon had mastered the art, and were turning their maps in a soldier-like manner to point north, with the compasses pointing neatly along the magnetic north line.

"That's it," I said. "Now they're oriented, and if we take them outside, and orient them again, we can establish our own

68

position on the maps, and then compare features on the maps with the things we actually see in front of us. Let's – yes, McAuslan?"

He was glowering at me in accusation. "Sur," he demanded. "These maps pointin' north?"

I admitted it, uneasily.

"But you," he remonstrated, "said *that* wis north." And he pointed to the wall behind me. "That's no' the way the maps is pointin'. Oh, no. They're pointin' ower there, an'—"

It was entirely my fault, of course, for using an arbitrary illustration. "I'm sorry, McAuslan," I said. "Before, what I meant was, *supposing* that wall *was* north; it isn't, really, but I was just trying to show . . . to find out . . . if everybody knew the points of the compass . . ."

He regarded me more in unwashed sorrow than anger. "Ye got it wrong," he said, tolerantly. "That wall's no' north at a'. That's north, where the maps is pointin', where the fellas has turned them, see, ower there, an'—"

"That's right!" I cried. "And we found out north by looking into our compasses, and turning them, and watching the numbers, the degrees, and – oh, God, everyone outside, Sergeant Telfer, and we'll do it again!"

I wouldn't have you think that I was callously abandoning McAuslan in his ignorance. After the lesson was over, and the rest of the platoon had shown that they could orient and take bearings competently, I took him aside for some special tuition. Sergent Telfer, while I was busy with the others, had shown him how to hold the compass to his eye, as a preliminary to taking a bearing, and McAuslan, having snivelled over it and complained that the bluidy thing widnae haud still, had attempted to level it out, and torn the metal cover off – a feat roughly equivalent to biting a rifle in two.

So when the others had gone I strove to impart to him the rudiments of map-reading, beginning with the fact that the sun rose in the east – yes, invariably, I said, because after half an hour of McAuslan's company you began to doubt even the verities. There it was, going down in the west, and up there was north. That, I eventually drove home, was where the compass needle always pointed, provided you stayed well away from heavy metal objects.

" 'Samazin' ", was his verdict, when I had finished; he regarded the compass with some of the satisfaction Galileo might have shown in identifying a new heavenly body. "A'ways the same way. It's a great thing, right enough."

"You can test it out when we go on a night exercise next week," I said. "We'll find the North Star, and you'll see that the needle always points to it. Okay, fall out, and tell the Cook-Sergeant I said you could get a late tea."

It was more, I reflected virtuously, than I would get myself; the officers' mess waiters would have removed the last curled-up sandwiches long ago. However, I was compensated by the glow of satisfaction at having taught McAuslan something – it didn't happen often, heaven knows, and when it did you felt like a don whose favourite student has got a starred first. I was so chuff with myself that I even boasted mildly about my triumph at dinner.

"Don't believe it," said the Colonel. "Fellow doesn't know right from left. Never did."

"That's a different thing, sir," I said. "A compass doesn't tell you that. But it does point north, and McAuslan knows it – now."

"You're not claiming McAuslan can *read* a compass?" said MacKenzie. "I won't have that."

"No," I said, "but he can look at a needle. Which is as much as most of your platoon can do, I'll bet. I don't see anybody in A Company giving Copernicus a run for his money, if it comes to that." For I was naturally defensive about McAuslan; the trouble was, everyone in the mess knew it.

"I'll grant you he can look at a needle," said the Adjutant, "but knowing McAuslan's capacity for lousing things up, I'm willing to bet that any compass that has been in his hands for two minutes will probably point south, strike twelve, and sound the alarm."

"You'd think McAuslan was the only dumb brick in this battalion," I said warmly. "When I think of some of the troglodytes I see shambling about headquarters – to say nothing of MacKenzie's shower of first-class minds in A Company, who have to be taught a drill for getting into bed—"

"My platoon," said MacKenzie, continuing the debate on the high level which I had set, "can map-read a ruddy sight better than yours can."

"Your platoon," I said, "have difficulty reading the *Beano*, because the words are too long, and don't have the syllables split up with hyphens, like *Chicks Own*."

"Like to bet?" snapped MacKenzie, and of course that did it. I was preparing to take him up on it when the Colonel, having heard the magic word "bet", said he was glad to see this spirit of healthy competition, because it augured well for the series of night exercises he was planning; having given orders that his battalion should become experts in map and compass work, he was all afire to test the results.

"We'll do the paratrooper stunt," said he, stuffing tobacco into his eager pipe. "You know, chaps taken out in closed trucks dropped in pairs at intervals, so that they haven't the foggiest where they are. Each pair has a map, a compass, and a box of matches, and they find their way home again. Test of skill and initiative; first-class, absolutely. Give platoon commanders—" he prodded his pipe-stem at MacKenzie and me "– like Kenny and Dand a chance to prove their points, eh?"

MacKenzie and I looked at each other, mentally computing what the harvest might be if our platoons were dropped by night in desert country and had to find their way back. I didn't fancy it, myself; night exercises are tricky at the best of times, but conducted on the edge of the Sahara, with people like McAuslan staggering about in circles unaided, they could be suicidal.

"Of course," said the Colonel, reading our thoughts, "we'd stick close to the coast, among the villages; don't want anyone striking out for the Congo by accident, do we?"

"Well, sir," I began cautiously, trying not to think of McAuslan let loose in an unsuspecting Arab village in the dark, "I'm not sure—"

"I am," said the Adjutant happily. "Your man McAuslan will never make it, for one. Dammit, he can get lost in the canteen. Drop him from a closed truck and he's liable to turn up twenty miles out to sea."

"Not he," said MacKenzie, derisively. "He can't stand water, which is why Dand's chaps have to wash him from time to time."

Which was true, but I was too busy thinking to resent it.

"You did say, sir," I addressed the Colonel, "that the idea would be to drop people in pairs?"

"No so fast," said MacKenzie. "I get it – you'll see to it that McAuslan is teamed up with some map-reading genius who'll find his way home for him. No soap, Dandy; you send him out with an ordinary member of your platoon, or there's no bet."

"What is the bet?" said the second-in-command, emerging from behind his decanter.

"That McAuslan, dropped from a closed truck at night, with an average Jock from Dand's platoon as his sidekick, won't find his way back to a given point within a reasonable time. Hang it all," he added, for despite being a MacKenzie and red-haired, he was a reasonable youth, "it isn't really a bet at all, it's a stone-cold cert. I'll go easy with you, you silly MacNeill," he went on to me. "I'll make it a straight hundred lire – or a slap-up dinner at the club. Well?"

I was nailed to the wall, of course; I'd talked myself into it. I rescued the port before the M.O. could get his hands on it, poured an inspirating glass, and thought, while they watched me.

"Stop looking so damned MacNeillish," grinned MacKenzie. "Put up or climb down."

"This would be a full-scale company exercise – three platoons, all ranks, dropped in pairs?" I looked at the Colonel, and he nodded. "Usual form," he said, which was all I wanted to know. MacKenzie leaped in, all suspicion.

"You can't partner McAuslan yourself, mind. It's got to be an average Jock—"

"Don't worry," I said. "I'll send him out with Wee Wullie."

The Adjutant looked surprised. "That's handicapping yourself a bit, isn't it? Wee Wullie's not exactly your brightest star. I mean, I concede that if you sent McAuslan out with Captain Cook, they'd both probably finish up at the bottom of a well, but . . ."

Wee Wullie, I should explain, was my platoon incorrigible, a rugged giant of extraordinary strength and evil temper, given to alcoholic excesses on a heroic scale which frequently involved him with the military police and provost staff. He would have been posted or locked up for ever long ago, for his crime sheet was encyclopaedic, but Wee Wullie had a fighting record from the war that counter-balanced his misdemeanours, and the Colonel, who had known him from way back, was as sentimentally protective as a mother-hen. He was eyeing me thoughtfully as the Adjutant spoke; like me, the Colonel knew that Wee Wullie had once performed an incredible solo march in the Western Desert in '42, carrying a German prisoner most of the way. But his feat had been distinguished for its sheer endurance, not for his sense of direction; he wasn't, I was ready to admit, the ideal choice to pilot such a walking disaster as McAuslan through desert country in the dark. But the Colonel had said that the exercise would take the "usual form"; I knew exactly what that meant, and MacKenzie either didn't or had forgotten.

"Wee Wullie's the man I want dropped with McAuslan," I said. "You can't complain that he's an above-average Jock for skill and intelligence. All right, Kenny, you're on for a hundred lire."

"Me too," said the Adjutant, with that innocent, sporting look that English gentlemen assume when they know they've got the opposition cornered. "I was in on this to start with; my jibes and taunts got MacNeill all steamed up, and I want my whack at his money."

"Wagering is sinful and an abomination," sighed the Padre. "Will ye be wanting odds, Dand?"

I absorbed as much of the anti-McAuslan money as I felt my £9 a week salary could afford – the Colonel for once hung back on a bet, which was comforting – and went away to think, avoiding the second-in-command, who had surfaced again from his port, and wanted to ask me if *Chicks' Own* wasn't that comic paper of his youth in which the animals wore clothes – there was some damned tiger in short pants, as he recalled . . . I made my excuses and slipped out to the verandah. I'd been a mug; McAuslan couldn't find his way out of a paper bag, and would undoubtedly get lost on an unprecedented, nay monumental, scale. It wasn't losing the lire I minded – well, not all that much, anyway – it was the credit of the thing. Subalterns are proud of their platoons, and I was obsessively proud of mine, McAuslan included. Unwashed, ugly, useless, accident-prone, illiterate, and altogether fit to be first stoker at Gehenna he might be, but he was one of my Jocks – and he'd been good enough to go in at Alamein and beyond. And he tried – he tried *me*, but that wasn't the point.

Could he conceivably chart a course across several miles of unknown country by night? No, he couldn't. Neither, probably, could Wee Wullie – but the Colonel had said "usual form", and therein lay the one gleam of hope.

The kind of exercise the Colonel envisaged, you see, isn't merely a test of map-reading skill. What happens is that a whole company, officers, N.C.O.s, Jocks and all, are loaded into trucks after dark, the tarpaulins are pulled down, and the trucks are driven away perhaps six or seven miles. The occupants are dropped in pairs, with maps, etc., at intervals of perhaps five minutes each, on an arc of a huge semi-circle whose centre is the home base to which they must find their way before dawn. But that's only the half of it. In between them and home another company is dropped, whose duty it is to prevent the first company getting through.

You can guess the results. I've played this particularly brutal game half a dozen times, in England, India, Palestine and elsewhere, and it invariably finished up as a series of fearful brawls in the dark. I recall one nightmare at Bangalore where I was teamed up with an enthusiastic Sikh cadet who believed that the best way of outwitting our fellow-students was to stalk them through the gloom and hit them with an entrenching-tool handle. And a similar exercise near Nazareth which ended as a pitched battle between Coldstream Guardsmen and the R.A.F. Regiment, with myself as an unfortunate umpire in between, firing Verey flares and futilely blowing my whistle.

In fact it has this virtue, that it is probably the best training for real warfare – night fighting, at any rate – that you can possibly get. There are those, like my Sikh, who treat it simply as an excuse for a good turn-up, which is really to miss the point. At their best, night exercises teach the young soldier that darkness, which he has learned to fear from childhood, is really a friend; that patience, and waiting, and lying doggo for hours if necessary, pay off far better than boldness and initiative. I wasn't exactly a cat-eyed Mohican myself, but by the time the Burma campaign was over I had learned that in the dark he who stays still stays longest. Twenty years later, when I woke up at home one chilly night, and thought I heard mysterious noises downstairs, I was delighted to find that I could still glide out into the gloom without a sound or even a creaking board, every nerve alert, totally self-possessed and controlled, right up to the moment when I missed by footing on the stairs and crashed roaring into the hall and broke my toe. But you know what I mean.

However, knowing what my company was like, I had a pretty fair idea that any night exercise was liable to end in mayhem, which was why I wanted to team McAuslan with Wee Wullie. Skilled map-readers and night guides they might not be, but any opposition who tried to bar their progress would be well advised to take a couple of Rugby League teams along; McAuslan could, in his own phrase, "handle himsel' ", but Wee Wullie, giving of his best, was about as manageable as a rogue elephant in steel-toed boots. He could, at least, preserve McAuslan from capture in the early stages of the exercise; meanwhile the rest of the platoon and I would be combing the African night for them, and would shepherd them safely in to base.

It was at least feasible, provided the eccentric pair, the idiot misfit and the Cowcaddens Caveman, didn't go badly astray, or break a leg, or start an Arab uprising, before we found them. That would be the dicey part, calling for some clever stalking and enormous luck; my hopes were not raised by their performance on the brief night lesson which I conducted for the platoon on the regimental football pitch on the eve of the exercise itself, to give them a refresher course on using the stars and night map-reading. Wee Wullie arrived on the parade about two-thirds drunk (his normal condition, I realised with sudden misgivings, on any night after the canteen closed) and with a piece of rusty barbed wire tangled round his right ankle; he had evidently picked it up by accident somewhere, without noticing, which gives you a notion of what Wee Wullie was like. He stood there, swaying gigantically in the gloom, like Talus the Man of Brass with a bonnet on top, breathing heavily and reeking like a spirit vault. McAuslan I identified in the dark by his hideous sniffing, and when they and the rest of the platoon had settled down, and all were craning obediently up at the beautiful starlit black sky, I started in.

"That's the North Star, there – easily identifiable because it never moves, and the two end stars of the Plough, just there, always point directly at it. Well, not exactly directly, but as near as dammit. You've got the Plough, McAuslan? That thing there, like a bloody great ladle – that's roughly how it'll be pointing tomorrow night, and since you'll be in the desert south of here, the North Star is roughly in the direction you want to make for. Okay?" I sought for some familiar allusion that might fix it in what passed for his memory. "That's north, see – in that direction. That's where Glasgow is, near enough. Right? Just remember, Glasgow's the direction you're heading if you go north."

It was risky, of course; I didn't want the night exercise to finish with McAuslan on Argyle Street, but that was a chance one had to take.

"Aye, right, sir. Ah've got it covered." Seen in dim profile, peering up into the heavens, he looked like some prehistoric moon-worshipper. "'At's a North Star, there – Ah'll find it the morra nicht, nae bother – cannae miss; it's right ower the Naafi."

"Oh, my God. You won't be standing here tomorrow night; you won't be able to see the Naafi. You'll be out in the desert; you'll have to find it from the Plough, don't you see?"

"Aw." He thought about this. "Lotta stars, in't there? See, there's the Constipation of O'Brien."

For a giddy moment I thought I had misheard him. Faintly I asked:

"What did you say?"

"The Constipation of O'Brien. See, up there—" he placed one sloth-like paw on my shoulder and pointed with the other. "'Ere it's. Thon's O'Brien – ye can see the star that's his heid, and they's his airms, an' his legs, an' they three wee stars is his belt, an' they ither stars is his—"

"Dear God," I said, "the Constellation of Orion. How the – yes, yes, that's it, McAuslan! That's splendid! Well done! But how on earth did you know that?"

"Och, the Padre showed me them, in a book he's got. Efter you wis tellin' me aboot the compass aye p'intin' north, an' said we wis gaunae look at the stars, Ah thought Ah micht as weel get genned up aforehand. So Ah asked the Padre." For a fleeting moment I wondered, why the Padre; was there in McAuslan's unfathomed mind a connection between religion and the astral bodies, between the cosmos and . . .? "Ah seen the book lyin' on his desk wan day when Ah had tae clean oot his office when

Ah wis on jankers," he went on, shattering my speculation. "So Ah asked him yesterday, an' he showed me a' aboot O'Brien, an' Gasser an' Bollocks, the Heavenly Twins, an'—"

To say that I was astonished is to say nothing; I was gratified, deeply. McAuslan taking so much interest as to conduct his own personal researches was something new, and highly encouraging. I congratulated him again on his zeal, and felt so uplifted that I expanded perhaps rather incautiously in answering a question from one of the other Jocks on the difference between True and Magnetic North. (One north, I felt, was probably as many as McAuslan could cope with, and I had skirted the subject previously.) I know that in answering the Jock I exceeded my remit by remarking that Columbus, on his great voyage, had been much disturbed to see that the compass needle gradually ceased to point directly to the North Star as he sailed west; this brought a horrified squawk from McAuslan, clamouring for a explanation of this heresy, and I would probably have been on that football pitch until 4 a.m., explaining with a sleeping platoon around me, but fortunately at this point Wee Wullie was resoundingly ill, and in the ensuing confusion I dismissed the parade. McAuslan, incidentally, lost the way back to his barrack-block, which was a full two hundred yards away – possibly he was still intent on studying the Constellation of Orion and its internal disorders – and Wee Wullie had to be carried to bed. Not good omens, however you looked at them.

There were even worse ones in store on the day of the exercise itself; the Colonel, with his genius for complicating things in the interests of keeping his soldiery up to the mark, and satisfying his insatiable regimental ego, had devised an additional wrinkle in the exercise. The place that we eager map-readers were going to have to find in the dark was the Yarhuna Road bridge, which lay about two miles south of the town, on the edge of the desert; on the bridge itself the defending company was to leave a red storm lantern, and anyone who got within sight of it undetected would be adjudged to have found his way home successfully. But that wasn't enough for the Colonel; to add to the sport, and prove how good we were, he had told the Artillery Commander who was providing the defending company that we would engage to stalk the lantern and extinguish it, all unseen and mysterious.

"He's been reading too many romantic novels about the

'Forty-five,'' I told the Adjutant. "That bridge'll be crawling with Gunners; you won't be able to get a mouse through."

"Come, come," he said, "where's your Highland craft and cunning? All you have to do is sneak through the gloom like Rob Roy, taking care not to stand on twigs and milk-bottles, gliding stealthily past the drowsing sentinels—"

"Are you taking part?" I demanded coldly.

"Not a prayer," he said. "I'll be in bed, dreaming about the goodies I'm going to buy with your hundred lire after McAuslan finds the source of the Nile. Have fun."

That reminded me that the real object of the exercise was simply to get McAuslan within sight of the lamp, which with good luck and management and Wee Wullie clobbering the opposition, might just be possible. Refinements like stalking the lamp over the last couple of hundred yards could take their chance – it might be fun to try it, though, and with that in mind I arranged that my own map-reading partner should be Lance-Corporal Macrae: he had been a professional ghillie and stalker in peace-time, adept at getting American tycoons and fat maharajahs within blasting distance of stags. Given sufficient time and darkness he could lift an eagle chick from its mother without her noticing, and as we rumbled out in the closed truck that midnight I explained to him that if he could exercise his talents by extinguishing the lamp undetected, it would probably earn him a weekend pass from a gratified Colonel.

"The rest of you," I told the close-packed mass of bodies in the darkened truck, "concentrate on getting within sight of the red light. If you get that far without being picked up by the Gunners, you'll have scored. Okay? After that, you can have a go at stalking the lamp, but that's just the icing on the cake. I don't suppose there'll be much chance of getting past the last guards near the bridge – it's pretty bare country, but have a try. But the main thing is to get within sight of it, so when you're dropped, in a few minutes' time, get a good bearing on the North Star, and start using your maps . . ."

"That's it, Wullie," McAuslan's voice sounded hoarsely out of the steaming press. "Gottae get a bearin'. See where north is. That's whit jiggered Columbus; didnae ken whaur he wis gaun, see, 'cos his compass wisnae p'intin'—"

"And remember," I said finally, "our password is 'Din', and

78

the password of the Artillery company who're trying to stop us is 'Gin'. So if anyone challenges you with 'Gin', just get the hell out of it, quickly. If they get hold of you – use your own initiative."

They gave happy growls in the dark, and McAuslan was heard to observe that he wid melt onybuddy that said "Gin" tae him. At this point the truck halted, and I peered under the tarpaulin at the silent African night; just a thin moon, fortunately, but enough to show the silent dunes and scrub, empty and desolate.

"First two out," I said, and two of the Jocks dropped over the tailboard. "I think we're somewhere west of the Yarhuna Road. Good luck."

We drove on, stopping every five minutes to drop another pair. Macrae and I were going to be last out, and I held Wee Wullie and McAuslan back as penultimate pair. Wee Wullie, who had cunningly been kept on fatigues that evening as long as decency allowed, to prevent him drinking the canteen dry in advance, had only had time for about eight pints before taps, so he was relatively sober and consequently morose. To McAuslan's repeated inquiries about whether he had the map, and the compass, and the matches, and could take a bearin', 'cos if we don't we'll be away for ile, he responded with irritable grunts; when the time came for him to drop, he went over the tailboard like a silent mammoth, swinging down one-handed from the overhead stanchion to land noiselessly in the sand, while McAuslan fell over me, muttering:

"Sure ye got the matches, big yin? Ah cannae see a bluidy thing – whaur's the tailboard, but? Och, ta, sur – there we are. Staun' frae under, big yin, Ah'm gaunae jump!"

He took a shambling dive over the tailboard, and the sound of rending cloth and an appalling oath split the night. As the truck jerked forward and their two dim figures receded into the gloom it appeared that McAuslan, his denim trousers in rags about his ankles, was grovelling at Wee Wullie's feet, complaining that his bluidy breeks wis tore; the trooser-erse, he lamented, wis oot o' them. I didn't hear any more, but with any luck McAuslan's semi-nudity would delay their exploration of the wilderness in which they had been left, and Macrae and I would have a chance to double back and find them.

It wasn't easy. The truck, on its last leg, doubled and turned bewilderingly – I wondered if MacKenzie had got at the driver – and Macrae and I were finally deposited on an utterly flat stretch of desert track with not a landmark in sight. A look at the stars confirmed that we were south-east of the Yarhuna Road bridge, and we ploughed confidently for home, but with no high hopes that our course would intersect that of the McAuslan–Wullie partnership, presumably labouring somewhere to westward.

We got our first definite fix after about twenty minutes, on a small Arab village called Qufra which I remembered from a route march. We were a good six miles from the Yarhuna Road bridge, but what was worse, Qufra had a Gunner patrol in it – we'd probably have walked into them, but a dulcet Liverpool voice drifting over the sand warned us in time. I hadn't expected them to be this far out; you don't usually reckon on meeting opposition until you're fairly close to home, where they can narrow the angle on you. We skirted the village, plodding through bad, shifting sand, and made another mile before we had to duck into a wadi to avoid more Gunners, camped out having a smoke near a palm grove.

It had been fairly placid thus far, and quite pleasant walking through the warm African night, admiring the moon shadows on the dunes, and pausing whenever a village or other landmark came in sight, to check our position on the map. But now the moon went down, leaving only the star-sheen, and ground black with shadows in visibility of about twenty yards. We went cautiously now, keeping apart, and presently received intimation that the exercise was warming up: sounds of tumult and combat came drifting out of the dark ahead, cries of "Din!" and "Gin, you bastard!", accompanied by a steady pounding which reminded me of balmy evenings on Chowringhee, Calcutta, when we used to take the air outside Jimmy's Kitchen and the Nip Inn, listening to the rhythmic thumping from the bushes on the darkened Maidan, where the Cameronians and Royal Marines were relieving the American Air Force of their wallets.

The battle ahead gradually faded into the distance, and we scouted forward to a low wall skirting what seemed to be an ancient Moslem temple. I thought I remembered it from the map, but it would have been too risky to strike a match, so we crouched in silence, listening and waiting.

That was a mistake. It gave me time to think, and my

imagination being what it is, the sight of that gaunt, eerie little ruin began to work on me. A slight wind had got up, rustling the weeds in the enclosure and sighing dolefully in the broken dome; it was suddenly chill and quiet, and the dark was closing in, bringing uncomfortable thoughts of deserted churchyards, with yawning graves, Black Masses, unholy conjurings, and satanic rites. It's fearful what a mixture of Highland atavism and Presbyterian upbringing can do at two in the morning; before I knew it I was muttering Forbidden Words like "Tripsaricopsem", and wondering perversely if the formula for raising Auld Horny in a kirkyard would charm up Mahound in a Moslem cemetery. Let's see, you mutter the Lord's Prayer backwards, and presently the Devil appears round the church in the form of a toad . . . inevitably I found the words going through my brain: "Amen ever and ever for glory the . . ."

A sudden hideous keening wail sounded from behind the ruin, Macrae dived beneath the cover of the wall, my hair bristled up on my scalp, and I stared horrified as the Devil suddenly came surging round the corner of the temple. For a dreadful moment I thought I'd unleashed the Powers of Darkness just by thinking about them, and then I realised that if this truly was His Infernal Majesty, he wasn't in the form of a toad; furthermore he was clad mostly in a pair of drawers, cellular, soldiers for the use of, and moving at a hell of a clip with three Artillerymen after him roaring "Gin!" By way of answer he was crying "Mither o' Goad!", which seemed out of character, and something in the way he attempted to leap the wall and failed, bringing down a hail of rock on Macrae and me, provided a positive identification.

"McAuslan!" I shouted, and then the Gunners came pounding over the top, with cries of triumph, and the night got interesting. I rolled down a sandy slope, locked in the arms of one of them, with McAuslan clutching at my leg and apparently trying to bite it. We snarled "Din!" and "Gin!" and "Aw, jeez, they tore ma bluidy shirt aff, an' me wi' nae breeks!" respectively, and I escaped possible gangrene only by shouting: "It's me, McAuslan! Worry him, boy!" We punched and wrestled blasphemously in the dark, McAuslan observing bitterly that he wis aboot sick o' this, and whaur wis Wullie wi' the bluidy compass, and then more Gunners came on the scene, and it

would have gone hard with us if the night had not also produced
Wee Wullie, in the nick of time. I had a Gunner sitting on my
chest, demanding my name and number, and had just played my
last desperate card, which was to threaten him with court-
martial for assaulting a superior, when something like a rushing
mighty wind swept away my oppressor, and presently Macrae
and I were sitting on the temple wall, panting and licking our
wounds, and listening to the appalling noise of our platoon giant
dealing with about a dozen frantic Artillerymen, and evidently
enjoying it.

We left him to it, and when we had found McAuslan crawling
about on all fours in the gloom alternately snuffling piteously
because he had lost a boot in the mêlée and mumbling to himself
that the North Star pointed to Glasgow, we took stock. Our
maps and compasses had gone, trodden into the field of battle
where Wee Wullie could be distantly heard singing "One-Eyed
Riley" with a ring of his slain presumably around him.

"He's an awfy man, yon," said McAuslan in an awed
whisper. "Like a wild beast, so he is. Cannae read a map for
toffee, but – an' Ah kept tellin' 'im, Ah did. 'Yer erse is oot the
windy, big yin,' Ah sez, but he had a flask o' rum in his pocket,
an' there wis nae pittin' sense intae 'im, an'—"

"Just as well," I said. "Now, listen, McAuslan. We haven't
far to go – a mile or so at most. All you have to do is keep quiet,
and let Macrae and me find the way. Right? Quiet, you understand, and stick like a limpet or so help me I'll brain you. If we
strike trouble, leave it to us; I want you to get within sight of that
red light, that's all – never mind about stalking it or doing
anything clever. Just stand up and yell for the nearest officer,
see?"

"Aw," he said, doubtfully, "but Ah thought—"

"Don't think! You're not paid to think! Just do as you're
told."

"Awright, sur. Awright. But Ah'm no wandered, me. Ah ken
the password, Ah can see the North Star, right enough, an' aw,
see there, there's ra Constipation o' O'Brien again, jist like in ra
Padre's book, an'—"

"Come on!" I snapped, and we set off into the night, two
desperate men and the amateur astronomer in his cellular
drawers, ambling behind with his eyes glued to the North Star,

blaspheming as he fell over things.

I was beginning to think we'd make it when we struck the Yarhuna Road, but some clever Gunner officer outguessed us; naturally we didn't follow the road itself, but kept to the scrubby country a couple of hundred yards off on one side, and that's where the crafty brute had planted his ambush. They came out of the ground like phantoms, chanting "Gin!", and we could do nothing but scatter and run, McAuslan gallumphing unevenly away into the gloom in his one boot, clutching his underpants in desperation and crying that it was a bluidy liberty. He had a stalwart Gunner in close pursuit, and was plainly done for; in the meantime, Macrae was nabbed, and I only escaped by selling a dummy to an assailant who must have been a Rugby player, because he bought it by sheer instinct. I ran my hardest for about a quarter of a mile, lay up in a dry ditch until the pursuit had tailed away, and then stole ahead.

It was easier now; apart from being on my own, I found I was moving into populated country, with people blundering through the night in all directions, occasionally muttering "Din" and "Gin" hopefully. It took just a little time and patience to get me to the top of a dune where I could look down on the road bridge, with its guttering red lamp. There were a few sentries staked out at a sporting distance from the bridge, and off to one side what looked like a group of umpires with a flashlight, and beyond them a couple of three-ton trucks with troops round them – captured map-readers who had surrendered their identity discs and been brought in. Another truck was coming down the road, headlights on, to pull up beside the first two and disgorge its disgruntled cargo. McAuslan, I reflected, would probably be among them.

However, so far as I could judge, fewer than half the company had been caught; the night must be full of skulkers like me, some of them lurking as I was within sight of the lamp. There wasn't much cover, but there were tongues of shadow right up to the bridge itself; if one could just take time, and crawl the furlong or so undetected . . . I cursed the luck that had put Macrae into the bag; if anyone could have got there, he could. Still, I could have a go; there was no disgrace in failing at this stage.

It took me about an hour, quite enjoyable in its way, to work my way down to within a stone's throw of the lamp. It was flat-on-your-belly stuff, an inch at a time, listening to the darkness, and twice some mysterious radar stopped me just in time while a shadow ahead resolved itself into a prone Gunner, waiting motionless for unwary stalkers. Each time I had to retreat painfully slowly and take a new tack, with my clothes full of itching sand and my stomach feeling as though it had been through a bramble bush. Then I struck what looked like a good line along a fold of dead ground, worming forward until I was close in to the bridge, snug in a patch of inky shadow, with the lamp not twenty yards ahead, just asking for it. Talk about your Chingachgook, thinks I, and was bracing myself to dive the last few yards when a voice out of the night offered me a cigarette. It was a Gunner captain, sitting still as a post within a yard of me; he had been watching my progress, he said, for several minutes.

"I'd have challenged, but you seemed to be having such fun. Gin, by the way."

"Din," I said, rolling over on my back and accepting his cigarette, "you rotten sadist. MacNeill, Lieutenant, D Company, and you're not getting my I.D. discs, either; I got within sight of your kindly light."

"Most of your chaps did, but everyone who tried to stalk the lamp has been nailed. Bound to be," he went on smugly. "I think we've got it pretty well sewn up. In fact, I'd say it's about time we called it a night, wouldn't you? Getting on for dawn, and I'm damned cold – can't see any of your latecomers doing any better . . . hullo, who's that?"

He was looking towards the bridge; in the dim glow of the red lamp a figure could be faintly seen, shambling uncertainly and pawing in a disoriented manner, like a baboon with a hangover. I stared with a wild surmise – I knew that Lon Chaney silhouette, even to the draggling outline of its cellular drawers . . .

"Hey, you!" cried the Gunner Captain, and the figure started, lurched, and stumbled; there was a clatter and a mouth-filling guttural oath – and the lamp was out, plunging the bridge into blackness. There were yells of astonishment, someone blew a whistle, the Gunner Captain swore horribly and started shouting for his sergeant, people ran around in the dark, and for about two minutes chaos reigned. Personally I just lay there and smoked, waiting for enlightenment.

It came when someone brought a torch and they focused it on

the figure which lay snuffling and swearing beside the wreckage of the lamp, bewailing the fact that he had got ile a' ower his drawers, an' them his only clean pair. He sat blinking and aggrieved in the spotlight while the Gunners regarded him with dismay, demanding to know who he was and where he had come from.

"Good Lord!" said one, "he's still got his tags on!" And sure enough, he still had his identity discs round his unwashed neck. Which meant he hadn't been picked up by the defenders – somehow he had avoided capture, and here he was in undisputed possession of the lamp which he had undoubtedly extinguished, glaring in baleful distress at his inquisitors and wiping his nose fretfully.

"Who the hell are you?" demanded the Gunner Captain in wrath. "And why the hell are you half-naked?"

I realised there were unplumbed mysteries here, and they must be played for all they were worth.

"He's McAuslan. One of my Jocks," I said, with just a hint of complacency. "Yes, as I hoped, he's bagged the lamp. He's pretty good at this sort of thing, of course." Good might not be the appropriate word, but it would do. "Well done, McAuslan. Yes, you see, he likes to wear as little as possible when he's stalking; in fact he usually does it entirely stark. He's—"

"Ah wis jist gaun ower the bridge for a—" McAuslan was beginning, but fortunately the rest was lost in Gunner upbraidings and demands for explanation. I hustled him to his feet, whispering sharply to him to keep his lip buttoned, for I knew the half had not been told unto me, and whatever it was I didn't want the Gunners to hear it. They weren't in the mood.

"How the blazes did he get through?" demanded the Captain. "Dammit, our posts were as tight as a tick – he couldn't have!" Aggrievedly he added: "Nobody saw him!"

"That", I pointed out, perhaps tactlessly, "is the object of the exercise. You confirm he's still got his tags, and he put out the lamp? Fine; let's go, McAuslan."

We left them recriminating, and I got him in the lee of a truck. "Right," I said. "Talk."

"Ah wis jist gaun ower the bridge for . . . tae do . . . Ah mean . . ." he began miserably, holding his drawers up. "Ah mean, Ah wantit fur tae relieve mysel'. Ah wis fair burstin', honest, so

Ah wis," he continued earnestly. "No kiddin', sur, Ah didnae mean tae break their lamp, straight up, but yon man roared at me, an' Ah jist couldnae help it. An' Ah wis burstin'—"

"That's all right, McAuslan; it doesn't matter. How in God's name did you manage to get in at all? The last thing I saw you were out yonder, with a Gunner breathing down your neck. Didn't he catch you?"

"Aw, him." He made a dismissive gesture, unwisely with the hand holding his pants up, and grabbed them just in time. "Big animal he wis. He got haud o' me, an' sat on ma heid, but Ah wis too fly fur 'im. Ye see, when he says 'Gin' tae me, Ah says 'Gin' back tae him. 'Whit's that?' says he. 'Gin', says Ah. 'Ah'm on your side, Jimmy.' An' the silly big soad let me up, an' Ah clattered 'im wan an' left 'im haudin' himsel'. He wis a right mug, yon," added McAuslan, with some satisfaction.

"Well I'm damned!" I said reverently. Talk about peasant cunning. "But how on earth did you get in – I mean, not only within sight of the lamp, but actually up to it? That was . . . well, marvellous – they had sentries everywhere!"

"Ah, weel, ye see," he said, hitching up his underwear and assuming a professorial pose, "it wis like this. When Ah got awa' frae the mug – 'Gin', says he, wid ye believe it? – Ah took a look fur ra North Star, but Ah couldnae see the bluidy thing. It must hiv gone oot, or somethin'. Onywye, Ah wis aboot fed up wi' the map-readin' lark – Ah mean, Ah could've done it nae bother, efter a' ye'd tellt me, but Wee Wullie had loast ra map, an' ra compass – och, he's a right big eedjit, yon," said McAuslan with feeling. "Nae sense, an' him half-fleein' wi' rum. He's an awfy man in drink, so he is. An' he's nae use wi' a map, onywye. He wis wandered. He wandered *me*, Ah don't mind tellin' ye," he added indignantly. "So when Ah got awa' frae the mug, Ah hid in a ditch fur a wee while, an' along comes a truck. It stoaped, so Ah crawled underneath, so's they widnae see me. They wis Gunners, an' soon they brought along some o' oor boys that they'd nabbed, an' pit them in ra truck, an' startit up. An' Ah wis fed up trampin' through the sand, so Ah jist catched hold o' the pipes unner ra truck, an' got me feet roon' them, an' they brung me in. An' when they stoapt by the brig Ah jist let go an' cam' oot, an' Ah wis burstin' somethin' hellish, so Ah went fur—"

86

"Stop, stop," I said, trying to take it in. By his own account he had travelled about a mile clinging to the bottom of a three-ton truck, with a desert road speeding by a couple of feet beneath his ill-covered rump. I shuddered, and looked at him with awe. Initiative, I was thinking, determination, endurance . . . map-reading and compass work not so hot, admittedly, but maps aren't everything.

"Ah'm sorry aboot the lamp, though, sur . . . it was a accident, Ah didnae see the thing, an' when he shoutit Ah jist breenged intae it, an' . . . Ah suppose," he added, wrinkling his urchin face dolefully, "that it'll mean anither stoppage oot ma' pey, an' Ah'm still payin' fur the tea urn Ah dropped on cookhoose fatigue, an' MacPherson's glasses, an' . . ."

"No," I said emphatically, "it won't be stopped out of your pay. Or if it is, you'll easily be able to pay for it out of the three hundred lire you've earned tonight. Never mind why." I looked at him, backed up defensively against the truck, clutching his revolting drawers, knuckling his grubby nose. "Son, you're great. Just don't tell anyone how you got through to the lamp, understand? They didn't spot you, so they're not entitled to know. Right – hop into the truck and we'll get you back to barracks, and you can change out of your evening clothes. Well done, McAuslan."

"Och, ta very much, sur. That's awfy good o' ye," said McAuslan – but he said it with a strained, worried look which puzzled me until he added, pleadingly: "Afore Ah get intae ra truck . . . Ah'm still burstin', no kiddin' . . ."

For the record, MacKenzie and the Adjutant and the Padre paid up like gentlemen – suspicious gentlemen, but I didn't enlighten them. I turned the money over to McAuslan, enjoining him to put it straight into saving certificates for himself and Wee Wullie. They didn't, I'm afraid. Instead they went on a magnificent toot the following Saturday, which concluded with Wee Wullie staggering back to barracks with McAuslan on his back finding his way, he alleged, by the stars. I might have taken more satisfaction in the success of his navigation if I hadn't been the orderly officer who met them at the gate.

The Sheikh and the Dustbin

When I was a young soldier, and had not yet acquired the tobacco vice (which began with scrounging cigarettes at route-march halts when everyone else lit up and I felt left out) I used to win cross-country races. This surprised me, for while I had been athletic enough at school I had never been fleet of foot; in the infants' egg-and-spoon race, and later in the hundred yards, I would come labouring in well behind the leaders, and as a Rugby full-back I learned to be in the right place beforehand because I knew that no amount of running would get me there in time if I wasn't. So it was a revelation, when the Army hounded us out in the rain to run miles across soggy Derbyshire in P.T. kit, to discover that I could keep up a steady stride and finish comfortably ahead of the mud-splattered mob, winning 7s. 6d. in saving certificates and having the Company Sergeant-Major (who was seventeen stone, all fat, and smoked like a chimney) wheeze enthusiastically: "Aye, happen lad'll mek a Brigade rooner! Good at all sport, are yeh, MacNeill? Play football, roogby, cricket, do yeh? Aye, right, yeh'll be left inner in't coompany 'ockey team this art'noon, an' report to't gym fer boxin' trainin' on Moonday. Welter-weight, are yeh – mebbe middle-weight, we'll see. Done any swimmin', 'ave yeh? 'Ow about 'igh joomp . . .?" That's the military mind, you see; if you're good at one thing, you're good at everything.

It didn't take long to convince him that I'd never held a hockey stick in my life and was a wildly unscientific boxer, but being a resourceful old warrant officer he made good use of my running ability, in a rather unusual way – and did much to advance my military education. For during those weeks of basic training I was detailed several times to escort prisoners to the military jail, the idea being that if during the journey by rail and road a prisoner somehow won free of the Redcap to whom he was handcuffed, I would run him down – what I was to do when I caught him was taken for granted. It never came to that; all our malefactors went quietly to the great grim converted factory at Sowerby Bridge which was the North Country's most feared and fearsome glasshouse and remains in my memory as one of the most horrible places I have ever seen. If my cross-country talents did nothing else, they won me a first-hand look at an old-style military nick which convinced me that, come what might, I was going to be a good little soldier.

The bleak walls and yards with their high wire-meshed gates, the lean, skull-faced guards screaming high-pitched, the crop-headed inmates doubling frantically wherever they went, our prisoner having to strip naked at high speed in the cold reception cell under the glaring eye of what looked like a homicidal maniac in khaki – all these were daunting enough, but what chilled my marrow was the sight of a single, everyday domestic object standing outside a doorway: an ordinary dustbin. Only this one had been burnished until it gleamed, literally, like silver; you could have shaved at it without difficulty. The mere thought of how it had got that way told me more about Sowerby Bridge than I wanted to know; think about it next time you put out the rubbish.

I don't suppose that military prisons are quite as stark as that in this enlightened age (where did they go, those gaunt, shrieking fanatics of staff men? Do they sit, in gentle senility and woolly slippers, watching *Coronation Street*?) but in their time they were places of dreadful repute – Stirling, and Aldershot (whose glazed roof is supposed to have inspired the name "glasshouse"); Heliopolis, outside Cairo, where prisoners were forced to run up and down the infamous "Hill", and Trimulghari, in India, home of the soul-destroying well drill in which wells had to be filled and emptied again and again and again. Perhaps rumour made them out worse than they were, but having been inside Sowerby Bridge, I doubt it. Reactionary old soldiers speculate wistfully on their reintroduction for modern criminals and football hooligans, forgetting that you can no more bring them back than you can bring back the world they belonged to; like conscription, they are just part of military history – for which the football hooligans can be thankful.

However, this is not a treatise on glasshouses, and if I have reflected on them it is only because they are part of the train of thought that begins whenever I remember Suleiman ibn Aziz, Lord of the Grey Mountain, who had no connection with them personally. But he was a military prisoner, and belongs in the same compartment of my memory as Sowerby Bridge, and barred windows, and Lovelace's poem to Lucasta, and "jankers", and McAuslan and Wee Wullie labouring on the rockpile, and the time I myself spent in cells as a ranker (the sound of that metal-shod door slamming is one you don't forget in a hurry, when you've been on the wrong side of it), and all my varied thoughts and recollections about what the Army used to call "close tack". Detention, in other words, and if it has two symbols for me, one is that gleaming dustbin and the other is old Suleiman.

He was quite the unlikeliest, and certainly the most distinguished prisoner ever to occupy a cell in our North African barracks. I won't say he was the most eccentric, because those bare stone chambers at the back of the guard-room were occasionally tenanted by the likes of McAuslan and Wee Wullie, but he was more trouble than all the battalion's delinquents put together – something, fortunately, which happened only on Hogmanay, when it was standing-room only in the cells and Sergeant McGarry's provost staff were hard pressed to accommodate all the revellers.

They were busy enough during the rest of the year, too, but not because our Jocks were rowdier than any other soldiers; if our cells were well used it was because the Colonel, unlike some commanders, refused to use the glasshouse as a dumping-ground for incorrigibles. To him, a man in Heliopolis was a dead loss to the regiment, and a failure, and he would move heaven and earth to keep our worst offenders out of the Big House – especially if they had been good men at war. Wee Wullie's record of violence and drunkenness should have put him on the Hill for years – but Wullie had played the soldier when it counted, in the Western Desert, and the regiment had a long memory. As it did for the remarkable Phimister, a genuine hero of Japanese captivity who must thereafter be forgiven for spending more time on the run from the Redcaps than he did on parade. It wasn't easy, and the Colonel had to do some inspired string-pulling on occasion, but no one doubted it was worth it. A

Highland regiment is a family, and settles its own differences within itself – if that sounds trite, it's true. So when Phimister went walkabouts yet again and was picked up trying to board a tramp steamer in Tunis, or Wullie overturned a police jeep and battled with its occupants, or McAuslan went absent and tried to pawn a two-inch mortar in the bazaar (so help me, it's a fact), there was no thought of shipping them to the glasshouse; they did their time in our own cells under the iron hand of McGarry, digging and carrying in sweltering heat, deprived of tobacco and alcohol, and safely locked in 'at night. It was genuine hard labour, they hated it, it kept them out of trouble, and as McGarry used to say:

"They come tae nae herm wi' me. What? They were never so weel aff in their lives! Wullie's sober an' McAuslan's clean, an' that's mair than ye can say when they're on the ootside. I don't gi'e them any bother – an' by God they don't gi'e me any."

Looking at McGarry, you might have feared the worst from that last remark. All provost staff tend to resemble galley overseers, and he was rather like an outsize Ernest Borgnine playing Ivan the Mad Torturer, but the appearance was deceptive. Despite barrack-room gossip, McGarry never laid hands on a man unless he was hit first, in which case he hit back – once. (The exception was Wee Wullie, who had to be hit several times.) For the rest, McGarry got by on presence and personality; the mere sight of that huge figure at the top of the guard-room steps, thumbs hooked in the top of his kilt as he coldly surveyed the scene, was the most potent disciplinary force in the battalion.

It was into this strange guard-room world that Suleiman ibn Aziz came unexpectedly on a summer night. I was orderly officer, and had just finished the routine inspection of prisoners to make sure they were still breathing and not trying to tunnel their way out. There were two in residence: McAuslan starting fourteen days after his brief career as a mortar salesman, and Phimister as usual. I was signing the book when I noticed that one of the four vacant cells was open – and within there was an undoubted rug on the floor, a table, chair, chest-of-drawers, jug and wash-basin, and in place of the usual plank and blanket there was a pukka bed, with sheets and pillows. I thought I must be seeing things.

"Who in the world is that for?" I asked. "Don't tell me you've got the Brigadier in close tack!"

"Nae idea, sir," said McGarry. "I just got word tae have a cell ready, an' then the Adjutant himsel' turns up tae see tae the furniture. It's no' a regular client, anyway."

"Somebody from outside? He must be pretty special. But why us?"

"Strongest jyle in the province, this," said McGarry, not without satisfaction. "God kens what kind o' sodgers Mussolini built this barracks for, but he wasnae takin' ony chances wi' his defaulters. These walls is six feet thick. There's tae be a special sentry on the door, too."

This was unprecedented – as was the appearance of the Colonel, Adjutant, and second-in-command at the main gate just after Last Post, when a staff car arrived bearing the Provost Marshal and a small figure in a black burnous and silver-trimmed *kafilyeh* handcuffed to a Redcap escort. He stood sullenly while the Colonel and the Provost Marshal conferred briefly, and then he was uncuffed and brought up the guard-room steps for delivery to McGarry; I had only a glimpse of a lean, lined swarthy face with an enormous beak of a nose and a white tuft of beard, and two bright angry eyes glaring under the *kafilyeh* hood. They hustled him inside, and the Adjutant, who had been hovering like an agitated hen, beckoned me to follow to his office, where the Colonel was sounding off at the Provost Marshal:

". . . and you can tell G.H.Q. that I don't take kindly to having my barracks turned into a transit camp for itinerant bedouin. What did you say the beggar's name was?"

"Suleiman ibn Aziz, sir," said the P.M. "Known in Algeria as the Lord of the Grey Mountain, apparently." He hesitated, looking apologetic. "In Morocco they call him the Black Hand of God. So I'm told, sir."

"Never heard of him," said the Colonel. "How long are we supposed to keep him?"

"Just a week or two, I hope – until the French come to collect him. I know it's a nuisance, sir, but there's really nothing to worry about; he's over seventy."

"I'm not in the least worried," snapped the Colonel, who didn't like the P.M. at the best of times. "Nor am I a damned

92

innkeeper. Why's he so important, anyway?"

"Well, sir," said the P.M., looking impressive, "I'm sure you've heard of Abd-el Krim . . .?" The Adjutant's head came up at that famous name; like me, he knew his P. C. Wren. The Colonel frowned.

"Krim? The chief who led the Riff Rebellion in Algeria, back in the twenties? Gave the French Foreign Legion a hell of a dance, didn't he? Yes, I've heard of him . . ."

"The Red Shadow!" said the Adjutant brightly, and the Colonel gave him a withering look.

"Thank you, Michael, you can play a selection from *The Desert Song* later." He turned back to the P.M. "I thought Krim surrendered to the French 20 years ago – what's this bird got to do with him?"

"Absolutely right, sir, Krim did surrender," said the P.M. "But Suleiman didn't. He'd been Krim's right-hand man from the start of the Riff revolt, near the turn of the century, commanded his cavalry – he was the man who drove the Legion out of Taza in '24, overran their forts, beat up their columns, played hell all over. Real *Beau Geste* stuff," he was going on enthusiastically, until the Colonel raised a bleak eye from scraping his pipe. "Yes, well . . . he had something like 20,000 Riffs behind him then, but when the French really went to town in '26 Krim packed in with most of 'em, and Suleiman was left with just a handful. Swore he'd never give up, took to the Moroccan mountains, and has been hammering away for twenty years, off and on – raiding, ambushing, causing no end of trouble. The French captured him twice, but he escaped both times." The P.M. paused. "The second time was from Devil's Island."

There was silence, and the Colonel stopped scraping for a moment. Then he asked: "Where did you learn all this?"

"Intelligence bumf, sir – it's all in the dossier there. Just came in this afternoon. Suleiman was picked up only two days ago, you see, by one of our long-range groups south of Yarhuna, acting on information from the French in Oran—"

"What the devil was he doing over here? We're more than a thousand miles from Morocco!"

The P.M. looked perplexed. "Well, it's rather odd, actually. When he escaped from Devil's Island it was early in the war, about '41. He managed to get back across the Atlantic, God knows how – he was nearly seventy then, and he'd had a pretty rough time in captivity, I believe. Anyway, he reached Morocco, got a few followers, and started pasting the French again, until our desert war was at its height in '42, when for some reason he came east and pitched in against Rommel." The P.M. spread his hands in wonder. "Why, no one knows . . . unless he regarded the Germans as allies of the Vichy Government. When the war ended the French were still after him, and for the past year or so he's been hiding out down south, quite alone. There was no one with him in the village where our people found him."

"And the French still want him? At this time of day?" The Colonel blew through his pipe. "What do they intend to do with him, d'you know?"

The P.M. hesitated. "Send him back to Devil's Island . . . so Cairo tell me, anyway. It seems the French regard him as a dangerous public enemy—"

"In his seventies? Without followers? After he's been on our side in the war?"

"It's up to the French, sir. We're just co-operating." The P.M. shifted in his chair, avoiding the Colonel's eye. "I ought to mention – there's a note in the dossier – that Cairo regards this as a top security matter."

"Indeed?" The Colonel's tone was chilly. "Then why don't they put him in Heliopolis, instead of my guard-room?"

The P.M. looked embarrassed. "Well, we're convenient here, of course – next to French territory. If they took him to Cairo, it would be bound to get talked about – might get into the papers, even." He glanced round as though expecting to find reporters crouched behind his chair. "You see, sir, the French want to keep it hush-hush – security, I imagine – and Cairo agrees. So the transfer, when it's made, is to be discreet. Without publicity." He smiled uneasily. "I'm sure that's understood."

The Colonel blew smoke, considering him, and just from the angle of his pipe I knew he was in one of his rare cold rages, though I wasn't sure why. The P.M. knew it, too, and fidgeted. Finally the Colonel said:

"We'll look after your prisoner, Provost Marshal. And if we don't come up to G.H.Q. Cairo's expectation as turnkeys, I suggest they do the job themselves. Convey that, would you? Anything else?''

The P.M., who wasn't used to mere Colonels who raised two fingers to Cairo, got quite flustered, but all he could think of to add was that Suleiman ibn Aziz spoke Arabic and Spanish but only a little French, so if we needed an interpreter . . .

"Thank you, my Adjutant speaks fluent French," said the Colonel, and the Adjutant, who had spent a hiking holiday in the Pyrenees before the war, tried to look like an accomplished linguist. The P.M. said that was splendid, and made his escape, and we waited while the Colonel smoked grimly and stared at the wall. The second-in-command remarked that this chap Suleiman sounded like an interesting chap. Enterprising, too.

"Imagine escaping from Devil's Island, at the age of 70!" The Adjutant shook his head in admiration. "Poor old blighter!"

"You can probably save your sympathy," said the Colonel abruptly. "From what I've heard of the Riffs' treatment of prisoners I doubt if our guest is Saladin, exactly." He gave a couple of impatient puffs and laid down his pipe. "Still, I'm damned if we'll be any harsher than we must. You're orderly officer, MacNeill? See McGarry has him properly bedded down and I'll talk to him in the morning – you *do* speak French, don't you, Michael? God knows you've said so often enough."

The Adjutant said hastily that he'd always managed to make himself understood – of course, he couldn't guarantee that an Arab would understand the Languedoc accent . . . why, in Perpignan they spoke French with a *Glasgow* accent, would you believe it, mong jew and tray bong, quite extraordinary . . . Listening to him babble, I resolved not to miss his interview with Suleiman next day. When the others had gone he began a frantic rummage for his French dictionary, muttering vaguely bon soir, mam'selle, voulez-vous avez un aperitif avec moi, bloody hell, some blighter's knocked it, and generally getting distraught.

"Never mind your aunt's plume," I said. "What's the old man so steamed up about?"

"I'll just have to speak very slowly, that's all." He rumpled his fair hair, sighing. "Eh? The Colonel? Well, he doesn't like having his guard-room turned into a political prison – especially not for the Frogs. You know how he loves *them*: 'Brutes let us down in '14, and again in '40—' "

"I know that, but what's wrong with having to look after an old buddoo for a week or two?"

"It's politics, clot. The Frogs want to fix this old brigand's duff, and no doubt our politicians want to keep de Gaulle happy, so the word goes to Cairo to co-operate, and we lift him and hand him over – but quietly, without fuss, so it doesn't get in the papers. See?"

"What if it does?"

"God, you're innocent. Look, the old bugger's past it, the Frogs are just being bloody-minded, we're co-operating like loyal allies – but d'you think Cairo wants to be *seen* helping to give him a free ticket back to Devil's Island? So we get the job, 'cos we're out here far beyond the notice of journalists and radicals – anti-colonialists and so on – who'd make a martyr of the old boy if they heard about it. Are you receiving me?"

"Well . . . sort of . . . but he's a rebel, isn't he?"

"Certainly, fathead, and ten years ago no one would have given a hoot about handing him over. But it's different now. Don't you read the papers? The old enemies are the new patriots. Gandhi's a saint these days . . . so why shouldn't this old villain be a hero? After all, he always has been, to some people – fighting for his independence, by his way of it. Suppose his name was William Wallace – or Hereward the Wake? See what I mean?"

It was new stuff to me, in 1947. Yes, I was an innocent.

"So that's why the Colonel gets wild," said the Adjutant. "Being used as a stooge, because Cairo hasn't got the guts to pass this Suleiman on openly – or to tell the Frogs to take a running jump. Which is what the Colonel would do – partly because he can't stand 'em, but also because he's got a soft spot for the Suleimans of this world. God knows he fought them long enough, on the Frontier, and knows what a shower they are, but still . . . he respects 'em . . . and this one's over the hill, anyway. That's why he's hopping mad at Cairo for giving him a dirty job, but it's a lawful command, and he's a soldier. So, incidentally, are you," added the Adjutant severely, "and you ought to have been in the guard-room hours ago, examining padlocks. I don't suppose *you* speak French? No, you ruddy wouldn't . . ."

All was well in the guard-room, and through the grille in his cell door I could see the prisoner on the bed, still wrapped in his burnous, snoring vigorously.

"By, but that's an angry yin!" said Sergeant McGarry. "Hear him snarl when I asked if he wantit anything? I offered tae get him some chuck, but I micht as weel ha'e been talkin' tae mysel'. Who is he, sir?"

I was telling him, when the gargoyle features of Private McAuslan appeared at the grille of the neighbouring cell, a sight that made me feel I should have brought some nuts to throw through the bars.

"Hullaw rerr, sur," said he, companionable as always. "Who's ra auld wog next door? See him, Ah cannae get tae sleep fur him snorin'. Gaun like a biler, sure'n he is."

"He's a reporter frae the *Tripoli Ghibli*, come tae interview ye an' write yer life story," said McGarry, and suddenly snarled: "Sharrap an' gedoon on yer cot, ye animal, or I'll flype ye!" McAuslan disappeared as by magic. I finished telling McGarry what I knew about his prisoner, and he shook his head as we stood looking through the grille.

"Black Hand o' God, eh? He's no verra handy noo, puir auld cratur. Mind you, he'll have been a hard man in his time."

That was surely true, I thought. In the dim light I could make out the hawk profile and the white stubble on the cropped skull where the *kafilyeh* had fallen away; he looked very frail and old now. The Lord of the Grey Mountain, who had led the great Riff *harkas* against the French invaders and fought the legendary Foreign Legion to a standstill, the drawn sword of Abd-el Krim, the last of the desert rebels . . . It was inevitable that I should find myself thinking of the glossy romance that had been shown at the garrison cinema not long ago, with its hordes of robed riders thundering over the California sandhills while Dennis Morgan sang the new words which, in the spirit of war-time, had been set to the stirring music of Romberg's Riff Song:

> Show them that surrender isn't all!
> There's no barricade or prison wall
> Can keep a free man enslaved . . .

It was pathetically ironic, looking in at the little old man who had been the anonymous inspiration for that verse, and had spent a lifetime fighting for the reality of its brave message, even taking part in the greater cause against Germany. The film fiction had ended in a blaze of glory; the tragic fact was asleep in a British Army cell, waiting to be shipped away to a felon's death in exile, the scourge of the desert keeping McAuslan awake with his snoring.

His interview with the Colonel next day was a literal frost, for during fifteen minutes' laboured interrogation by the Adjutant he spoke only once, and that was to say "Non!" Seen in daylight he was a gaunt leathery ancient with a malevolent eye in a vulpine face whose only redeeming feature was that splendid hooked nose, but he carried himself with a defiant pride that was impressive. Seated in his cell, refusing even to notice his visitors, he might have been just a sullen little ruffian, but he wasn't; there was a force in the spare small body and a dignity in the lifted head; whether he understood the Adjutant's questions about his welfare (which sounded like a parody of *French without Tears*, with such atrocities as "Etait votre lit tendre . . . suffisant douce, I mean", which I construed as an inquiry about the comfort of his bed) it was hard to say, since he just stared stonily ahead while the Adjutant got pinker and louder. That he was getting through became apparent only with the last question, when the Colonel, who had been getting restive, interrupted.

"Ask him, if we give him the freedom of the barracks, will he give his word of honour not to try to escape?"

This was the Colonel sounding out his man, and it brought the first reaction. Suleiman stiffened, stared angrily at the Colonel, and fairly spat out "Non!" before standing up abruptly and turning on his heel to stalk across to the window, thus indicating that the palaver was finished.

"Well, he can give a straight answer when he wants," said the Colonel. "He doesn't lie at the first opportunity, either. Keep his cell locked at night, McGarry, with a sentry posted, but during the day he can sit on the verandah or in the little garden if he likes. The more he's in open view, the easier he'll be to watch. And he's not to be stared at – see that that's understood by all ranks, Michael. Very well, carry on."

So we did, and in the following days the small black-robed figure became a familiar sight, seated under an arch of the guard-room verandah or in the little rock-garden at the side, the armed sentry at a tactful distance and McGarry as usual at the head of the steps. According to him Suleiman never uttered a word or showed any emotion except silent hatred of everything around him; at first he had even refused to sit outside, and only after McGarry had taken out the chair two or three times, leaving the cell door open, had he finally ventured forth, slowly, making a long survey of the parade square before seating himself. He would stay there, quite motionless, his hands folded before him, until it was time to go to his cell to pray, or the orderly brought his meals, which were prepared at an Arab eating-house down the road. He never seemed to see or hear the sights and sounds of the parade-ground; there was something not canny about the stillness of the small, frail figure, his face shaded from the sun by the silver-trimmed *kafilyeh*, as though he were under a spell of immobility, waiting with a furious patience for it to be lifted.

The Provost Marshal must have got word of the freedom he was being given, for he called to protest to the Colonel about such a focus of nationalist unrest being in full view from the gate where local natives were forever passing by. What the Colonel replied is not recorded, but the P.M. came out crimson and sweating, to the general satisfaction.

For there was no doubt of it, in spite of his hostile silence and cold refusal even to notice us, a sort of protective admiration was growing in the battalion for the ugly little Bedouin warlord. Everyone knew his story by now, and what was in store for him, and sympathy was openly expressed for "the wee wog", while the French were reviled for their persecution, and our own High Command for being art and part in it.

"Whit wye does the Colonel no' jist turn his back an' let him scarper?" was how Private Fletcher put it. "So whit if he used tae pit the hems oan the Frogs? A helluva lot we owe them, an' chance it. Onywye, they say the wee fellah got tore in oan oor side in the war – is that right, sur? Becuz if it is, then it's a bluidy shame! We should be gi'in' him a medal, never mind sendin' him back tae Duvvil's Island!"

"Sooner him than me," said Daft Bob Brown. "Ever see that fillum, *King o' the Damned*? That wis aboot Duvvil's Island – scare the bluidy blue lights oot o' ye, so it wud."

"We should gi'e him a pound oot the till an' say 'On yer way, Cherlie'," said Fletcher emphatically. "That's whit Ah'd dae."

You and the Colonel both, Fletcher, I thought. Scottish

soldiers have a callous streak a mile wide, compensated by a band of pure marshmallow, and either is liable to surface unexpectedly, but if there is one thing they admire it is a fighting man, and it doesn't matter whether he's friend or foe, fellow or alien. Suleiman ibn Aziz was a wog – but he was a brave wog, who had gone his mile, and now he was old and done and alone and they were full of fury on his behalf. Barrack-room sentimentality, if you like, which overlooked the fact that he had been a fully-paid-up monster in his time; that didn't matter, he wis a good wee fellah, so he wis.

Their regard showed itself in a quite astonishing way. It was a regimental tradition for Jocks entering or leaving barracks to salute the guard-room, a relic of the days when the colours were housed there. Now – and how it began we never discovered – they started to extend the time of their salutes to cover the small figure in the burnous seated in the garden; I even saw a sergeant give his marching platoon "Eyes left!" well in advance so that Suleiman was included, and the Regimental Sergeant-Major, who happened to be passing (and missed nothing) didn't bat an eyelid. Highland soldiers are a very strange law unto themselves.

I doubt whether Suleiman noticed, or was aware of the general sympathy. His own obvious hostility discouraged any approaches, and the only ones he got came from his fellow-prisoner McAuslan. The great janker-wallah was never one to deny his conversation to anybody unlucky enough to be within earshot, and since his defaulters' duties included sweeping the verandah and weeding the garden, Suleiman was a captive audience, so to speak; the fact that he didn't understand a word and paid not the slightest heed meant nothing to a blether of McAuslan's persistence. He held forth like the never-wearied rook while he shambled about the flower-bed destroying things and besmirching himself, and the Lord of the Grey Mountain sat through it like a robed idol, his unwinking gaze fastened on the distance. It was a pity he didn't speak Glaswegian, really, because McAuslan's small-talk was designed to comfort and advise; I paused once on a guard-room visit to listen to his monologue floating in through the barred window:

". . . mind you, auld yin, there's this tae be said for bein' in the nick, ye get yer room an' board, an' at your time o' life the Frogs arenae gaun tae pit ye tae breakin' rocks, sure'n they're no'? O' course, Ah dae ken whit it's like in a French cooler, but ach! they'll no' be hard on ye. An' ye never know, mebbe ye'll get a chance tae go ower the wa' again. They tell me ye've been ay-woll twice a'ready, is that right? Frae Duvvil's Island? Jings, that's sumpn! Aye, but – mah advice tae ye is, don't try it while ye're here, for any favour, becuz that big bastard McGarry's got eyes in his erse, an' ye widnae get by the gate. Naw, jist you wait till ra Frogs come for ye, an' bide yer time an' scram when their back's turned – they're no' organised at a', ra Frogs. Weel, ye ken that yersel'. Here, but! it's a shame ye couldnae tak' Phimister wi' ye – him that wis in the cell next door tae me, the glaikit-lookin' fella. He's no' sae glaikit, Ah'm tellin' ye! Goad kens how many times he's bust oot o' close tack – he wid hiv ye oan a fast camel tae Wogland afore ra Frogs knew whit time it wis! Jeez, whit a man! Aye, but ye'll no' be as nippy as ye were . . . ach, but mebbe it'll no' be sae bad, auld boy! Whitever Duvvil's Island's like, it cannae be worse'n gettin' liftit by the Marine Division in Gleska, no' kiddin'. See them? Buncha animals, so they are. Did Ah no' tell ye aboot the time Ah got done, efter the Cup Final? It wis like this, see . . ."

To this stream of Govan consciousness Suleiman remained totally deaf, as he did to all the sounds around him – until the seventh day, when the pipe band held a practice behind the transport sheds in preparation for next day's Retreat: at the first distant keening note his head turned sharply, and after a moment he got up and walked to the edge of the garden, evidently trying to catch a glimpse of the pipers. For a full half hour he stood, his hawk face turned towards the sound, and only when it ended did he walk slowly back to the guard-room, apparently deep in thought. There he suddenly rounded on McGarry, growling: "L'Adjutant! Monsieur l'Adjutant!". The Adjutant was summoned forthwith, and presently came to the mess with momentous news: Suleiman ibn Aziz had demanded curtly that he be allowed to witness the band's next performance.

I have written elsewhere of the Arabs' delight in the sound of bagpipes, and how they would flock to listen whenever the band appeared in public. But Suleiman's interest was so unexpected and out of keeping with his grim aloofness that there was something like delight in the mess, and there was a big turn-out next day when the Adjutant conducted him to join the Colonel before H.Q. Company, where a chair had been provided for him. He went straight to it, ignoring the Colonel's greeting, and sat erect and impassive as the band swung on in full fig, the drums thundering and the pipes going full blast in "Johnnie Cope"; they marched and counter-marched, the tartans swinging and the Drum-Major, resplendent in leopard-skin, flourishing his silver staff, through "Highland Laddie", "White Cockade", and "Scotland the Brave", and he watched with never a flicker on his lined face or a movement of the fingers clasping his burnous about him. When they turned inwards for their routine of strathspey and reel he lifted his head to the quickening rhythm, and when they made their final advance to "Cock o' the North" he leaned forward a little, but what he was making of it you couldn't tell. When the Drum-Major came forward to ask permission to march off, the Colonel turned to him with a smile and gesture of invitation, but he didn't move, and the Colonel returned the salute alone. The band marched away, and the Adjutant asked if he'd enjoyed it; Suleiman didn't reply, but sat forward, his eyes intent on the band as they passed out of sight.

"Oh, well, we did our best," muttered the Adjutant. "Don't suppose we could expect him to clap and stamp. At least he didn't walk out—"

Suleiman suddenly stood up. For a moment he continued to stare across the parade ground, then he turned to the Colonel, and for the first time there was a look on his face that wasn't baleful: his eyes were bright and staring fiercely, but they were sad, too, and he looked very old and tired. He spoke in a harsh, husky croak:

"La musique darray maklen! C'est la musique, ça!"

It was the first time he'd ever offered anything like conversation – whatever it meant. "What did he say?" the Colonel demanded. "Music of what?"

The Adjutant asked him to repeat it, but Suleiman just turned away, and when he was asked again he shook his head angrily and wouldn't answer. So the Adjutant took him back to the guard-room while the rest of us argued about what it was he'd said; he seemed to have been identifying the music, but no one could tell what "darray maklen" meant. The first word might be "arrêt", meaning anything from "stop" to "detention", but

102

the Adjutant's dictionary contained no word remotely like "maklen", and it wasn't until the end of dinner that the Colonel, who had been repeating the phrase and looking more like an irritated vulture by the minute, suddenly slapped the table. "Good God! That's it, of course! Morocco! It fits absolutely. Well, I'll be damned!" He beamed round in triumph. "The music of Harry Maclean! That's what he was saying! Talk about a voice from the past. Oh, the poor old chap! The music of Harry Maclean . . ."

"Who's Harry Maclean?" asked the Adjutant.

"Kaid Maclean . . . oh, long before your time. Came from Argyll, somewhere. One of the great Scotch mercenaries . . . packed in his commission in the '70s and went off to train the Sultan of Morocco's army, led 'em against all sorts of rebels – of whom our guest in the guard-room would certainly be one: Maclean was still active when the Riffs broke loose. Amazing chap, used to dress as a tribesman (long before Lawrence), got to places no European had ever seen. Oh, yes, Suleiman would know him, all right – may have fought with *and* against him. And he remembers the music of Harry Maclean . . . you see, Maclean was a famous piper, always carried his bags with him. I heard him play at Gib., about 1920, when I was a subaltern – piped like a MacCrimmon! He was an old man then, of course – big, splendid-looking cove with a great snowy beard, looked more like a sheikh than the real thing!"* The Colonel laughed, shaking his head at the memory, and then his smile faded, and after a moment he said: "And we've got one of his old enemies in the guard-room. An enemy who remembers his music."

There was quiet round the table. Then the second-in-command, who seldom said much, surprised everyone by remarking: "We ought to do something about that."

"Like what?" asked the Colonel quickly.

"Well . . . I'm not sure. But if this fellow Suleiman did know Maclean, it would be interesting to get him talking, wouldn't it?

* Sir Harry Aubrey de Vere Maclean (1848–1920), joined the Army in 1869, fought against Fenian raiders in Canada, and in 1877 entered the service of Sultan Mulai Hassan of Morocco as army instructor. In an adventurous career lasting more than thirty years "Kaid Maclean" became something of a North African legend: he was the trusted adviser of the Sultan and his successor, campaigned against rebel tribes, survived court

Not that he's shown himself sociable, but after today . . . well, you never know."

"Oh, I see." The Colonel sounded almost disappointed. "Yes, I suppose it would."

"Have him into the mess, perhaps," said the Senior Major. "Dinner, something like that?"

"He wouldn't come," said Bennet-Bruce.

"No harm in asking," said the second-in-command.

"That's what you think," said the Adjutant bitterly. "Every time I speak to him he just glares and turns his back – I'm beginning to think I've got B.O."

"Then don't ask him," said the Senior Major. "Just bring him along, and once he's here, chances are we can thaw him out."

"Ye daurnae offer him drink!" protested the M.O.

"Of course not – but we can lay on Arab grub, make him feel at home . . . well, it would be a gesture," said the second-in-command. "Show him that we . . . well, you know . . . I don't suppose he'll get many invitations, after he leaves here." He glanced at the Colonel, who was sitting lost in his own thoughts. "I move we ask him to the mess. What d'you think, sir?"

The Colonel came back to earth. "Certainly. Why not? Have him in tomorrow – make it a mess night." He pushed back his chair and went out, followed by the seniors.

"Sentimental old bird, the skipper," said Errol.

"How d'you mean?" said MacKenzie.

"Well, he's been on the wee wog's side all along – who hasn't? Now this Harry Maclean thing . . . it just makes having to turn Suleiman over to the French that much harder, doesn't it?"

"You're a perceptive chiel," nodded the Padre.

"It doesn't make much odds," said the Adjutant gloomily.

---

intrigues, journeyed throughout Morocco and visited the forbidden city of Tafilelt, and was once kidnapped (at the second attempt) and held to ransom by insurgents. Although unswervingly loyal to his employer, he was recognised as an unofficial British agent, and was created K.C.M.G. when he attended King Edward VII's coronation as one of the Moroccan delegation. Maclean was a genial, popular leader although, as his biographer remarks, "being of powerful physique he was able to deal summarily with insubordinate individuals". He was an enthusiastic piper who also played the piano, guitar, and accordion. (See the *Dictionary of National Biography*.)

"It's rotten whichever way you look at it." He glanced across at Errol who was flicking peanut shells at the Waterloo snuff-box. "What would you do . . . if it was you?"

"If I were the Colonel – and felt as sorry for old Abou ben Adem as he does?" Errol gave his lazy smile. "I certainly wouldn't connive at his escape – which is the thought at the back of everyone's mind, only we're too feart to say so. I might write to G.H.Q., citing his war service and decrepitude, and respectfully submitting that the French be told to fall out—"

"He's already done that," said the Adjutant. "Got a rocket for not minding his own business."

"Well, *shabash* the Colonel sahib! But that's all, folks. He's done his best – so all we can do is give Suleiman the hollow apology of a dinner to show our hearts are in the right place, and wish him bon voyage to Devil's Island."

"That's a lousy way to put it!" snapped MacKenzie.

"Only if you feel guilty, Kenny," said Errol. "I don't. He's a tough old bandit, down on his luck . . . and a damned bad man. No, I'd hand him over, with some regret, as the Colonel will. But unlike the Colonel I won't vex myself wondering what Harry Maclean would have done."

"That's a bit mystical," protested the Adjutant.

"Is it? You're not Scotch, Mike. The Colonel is – so he gets daft thoughts about . . . oh, after the battle . . . kinship of old enemies . . . doing right by the shades. Damned nonsense, but it can play hell with a Highlander in the wee sma' hoors, especially if he's got a drink in him. Read between the lines of *The Golden Bough* sometime." Errol stifled a yawn and got up. "It was written by a teuchter, incidentally."

"Interesting," said the Padre. "Well, what *would* Harry Maclean do about Suleiman?"

Errol paused at the door. "Shoot the little bugger, I should think. He probably spent half his life trying."

Acting on the Senior Major's advice, the Adjutant didn't invite Suleiman formally, but simply conducted him to the mess, where we had assembled in the dining-room. The table was blazing with our two centuries' worth of silver, much of it loot – Nana Sahib's spoons, the dragon candlesticks from the Opium Wars, the inlaid Ashanti shield (now a fruit-bowl), the silver-gilt punchbowl presented by Patton in Normandy, the snuff-box made from the hoof of the Scots Greys' drumhorse, the porcelain samovar given to a forgotten mercenary who had helped to stop the Turks at Vienna and whose grandson had brought it to the regiment. It was priceless and breathtaking; Suleiman could not doubt that he was being treated as a guest of honour. The Pipe-Sergeant had even bullied the Colonel into letting him compose a special air, "The Music of Suleiman ibn Aziz" – it was impossible to stop the pipey creating new works of genius, all of which sounded like "Bonnie Dundee" or "Flowers of the Forest", depending on the tempo; it remained to be seen which had been plagiarised when the pipey strode forth to regale us after dinner.

Poor soul, he never got the chance. Suleiman took one look at the gleaming table, the thirty expectant tartan figures, the pipers ranged against the wall, the Colonel welcoming him to his seat – and straightway stormed out, raging and cursing in Arabic. Why, I'm still not sure; he must have known it was kindly meant, and we could only assume that he regarded all Franks as poison and any overture from them as an insult. The mess reaction was that it was a pity, but if that was how he felt, too bad. Strangely enough, it didn't diminish the sympathy for him, and it was a reluctant Adjutant who had to tell him next day (Sunday) that the French were coming earlier than expected, and he would be leaving the following Thursday. Either because he was taken aback, or was still in a passion over the dinner fiasco, Suleiman let fly a torrent of abuse in *lingua franca*, shook his fist in the Adjutant's face, and rounded things off by spitting violently on the floor.

Which was distressing, and hardly reasonable since he'd known he was going sooner or later, but the explanation emerged three nights after. On Monday he was still in a villainous temper, but McGarry thought he looked unusually tired, too, and he wouldn't leave his cell to sit on the verandah. On Tuesday he kept his bed, sleeping most of the day. In the small hours of Wednesday morning he broke out.

He must have been working at the single bar of his cell window since his arrival, presumably calculating that he would have it loose by the end of the second week. The advance of the French arrival had upset his plans, and he had spent two and a half nights digging feverishly at the concrete sill – with what tool, and how he had not been detected, we never discovered. Only a chance look through the grille by the sentry discovered the bar askew, and thirty seconds later the guard were doubling out of barracks in the forlorn hope of catching a fugitive who had the choice of melting into the alleys of the city not far off, or vanishing into the Sahara which stretched for two thousand miles from our southern wall.

It was sheer blind luck that they came on him hobbling painfully along a dry ditch on the desert road; being reluctant to lay hands on an old man who was plainly on his last legs, they called on him to stop, but he just kept going, panting and stumbling, until they headed him off, when he turned at bay, lashing out, and after a furious clawing struggle he had to be carried bodily back to the guard-room, literally foaming at the mouth. Taken to a new cell, he collapsed on the floor, too exhausted to resist an examination by the M.O. which revealed what was already obvious – that he was an unusually hardy old man, and dead beat. Even so, an extra sentry was posted under his window.

There was no point in reporting the incident to the Provost Marshal, and for the last twenty-four hours before the French were due he was just confined to his cell, sitting hunched up on his cot, ignoring his food; having made his bid and failed he seemed resigned, with all the spirit drained out of him.

Then, late in the afternoon, he began to sing – or rather to chant, a high wailing cry not unlike the *muezzin*'s prayer call, but with a defiant note in it – the kind of thing which prompts the Highlander to remark: "Sing me a Gaelic song, granny, and sing it through your nose." It reminded me of something else, but I wasn't sure what until the Padre, who happened to be in our company office, cocked an ear to the distant keening sound and quoted:

"'The old wives will cry the coronach, and there will be a great clapping of hands, for I am one of the greatest chiefs of the Highlands.'"

"I never knew that," said Bennet-Bruce. "I always thought you were a clergyman from Skye."

"Pearls before swine," said the Padre. "I'm telling you what old Simon Fraser said before they took the head off him on Tower Green." He listened, eyes half-closed. "I wonder if our old buddoo isn't saying the same thing."

"Why should he? No one's going to cut his head off."

"Perhaps not," said the Padre. "But if that's not a coronach then I never heard one."

Whatever it was, it didn't exactly set the feet tapping; the high wavering cry raised the hairs on my neck – and not on mine alone. The Colonel left his office early to get out of earshot, and the Adjutant, kept at his desk, was noticeably not his usual Bertie Woosterish self: he tore my head off over some routine inquiry, slammed his window shut, and gave vent to his feelings.

"Gosh, I'll be glad to get shot of him! Nothing but trouble! We didn't *ask* to be landed with him, we've tried to make things as easy for him as we can, tried to be decent – and the little bastard spits in our eye, gets the Colonel in the doghouse with Cairo, treats *me* like dirt, tries to bust out—"

"Well, you can't blame him for that, Mike."

"— and generally gets right on the battalion's collective wick! Of course I don't blame him." The Adjutant stared gloomily out of the window. "That's the trouble. I'm all *for* him. We all are – and he doesn't even know it. He thinks we're as big a shower as the French and G.H.Q. He hates our guts." He brooded at me in a pink, bothered way. "Why shouldn't he? And why the hell should we worry if he does? You think I need a laxative, don't you?"

"I think you need some tea," I said. But I thought he was right: Suleiman, somehow, had got in among us, and it would have been nice to think that he knew we were on his side – for all the good *that* would do him. A selfish, childish wish, probably, but understandable.

Because I wanted to be there when he left, I had arranged to be orderly officer next day, and after dinner I went to tell McGarry that the French probably wouldn't take him before noon. McGarry promised to have him ready; the few belongings that had come with him were in an unopened bundle in the office safe, and the man himself was asleep.

"Nae wonder, after the fight he pit up. No' the size o' a fish supper, but it took four o' them tae carry him in, an' him beatin' the bejeezus oot o' them. Say that for him," McGarry nodded admiringly. "He's game."

Just how game we discovered next morning when the orderly

took breakfast into the cell, and Suleiman came at him from behind the door like a wildcat, knocked him flying, ducked past McGarry, and was heading for the wide blue yonder when he went full tilt over McAuslan, who was scrubbing the floor. In the ensuing mêlée which involved two sentries (with McAuslan wallowing in suds imploring all concerned to keep the heid) Suleiman managed to grab a bayonet, and murder would have been done if McGarry had not weighed in, clasping both of Suleiman's skinny wrists in one enormous paw and swinging him off his feet with the other. Even then the little sheikh had fought like a madman, struggling and kicking and trying to bite until, to the amazement of McAuslan:

". . . a' the fight seemed tae go oot o' him, an' he lets oot sich a helluva cry, an' ye know whit? He jist pit his heid on big McGarry's chest, like a wean wi' his mither, an' grat. No, he wisnae bubblin' – no' that kinda greetin', jist shakin' an' haudin' on like there wisnae a kick left in him. An' big McGarry pit him on his feet, an' says: 'Come on, auld yin', an' pits him back in the cell – an' then turns on me, fur Goad's sake, an' starts bawlin' tae get the flair scrubbit an' dae Ah think Ah'm peyed tae staun' aboot wi' no' twa pun' o' me hingin' straight! Ye'd think it wis me had been tryin' tae murder hauf the Airmy an' go absent, no' the wee wog!''

All this I learned when I checked the guard-room at nine – the facts from McGarry, the colour from Our Correspondent on Jankers. Suleiman had stayed quiet in his cell.

The French arrived at eleven in the Provost Marshal's car and an escorting jeep: a major and captain in sky-blue kepis, a sous-officier in the navy tunic and red breeches of the Légion Etrangère, two privates with carbines, and a Moorish inter-preter. The officers and the P.M. were escorted to the mess for hospitality while the rankers stayed with their vehicles; the sous-officier, a moustachioed stalwart with a gold chevron and no neck, paced up and down exchanging appraising glances with McGarry on the guard-room verandah.

There seemed to be more casual activity than usual in the vicinity that morning: several platoons were drilling on the square, various Jocks had found an excuse for moving to and from the nearer buildings, and others were being unobtrusive in the middle distance; nothing like a crowd, just a modest gathering, not large enough to excite the displeasure of R.S.M. Macintosh as he made his magisterial way across the parade, pausing to survey the platoons who presently stopped drilling and stood easy, but did not dismiss. It was all very orderly, but in no way official; they were waiting to see Suleiman ibn Aziz go, without being too obvious about it. The windows and verandahs of the farther barrack-blocks had their share of spectators, and the Padre and M.O. were coming through the main gate and mounting the guard-room steps, returning the magnificent salute of the sous-officier – he was a slightly puzzled sous-officier, judging by the way he was studying the square: why so many Ecossaises about, he might well have been wondering. Was this how les Dames d'Enfer kept discipline, by example? What would Milor' Wellington have said? He shook his head and resumed pacing, and the Ecossaises regarded him bleakly from under their bonnet-brims.

"Now's the time for the English to attack," observed the M.O.

"Right enough, Lachlan," agreed the Padre. "The Auld Alliance is looking gey fragile." He consulted his watch. "Band practice shortly, I think – there, what did I say?"

From behind the band office came the warm-up notes of a piper, and then the slow measured strains of "Lovat's Lament", the loveliest and most stately of slow marches. The Padre nodded approval.

"Aye, that's pipey. Not bad, for a man that never set foot on Skye."

"Who's idea's this?" I asked. "The Colonel's?"

"Why don't you ask him?" said the M.O. "Here he is, wi' the Comédie Française."

The Colonel and Adjutant were emerging from the tamarisk grove that screened the mess, with the French officers and the P.M. The R.S.M. let out a splendid Guards-trained scream of "Attain-shah!" and there was an echoing crash of heels on the square. The Padre chuckled.

"Canny Macintosh! You notice he didn't say 'Parade–shun!' Because there is no parade, of course. A nice distinction."

I followed the Colonel's party into the guard-room, the sous-officier and the Moorish interpreter bringing up the rear. Suleiman, with McGarry standing by, was sitting beside the table,

110

very composed, the lean brown face impassive under the silver-edged *kafilyeh* – it was hard to believe that this frail, quiet little man had twice tried to break out, fighting like a wild beast and trying to stab a sentry with his own bayonet. He didn't get up, and the French Major smiled and turned to the Colonel.

"I am pleased he has caused you no inconvenience, sir." He spoke English with barely a trace of accent.

"None whatever," said the Colonel. "All ready, Sarn't McGarry? Very well, sir."

The Major nodded to the sous-officier, who strode across and snapped an order. Suleiman didn't stir, and the sous-officier repeated it in an explosive bark that was startling in its unexpected violence. But not as startling as what followed. McGarry stiffened to his full height and rasped:

"You don't talk tae the man like that, son!"

The sous-officier didn't speak the language, but he knew cold menace when he heard it, and gave back as though he'd been hit – which, in my opinion, he nearly had been. The others stared, all except the Colonel, who had tactfully turned aside to listen to something that the Adjutant wasn't saying. There was an embarrassed pause, and then Suleiman glanced up at McGarry and, with the smallest of deprecating gestures, rose to his feet. He turned his back on the sous-officier, looked McGarry full in the face, and made the quick graceful heart-lips-brow salutation of the *salaam*.

For once McGarry was taken flat aback, and then he did the only thing he could do – stamped his heel and nodded. Suleiman turned away and calmly surveyed the waiting officers; he looked for a moment at the Colonel and then said something in Arabic to the interpreter, who passed it on in French to the Major, indicating the bundle of coarse cloth on the table which contained Suleiman's belongings. The Major looked surprised, shrugged, and turned to the Colonel.

"It seems there is something he wishes to leave with you."

He gave an order to the sous-officier, and we waited expectantly while the bundle was unwrapped. Outside the pipey could still be heard running through his repertoire; he was on to the marches now, with a kettle-drum rattling accompaniment, but you couldn't tell whether Suleiman was hearing it or not. He was standing absolutely still, his hands clasped before him, looking straight ahead at the Colonel, but he must have been watching out of the corner of his eye, for as the sous-officier began to take out the bundle's contents – a packet of papers, a bunch of keys, a couple of enamelled boxes, a few rather fine-looking ornaments which were probably gold and silver, one or two strands of jewellery – he gave another grunt in Arabic and thrust out his hand, palm up. The sous-officier was holding a packet about a foot long, wrapped in red muslin; he passed it to the interpreter, who handed it nervously to Suleiman.

You could have heard a pin drop while the little man flicked a hand to indicate that the rest of his goods should be parcelled up again, and then stood looking down at the red packet, turning it in his hands, clasping it as though reluctant to let it go. Then his head came up and he walked across to the Colonel and held it out to him with both hands. The Colonel took it, and as he did so Suleiman suddenly clasped both his hands over the Colonel's on the package, holding the grip hard and staring fiercely into the Colonel's face. Then he let go, inclined his head gravely, and stepped back. The Colonel said "Thank you", and Suleiman ibn Aziz walked out of the guard-room.

On the verandah he paused for a moment, looking at the Jocks in the square who were waiting to see him go. The unseen Pipe-Sergeant and the kettle-drums were waking the echoes, and I heard the Padre murmur to the M.O.:

"That'll be 'The Music of Suleiman ibn Aziz', I daresay – it sounds just like 'The Black Bear' to me, but then I haven't the pipey's imagination."

Suleiman ibn Aziz went down the steps and into the waiting car, the French officers exchanged salutes with the Colonel and climbed in, the legionnaires piled into the jeep, the sous-officier exchanged a last stare with McGarry, the sentry on the gate presented arms as the vehicles drove through, and the Jocks on the square began to drift away.

The Colonel was holding the red muslin package. "Right, let's have a look at it," he said, and led the way back into the guard-room, for he knew McGarry would be as curious as the rest of us. We all stood round as he unwrapped the cloth, and when the contents lay on the table nobody spoke for quite some time. We just looked at it and let the thought sink in.

It was an Arab dagger, and not a rich or ornamental one. The sheath was cracked and discoloured, and while the blade was classically curved and shone like silver, it was pitted with age, the brass cross-hilt was scarred, the pommel had lost its inlay, and the haft was bound with wire in two places. You wouldn't have given two ackers for it on a bazaar stall – unless you had laid it across your finger and noted the perfect balance, or lowered its edge on to a piece of paper and watched it slice through of its own weight.

The Colonel fingered his moustache, gave a little cough, said "Well," and was silent. He picked the dagger up again, weighed it in his hand, and said at last: "Not the most valuable of his possessions, I daresay. But certainly the most precious."

"He must have had it a long time," said the Adjutant. In a wondering tone he added: "He gave it to us."

The Colonel pushed the blade home. "Right. Get it cleaned up and sterilised – God knows who it's been in. It can go with the mess silver." He caught the Adjutant's doubtful frown. "Well, why shouldn't it? If some cavalry regiment can use Napoleon's brother's chamber-pot as a punchbowl, I see no reason why you shouldn't cut your cheese with a knife that's been through the Riff Rebellion."

"Absolutely, sir!" agreed the Adjutant hastily. "I'll see the mess sergeant looks after it right away." Then he looked worried. "I say, though – we ought to have given old Suleiman some cash for it – you know, bad luck not to pay for a knife. Cuts friendship, my aunt used to say."

The Colonel paused in the doorway. "I'm afraid his luck can't get much worse, Michael." He frowned, considering. "And I'm not sure that we were ever friends, exactly. Put it with the silver anyway."

113

McAuslan, Lance-Corporal

To hear him talk, usually at the top of his raucous voice, you might have thought that Private McAuslan was a violent man, but he wasn't, really, except under extreme provocation. Being unclean, dim, handless, illiterate, and ugly, he attracted a good deal of abuse from comrades as well as superiors, but while he didn't take it gladly his response seldom went beyond verbal truculence. Any day you might hear his warning roar of "Watch it, china!" floating from the windows of 12 Platoon barrack-room, followed by furious threats to melt, claim, sort out, or banjo his critic, but there it would end, as a rule; his associates knew just how far it was safe to rib him, and that there were some subjects best left alone. His intelligence, for example: he was used to being called dumb, dozy, clueless, and not the full hod of bricks, and that was all right, being the small change of military conversation; only if the ridicule went too far, or became too penetrating, was physical eruption liable to follow, as young Corporal Crawford learned to his cost.

He was a weapons instructor who, during a lecture, was unwise enough to make fun of McAuslan's inability to see through a well-known optical illusion. Bren gun magazines are kidney-shaped; lay them side by side and one looks larger than the other because its convex edge is longer than the concave edge of the magazine beside it; change them over, and the one which looked smaller now appears to be the bigger . . . a simple trick which causes much hilarity among five-year-olds.

Whether McAuslan had reached that stage, intellectually, was debatable, but he wasn't amused. I wasn't present, but according to my informant, Private Forbes, Crawford had been squatting over the magazines on the floor, switching them round and jeering at McAuslan's failure to see that they were identical, and McAuslan, having glowered at them in genuine baffled fury, had suddenly kicked Crawford full in the solar plexus, lifting him several feet and laying him out cold. Which had earned McAuslan fourteen days in the cooler, as well as demonstrating that there are few things more dangerous than presenting a primitive mind with an insoluble problem, never mind mocking it. Good teachers know this; bad ones, like Crawford, are appalled when they learn it the hard way.

The only other time I knew McAuslan moved to calculated assault (occasional canteen disturbances don't count, in Scottish regiments) was when he attacked an Arab vendor who had been threatening Ellen Ramsay on a shopping expedition, but that had been simple gallantry. Any normal – or in McAuslan's case, sub-normal – man would have been glad to play knight-errant to the fair Ellen, although in justice to the lad I believe he would have been just as forward in the defence of Gagool the Crone. For there was a champion inside McAuslan's ill-made frame, and a strong sense of fair play – his concept of what was, in his own words, "no' fair", got him court-martialled once. But, as I say, he wasn't normally given to hitting people, and when I heard that he and Private Chisholm were in cells for fighting in (and incidentally wrecking) the battalion's modest library, I was moved to do some preliminary investigating before their inevitable appearance in front of the Colonel.

For one thing, the locale was unusual, and for another, Chisholm was a civil, sober, and well-bred lad, the product of an Edinburgh public school, and a most unlikely antagonist for McAuslan, if only because each probably had difficulty understanding what the other was saying, a common prerequisite to disagreement. I visited them in the guard-room, starting with Chisholm as the more likely to provide a coherent explanation.

He didn't, as it turned out. Indeed, he was reticent to the point of embarrassment, and would say only that there had been a private difference of opinion, which since he was sporting a splendid black eye was an obvious understatement. I warned him that the Colonel would require rather more detail, and passed on to intrude on Private Grief in person; he was sitting on his cell floor, bruised and foul, moodily pulling threads from a blanket and looking like a disgruntled cave-dweller.

"Chisholm made a pretty good job of you," I observed, breaking the ice tactfully.

"Chisholm's a ——", he said, with unusual venom, and then rose and crouched apologetically to attention. "Ah beg yer pardon, sur; Ah shouldnae hiv said that. Awfy sorry. Aye, but he should've knowed better, so he should. Ah mean, he's no' a yahoo, is he? Chisholm, he's meant tae be eddimacated, fella that's been tae a posh school, an' that—"

"All right, McAuslan," I said patiently. "What happened?"

He scowled, with an indignant snuffle. "He insultit me."

"Insulted you?" It seemed unlikely, if not impossible. "How?"

"Aye, weel, ye see. It wis because o' because. That's whit startit it."

Not for the first time with him, I found myself doubting my senses. "I'm sorry, you'll have to say that again. It was because of what?"

"Because. Whit he said aboot because."

"I'm not with you, McAuslan. Why do you keep saying because?"

"Because that's whit it wis aboot. Because."

I felt that if I asked "Who's on first?" he would reply "No, he's on third," like Abbot and Costello, so I tried a new line.

"Shut up, McAuslan. Now, we'll start again. Why were you in the battalion library?"

"Tae listen tae because."

"So help me God, if you use that word again I'll forget myself. *What* were you listening *to*?"

"Ah'm tellin' ye, sur! Because!" His simian brow was bedewed with sweat, and he was plucking lumps from the blanket as he strove to enlighten me. "Ah wis listenin' tae because! Onna gramyphone. Ye know, Because Goad made thee mine Ah'll cherish thee, but. Itsa song onna record onna gramyphone. Ye must hae heard it, sur!" He regarded me in desperate appeal. "Because?"

It dawned. In the library the Padre maintained a portable gramophone and a selection of records for the battalion's music-lovers, of whom the battered wretch before me was apparently one – and that was enough to beggar belief, but that's McAuslan for you.

"I see," I said. "I'm sorry, McAuslan, I didn't understand. I must be slow today. You went to the library to listen to a record of the song entitled 'Because', and—"

"Onna gramyphone."

"As you say, on the gramophone. Then what happened?"

"Aye, weel, like Ah'm sayin', Ah'm listenin' tae ra record – here it's a smashin' record, but! Ye know it, sur? Yon man Tawber – he's a Hun, but jeez, whit a voice!" His pimpled countenance took on a look of holy rapture. "He minds me a bit o' Jackie O'Connell that used tae be in C Company, ye mind him? Irish boy, sang like a lintie, 'Ah'm on'y a Wanderin' Vagabond' an' 'Bless this Hoose' an'—"

"Hold it, McAuslan! You were listening to 'Because', sung by Richard Tauber. Fine. Then what happened?"

"Aye, weel, sur, like Ah tellt ye, Ah'm listenin' tae ra record, an' wee Tawber's givin' it lalldy, when Chisholm comes in an' starts pickin' oot some o' the ither records that's there – there's some right bummers, Ah'm tellin' ye, bluidy screechin' Eyeties, ye widnae credit it – an' efter a bit he sez: 'Ye gaunae play that record a' night, then?' 'Take yer time, pal,' Ah sez, 'Ah'm listenin' tae ra music here.' So he stauns aroon' an' then sez: 'Ye've played it hauf a dozen times a'ready. Hoo aboot givin' some ither buddy a chance?' 'Look, mac,' sez Ah, 'just haud on an' ye'll get the gramyphone when Ah'm finished, see? Whit ye in such a hurry to play, onywye?' 'Ah've got some *music* here,' sez he, nasty-like, 'jazz classics an' chamber music, for your information.' 'Jazz classics?' sez Ah. 'There's no such thing, an' Ah can mak' better chamber music in a latrine bucket.' 'Ah suppose ye think that cheap syrup ye're playin' is music?' sez he. 'Cheap syrup?' sez Ah – an' that wis when Ah stuck one oan him."

As Wagner used to say, no doubt. Well, it was fascinating, all right, and revealed a side to McAuslan which I had never dreamed of. And yet why not? Breasts didn't come any more savage than his, and if Tauber soothed it, splendid. But that wasn't really the point.

"In other words, you were hogging the gramophone, and he objected, and you belted him. You're just a hooligan, aren't you?"

"Oh, haud on, sur, it wasnae that, but!" he protested. "Ah'd hiv let him hiv the gramyphone if he hadnae been so sniffy, the toffy-nosed Embro git! But Ah wisnae havin' him sayin' that aboot the greatest song ever wrote! No' on yer life!" His unwashed face quivered with outrage. " 'Cheap syrup', sez he! That wis why Ah clocked him, an' then he clocked me, an' we got tore in, an' then the Gestapo came an' beltit the both o' us an' pit us in the tank." He snorted and sat down abruptly, plainly much moved. "The cheek o' him! No, Ah wisnae havin' that, no' aboot 'Because'." He gave a rasping sigh, scratching himself in a way that determined me to have a shower presently. "Think mebbe Sarn't McGarry'd gi'e us a cuppa chah, sur?"

"Try asking him and see what you get," I suggested, and he shuddered. He and the Provost Sergeant were old acquaintances. "But, look here, McAuslan, you can't clock people just because they don't like 'Because'." Now I was doing it. "People are entitled to express their opinions – I mean, it's a nice song, but—"

"Itsa greatest music onybody ever made up." He said it with a grim intensity that quite startled me. "It's marvellous. Nuthin' like it. No' even in Church."

"That's your opinion, but the fact that Chisholm doesn't share it is no reason to start a brawl and break up the library. Or for getting a man with a clean sheet into trouble, you horrible article. Not that he isn't to blame, too. Anyway, whatever the Colonel gives you – and I hope it's plenty – the first thing you and Chisholm do when you get out is apologise to the Padre, pay for the damage, and put in seven nights fatigue at the Church. Got that?"

"Yessur, rightsur! But Chisholm shouldnae hiv insultit—"

"Shut up about Chisholm! Anyway, what the hell's so special about 'Because'?" I asked out of irritated curiosity, and was given the brooding, reproachful stare of the great anthropoid at zoo spectators; he even stopped scratching.

"It's bluidy great," he said solemnly. "Wonderfullest song ever wrote. 'Atsa fac', sur."

He really meant it, and I knew McAuslan well enough to be aware that when he believed something, it was engraved on marble, or whatever his brain was made of. And while musical obsession was something new, well, different strains work their magic on different ears, and if he was enthralled by "Because", I wasn't going to argue – on his recent showing, it wouldn't have been safe. I left his cell thinking there were many things that I

118

knew not, and the deeps of McAuslan's mind was the first of them. Why "Because"? Was I missing something? I whistled the tune absently, and paused, repeating the words under my breath.

> Because you come to me
> With naught save lo-ove . . .

"Beg pardon, sir?" said Sergeant McGarry anxiously, and I left hurriedly, still pondering why that ordinary (even syrupy, as Chisholm had said) little tune should stir such passion in my platoon's answer to Karloff. Tauber sang it beautifully, to be sure, but hardly well enough to justify battery. Having nothing better to do, I turned off to the library, which was empty at that time of night and still bore signs of the evening's discord; "Because" was still on the gramophone, so I cranked the handle and let her rip, and Tauber hadn't unleashed more than a couple of sobs before there was a cry of alarm from the inner office and the Padre shot out, pale-faced and hiding his spectacles; he stopped with a gasp of relief and subsided on a chair.

"Thank God it's yourself – for a minute I thought it was yon Gorbals troglodyte back again. Has McGarry bound him with fetters of brass, I hope?"

"Sorry I startled you, bishop. Just doing some research on Tauber."

The Padre cocked a critical ear. "Ah, the Cherman lieder. Chust so. Fine voices, but they aye sound to me as though they've got something trapped. I'm an Orpheus Choir man myself, and a wee bit of Brahms, but I've no taste. 'Because', eh? I once knew a tenor who sang it in the Gaelic . . . mind you, he was from Tiree . . ."

"Wonder why it appeals to McAuslan?"

"Who can say?" The Padre prepared to go into a Hebridean philosophic trance. "Barrack-room sentiment? Childhood memory? Maybe his mother sang him to sleep wi' it." He shivered. "Can ye picture such a woman? Mrs Medusa McAuslan. Aye, well, I could have seen her son far enough this night, the ruffian. And yet," he gave a reflective sigh, "there's consolation in it, too. Better that he and Chisholm should thrash each other over music than over cards or drink or the Rangers

119

and the Celtic. D'ye not think so, Dand?"

One who didn't was the Colonel. He gave them three days in close tack, with stoppage of pay for damages. The platoon, when the cause of the brawl became known, waxed hilarious over McAuslan's Orphean tendencies, but when I heard that Private Fletcher had serenaded beneath his cell window with a ribald version of "Because", I thought it time to warn them that they were playing with dynamite, and added that if in future McAuslan was provoked to violence by musical humour, the joker could expect no mercy, d'you get that, Fletcher? I probably needn't have bothered, for soon after his release the episode was forgotten in a new sensation from which McAuslan emerged, briefly, as something of a celebrity.

I have described the great Inter-Regimental Quiz elsewhere. What happened was that, to settle a bet between our colonels, a team from the neighbouring Fusiliers was matched against one from our battalion in a general knowledge competition, held in the presence of the Brigadier, garrison society, and a baying mob of supporters from both regiments. After a gruelling struggle in which I, for one, was drained of my great store of trivia, and the Padre was reduced to the point where he couldn't tell the Pentateuch from the Apocrypha, the contest ended in a tie, at which stage the Brigadier, who was the biggest idiot ever to wear red tabs, said the thing should be settled by one sudden-death question which he would put to both sides and, if they couldn't answer, to their supporters. Naturally we all cried sycophantic agreement, and the Brigadier, bursting with self-satisfaction, propounded the most fatuous hypothetical trick-question you ever heard: how can one player score three goals at football without anyone else touching the ball in between?

We didn't know, of course, and suggested politely that the thing was impossible. Not so, said the Brigadier smugly; it was unlikely, granted, but theoretically possible – and that was the great moment when McAuslan, eating chips in the audience, rose from his seat like a fly-blown prophet and gave the right answer.* It seemed he had once heard it in a Glasgow pub; what that says about the Brigadier's intellectual circle you must judge for yourselves. Anyway, the Brigadier was delighted, and con-

* Which is long and complex, and may be found in *McAuslan in the Rough*.

gratulated McAuslan, who won a box of Turkish Delight for his pains.

A harmless incident, apparently, but pregnant with disaster. For the Brigadier, gratified that his ridiculous question had broken the deadlock, remarked to our Colonel in the mess afterwards that he'd been impressed by that odd-looking bird who'd come up with the answer. What was his name again? McAuslan, eh? Not the kind, from his appearance, whom you'd expect to be able to solve a knotty problem like that – why, the Brigadier had been stumping people with it for years. Well, it just went to show, you couldn't judge a sausage by its . . . by its . . . oh, dammit, he'd forget his own name next . . . yes, by its skin, that was it.

"Kind of chap I used to watch out for in my battalion days," mused the Brigadier. "Chaps with potential often look a bit . . . well, strange. Wingate, for instance." I had a brief dreadful vision of McAuslan leading the Chindits, and then the Brigadier dispelled it with one of the most shocking suggestions ever made.

"This chap McAuslan," he asked the Colonel, "ever thought of making him an N.C.O.?"

The Colonel admitted later that he hadn't been so shaken by a question since the Japanese interrogated him on the Moulmein railway – and at least he'd been able to tell them to go to hell. With the Brigadier – whom he'd been heard to describe as an ass who ought to be put in charge of a company store and excused boots – he decided to employ controlled sarcasm.

"Interesting idea, sir," he said smoothly. "Of course, we've thought long and hard about McAuslan. Haven't we, MacNeill? We don't overlook men of his calibre, not in this battalion. But as you know, sir, there are some men who simply won't accept promotion. Pity, but what can one do? Waiter, another round here." Perfectly true, and totally misleading – there *are* men who won't take promotion, but McAuslan was the last who was likely to get the chance.

The Brigadier frowned and said exceptional men should be persuaded; it was the Army's duty to make them realise their full potential. The Colonel smiled – I guessed he was on the point of suggesting innocently that the Brigadier should take McAuslan into Brigade H.Q., possibly in Intelligence, but fortunately someone came up at that moment and the subject was changed.

"That's what they put in command of brigades nowadays," observed the Colonel, when the Brigadier had gone. "Well, thank God they kept him in Cairo during the war. Waiter, bring me another – and you can stop smirking, young Dand, and concentrate on keeping that blot McAuslan out of the public eye in future."

That was easier said than done at the best of times, and now a combination of circumstances arose to make it impossible. First, Bennet-Bruce went off on yet another of those luxurious courses that seem to come the way of military Old Etonians – if it wasn't Advanced French at Antibes it was water-skiing at Djerba – and our company came under the temporary command of that debonair and dangerous exquisite, Captain Errol. Secondly, the rest of the battalion, Colonel, H.Q., Support Company and all, went off on a seven-day exercise in the big desert, leaving only D Company to rattle about in the deserted barracks; officially we were maintaining a military presence, but in fact we were cleaning and decorating the transport sheds for the big occasion of the regimental year, Waterloo Night, which would be celebrated with dance and revelry on the evening of the battalion's return. Thirdly, Private McAuslan went with a fatigue party to collect extra furniture for the dance from the Brigade quartermaster.

All innocent events in themselves; it was their coincidence that made them lethal.

The Brigadier, returning from what must have been an unusually excellent lunch, happened by just as the fatigue party were loading their truck, and recognised McAuslan (as who wouldn't) among them. Feeling paternal, he summoned the toiler and asked him what was all this nonsense about refusing promotion, eh? What McAuslan said is not recorded; no interpreter was present, and he was presumably in his usual state of stricken incoherence before High Authority. The Brigadier shook his head kindly and spoke of ambition and advancement; he may even have told McAuslan there was a baton in his knapsack (it was his good luck he couldn't see inside McAuslan's knapsack, not after lunch). Finally, he said why didn't McAuslan change his mind and accept a lance-corporal's stripe as the first step to higher things. I assume that at this point McAuslan made some noise which was taken for assent, for the Brigadier cried capital, capital, he would see to it, and "Carry on, Corporal!"

Most great military blunders stem from the good intentions of some high-ranking buffoon, but in fairness it has to be said that the Brigadier was seeing McAuslan at his best – awestruck dumb, naked save for identity discs and khaki shorts which gave no real idea of how revolting he looked in uniform, and engaged in the only work of which he was capable: to wit, carrying heavy and unbreakable objects across level ground under supervision. Even so, one good look at that neanderthal profile should have warned even a staff officer; perhaps he was short-sighted, and the lunch had been quite exceptional.

Strictly speaking it isn't a Brigadier's business to interfere in minor promotions, and if when he phoned the barracks he'd got the Colonel or Bennet-Bruce they would have thanked him for his recommendation and then forgotten about it. But in their absence he got Errol, who could have given lessons in mischief to Loki, and when the Brigadier said that a tape should be stuck on McAuslan's arm forthwith, our temporary commander said he would be delighted to comply; he'd often thought McAuslan was due for a boost upstairs, and he would take the liberty of congratulating the Brigadier for having spotted talent from his Olympian height, or words to that effect. Knowing Errol's line of oil, I imagine the Brigadier may have wondered if he shouldn't have put McAuslan straight up to sergeant.

So there it was: the appointment of 14687347 McAuslan, J., to lance-corporal (acting, unpaid) went on company orders that afternoon, and my reaction, on returning from a hard day in the transport shed and suffering a minor apoplexy when I heard the news, was to inquire of Errol if he had gone doolaly, and if not, what was he playing at?

"Respecting the wishes of my superiors," he said languidly, with his feet on the desk. "Have some tea."

"Are you kidding? Look – hasn't anyone told you about McAuslan? The brute's illiterate, his crime sheet's as long as a toilet roll, he's had to be forcibly washed God knows how often, he doesn't know left from right, can't tell the time of day, and is, at a conservative estimate, the dirtiest and dumbest bad bargain His Majesty's made since Agincourt!"

"You paint a pretty picture," he said. "Care to argue with the Brigadier, Mr MacNeill?"

"Care to explain to the Colonel, Captain Errol? He'll have your guts for garters."

"I'm just the slave of duty. When Brigadiers say unto me, go – I've gone already."

"Look," I said, "it isn't on. For one thing, my Jocks won't wear it. Can you see them taking orders from that . . . that walking tattie-bogle? They'll mutiny."

"I doubt it," he said. "Anyway, he's been promoted. What d'you want me to do – bust him straight back? Without a reason?"

"I've just given you about seventeen!"

"For not promoting him, yes. Not for busting him. There's a difference. The deed's been done, he's got his stripe, and he's entitled to his chance." He raised a mocking eyebrow. "You ought to appreciate that – you've been a lance-jack yourself, and see where it got you."

"You're a bastard, you know that?"

"So they tell me," said Errol complacently. "Come on, let's have a drink and I'll play you fifty up before dinner."

It was only when my initial outrage at the Brigadier's folly (and Errol's malicious acquiescence) had subsided that the enormity of the thing really sank in. McAuslan simply couldn't begin to be a lance-corporal. You just had to picture the sequence of events when he shambled out, looking as though he'd just been cut down from the Tyburn gibbet, with a new stripe on his sleeve: the Jocks would collapse in mirth, McAuslan would give an order, it would not be taken seriously, and he would charge someone with disobedience – assuming he knew how. Then what? How could I, with a straight face, punish an honest soldier for ignoring an order given by a deadbeat whose military unfitness was a battalion byword? It might even be argued that McAuslan, whose imperative vocabulary consisted mainly of "Sharrup!" and "Bugger off!" was incapable of giving a lawful command. Suddenly the Nuremberg trial took on a whole new aspect, and I had to fight down a vision of the Tartan Caliban sitting in the dock scratching himself while the Nazi war criminals scrambled to keep away from him. More immediate pictures presented themselves: McAuslan, whose mere touch brought rust, inspecting rifles . . . McAuslan reprimanding someone for slovenliness . . . McAuslan calling

124

the roll when he couldn't even read. It was all a nightmare, impossible.

The effect on discipline would be disastrous. It was also, incidentally, most unfair to the man himself. Lance-corporal (which is an appointment, without even the dignity of a rank) is the most thankless number you can draw in the Army, a dogsbody's job with responsibilities but no real power, as I knew from experience of which Errol had reminded me, although he probably didn't know that I'd been a lance-jack no fewer than four times and been busted back to private on three of them – for losing, on different occasions, a tea-urn, a member of my section, and a guard-room.* I had painful memories of trying to take charge, at the age of nineteen, of ten men all older and longer served than I was, of being the butt both of superiors and subordinates, and of the shame of those three reductions to the ranks. The fourth promotion, in Burma, was different; then it was life or death, with no time for doubts or indecisions, and I had kept my stripe. But it's no fun, having that one tape (look what it did to Hitler) and for McAuslan, with all his natural handicaps, I could see it being traumatic.

I was dead wrong. Whoever suffered from that promotion, it wasn't him. He took to that stripe like a Finnish sailor to schnapps; you'd have thought he'd been born with it. With the help of a new suit of khaki drill (issued, I later discovered, on the orders of the unpredictable Errol) he managed to look semi-human for his first few hours in authority, and in that time he became, in his own mind at least, a lance-corporal. He didn't look, act, or sound like one, but he plainly *felt* like one, God help us. The presence of that newly-blancoed white chevron on his ill-fitting sleeve seemed to fill him with aggressive confidence, and he lumbered around like a badly-wrapped mummy bellowing irrelevant orders at anything that moved. And like many a dim-wit before and since he got by on the sheer force of his own ignorance and the tolerance of those around him. Greeted with

---

* The tea-urn is presumably still lying somewhere near the summit of Scafell Pike. The man who went missing from my section, on a night exercise in Norfolk, turned up the following day, drunk. The guard-room was an enormous bell-tent which was removed from over my sleeping head by Royal Scots Fusiliers and Cameronians celebrating Hogmanay at Deolali, India.

derision by his section, he didn't seem to notice; having reduced the elementary business of marching them to the transport sheds to a shambolic rout, he simply blared abuse – and they got there, eventually; after all, they knew the way. With no idea of how to organise a work-gang, he just repeated, with coarse embellishments, the orders of the full corporal in overall charge, and since no one paid any attention, no harm was done. He thought he was doing fine.

He wouldn't have survived ten minutes of normal military duty, but supervising men as they heave planks and trestles around is simple stuff, and with the battalion away there was a relaxed and informal atmosphere undisturbed by parades, bugle calls, sergeant-majors, and the usual disciplinary apparatus with which he couldn't have begun to cope.

To our shame, Sergeant Telfer and I kept out of the way. Our unspoken excuse was that we had to oversee the hanging above the bandstand of the Waterloo Picture, a gigantic oil painting (by Lady Butler, I think) which normally hung in the mess but was publicly displayed on this annual occasion. It showed the great moment which was the regiment's pride, when our predecessors, having taken everything the French could throw at them, had caught hold of the stirrup leathers of the advancing Scots Greys and launched themselves against the overwhelming strength of Napoleon's army in what posterity calls the Stirrup Charge; there has never been anything like it in war, and the Emperor himself is said to have stared in disbelief at "those Amazons" and "the terrible grey horses". We hung it just so, in its massive gilt frame, and as we worked we could hear, from the far end of the great echoing shed, sounds of the New Order being imposed on Three Section: McAuslan's raucous bellows of "Moo-ove yersels, ye idle bums, or Ah'll blitz ye!" and "Ah heard that, Fletcher! Whit d'ye think this is on mah sleeve – Scotch mist?" responded to with derisive obscenities. Obviously the section thought him a great hoot.

I knew that wouldn't last long. Being ordered about by McAuslan might be an amusing novelty for a few hours, especially when the orders were superfluous, but they'd get fed up fast enough when the orders mattered and had to be obeyed, and the total unfitness of the thing came home to them. We had an example of this when Telfer put Three Section to tidying up the

126

outside approaches to the sheds and I suggested that the stone borders of the paths could do with a lick of whitewash. Before Telfer could translate this into an order, Lance-Corporal Grendel, who had been lurking attentively, sprang into executive action.

"Whitewash, sur! Right, sur, right away!" He lurched forward, tripping on his untied laces, full of martial zeal. "Youse men – Forbes, Fletcher, Leishman! Get yersels doon ra Q.M. store! Get ra whitewash'n'brushes! C'moan, c'moan, c'moan, Ah'm no talkin' tae mysel'! Moo-ove, ye shower, or Ah'll be havin' ye!"

The sheer volume and violence of it was paralysing. For a moment they stared in disbelief; then, as it dawned that the joke was no longer a joke, and the Despised Unwashed was become the Voice of Authority, Fletcher's jaw tightened angrily and I caught his eye just in time.

"Right, off you go," I said. "Three cans should do, and six brushes. Carry on, you three." They went, Fletcher casting a baleful glance at McAuslan who, ill-dressed in a little brief and insanitary authority, pursued them with invective. It was like listening to a Guards Drill Sergeant finally cracking up.

"Ye hear that, ye middens? Three drums'n'six brushes, an' don't be a' bluidy day aboot it! Ah'm watchin' ye, Fletcher! Ah've got your number, boy! Double, ye horrible heap, ye! Keep the eye doon, Forbes, or yer feet won't touch! Moo-ove yer idle body, Leishman, Ah can see ye—"

"Take it easy, Corporal," I said, "they're going." He wheeled round obediently, falling over himself and scrambling to disorderly attention, and I was about to advise him to moderate his word of command when I caught the glazed fanatical gleam in his eye and realised that the brute was drunk with power; the heady wine of authority was coursing through his system, and he was ready to decimate whole armies. It was quite frightening, in a bizarre way: McAuslan as Captain Bligh. A new and alarming prospect opened up – mutiny, for if this personality change was permanent it could only be a matter of time before Fletcher or some other indignant soul planted the tyrant one and qualified for a court-martial. Already I could hear the Colonel's incredulous question: "You say Fletcher assaulted a superior? Who, for heaven's sake?" and my hollow reply:

127

"Lance-Corporal McAuslan, sir . . ." No. Something would have to be done, and speedily, whether the Brigadier and Errol liked it or not.

I was still debating the possibility of sending McAuslan on leave, or hiring Arab thugs to kidnap him, when we finished work for the day. Three Section, I was relieved to see, fell in of their own accord and marched back to the barrack-block paying no heed to Mad Lejeaune of the Legion, who lumbered in their wake, bawling the step – not only out of time with the squad, but with himself, too. His new uniform was fit only for the incinerator by this time, and his stripe was starting to come loose, which I hoped was an omen.

And then in a moment it was all out of my hands and forgotten about. Errol was just coming off the phone when I entered the company office, and before I could begin an impassioned plea for McAuslan's reduction to the ranks on whatever pretext, he was issuing orders.

"You know Bin'yassar Convent, don't you? The Mother Superior's been on the line to Brigade – it seems a big caravan of desert buddoo have shown up at the oasis, and she doesn't like the look of them. You'll take Eleven Platoon, battle order, three days' rations, they'll wear their tartans, and I'm giving you a piper. Get out there right away, sit down in the convent, and show the flag – you know the drill. It's almost sure to be a false alarm, but we've got to keep the old girl happy. Right, move!"

It was a routine operation I had performed before, which was presumably why I'd been picked this time. The convent was about thirty miles away, on the very edge of the big desert, a relic of the days when the Crusaders patrolled the caravan trails. From time immemorial it had been occupied by the Sisters of some Order or other, and since it was in our protected zone we were occasionally called on to ferry supplies, make road repairs, and stand guard against possible emergencies. The North Sahara is one of the last lawless places on earth, or was then, and its inhabitants spend much of their time moving around; they may be anything from the gentlest of nomad herdsmen to Hoggar slavers and Targui gun-runners, and when they suddenly materialise on your doorstep it is as well to take precautions. The Mother Superior wasn't a nervous woman, but as she explained in broken English when the platoon and I arrived that evening, some of her nuns were, and would we please play our music to reassure them and warn off these desert intruders.

Looking south from the high convent wall I couldn't blame the nuns; there must have been two or three hundred black or red tents pitched round the palms of the oasis a mile away, with camel and horse herds as well as the usual goats. A reek of bitter smoke and other interesting African aromas drifted across the low sandhills, with the murmur of a great multitude. Through my binoculars I could make out groups of armed riders swathed in black, but whether they were wearing the veils which would have identified them as Touareg I couldn't be sure. It was unlikely, so close to the coast. In fact, it all looked a good deal more romantic and sinister than it was; I doubted if tribesmen had laid a finger on Bin'yassar Convent in seven centuries, and the greatest danger from the present incursion was the cholera with which they would undoubtedly contaminate the local wells.

However, there was the drill to go through, starting with the piper playing on the wall at sunset to let the Bedouin know we were in residence, and a parade outside next morning, with kilts and fixed bayonets. Highlanders are the most conspicuous troops there are, which was why we got this sort of job; the wildest of wild men in North Africa (or anywhere else for that matter) can recognise "Cock o' the North" when they hear it, and know they are in touch with the Army – it's not a threat or even a warning so much as a signal, and unless they are really looking for trouble it has only one practical effect: they come closer to gaze silently on these strange northern barbarians in their weird green skirts and funny hats, and to listen to the eerie thrilling sound which fascinates the native ear from Casablanca to the South Seas. (Maybe we *are* one of the Lost Tribes; I wouldn't be surprised.)

So during our stay there was a permanent semi-circle, thousands strong, a few hundred yards from the walls, staring in dead silence at the kilted sentries and waiting for the piper to start up again. They were entirely peaceful, but I suppose our presence may have spared the nuns some pilfering and annoyance. That was all there was to it, except that I had to spend every spare hour in attendance on the ancient Mother Superior, who was a clock-golf freak and counted all time lost when she wasn't beating the daylights out of visitors with her

129

putter. Constant practice had sharpened her game to the point where she could have given Greg Norman a stroke a hole, and after two days of watching her sink fifteen-footers I didn't care if I never saw a golf ball again. (You were called on to do some peculiar things in the old British Army, but I can't recall many stranger than following that bird-like little old woman in her white robe and wimple as she hopped round the clock-golf layout, rattling her putts across the baked earth with invariable accuracy and chirping triumphantly in Italian. Beaten seven and five in a Garden of Allah in the Sahara Desert. I wonder if it's still there.)

On the third morning the oasis was deserted; the buddoo had vanished back into the big desert. The Catholic members of Eleven Platoon went to an early Mass while the Protestants stood about outside with arms folded, sniffing; I thanked the Mother Superior for her marathon putting lesson; the entire convent staff stood on the walls waving as we left, apparently convinced that we alone had saved them from sack and pillage – and only as we drove back into town did I recall that other minor crisis I had left behind in barracks three days ago. Had the iron discipline of Lance-Corporal McAuslan provoked a mutiny yet? Had he perhaps failed in some duty and been reduced to the ranks – the battalion would have been back home for two days now (I had missed the Waterloo Ball the previous night) and I couldn't believe that the Colonel would lose much time in returning him to private life, so to speak. Yet with McAuslan, you never knew; he might have got himself recommended for a commission by now, or deserted.

I was not kept in suspense. Almost the first thing I saw as our lead truck turned into the barrack gate was the familiar unkempt figure crouching in the little rock-garden outside the guard-room, apparently foraging for bugs under stones. He had all the appearance of a defaulter on fatigues, which suggested that he was a private again, but with the sleeve of his denims in its usual mouldering state it was hard to tell whether there was still a stripe there or not. I got out, told the trucks to carry on to the barrack-block, and addressed him.

"What happened to you?"

He rose, shedding loose soil and debris, and gave me cordial greeting. "Aw, hullaw rerr, surr. Ye got back. The Fenian wimmen a'right, then?"

I assured him that the convent was safe, and repeated my question, and he wiped his nose audibly with a hand covered in compost; it didn't make him a whit dirtier than he already was.

"Ah got stripped," he announced, and heaved a sigh of deep resignation. "Bustit."

"Oh dear, that's a shame," I lied. "How did it happen?"

"Aye, weel, ye see." He frowned, meditating, and passed a hand through his tangled hair, dislodging a well-built earthworm. "It wis because o' MacGonagal."

For a wild moment I thought he meant the poet. You see why: from taking up the cudgels in one branch of the arts, music, it would be a short step to brawling on the slopes of Parnassus – and then I remembered there was a MacGonagal in Three Section, a pugnacious Glaswegian recently posted to us from the Highland Light Infantry.

"He got impident, an' Ah belted him." That settled which MacGonagal it was, anyway. "It was just last night, efter the Waterloo Ball, when we were clearin' up on the bandstand, pittin' the furniture away, an' that—"

"Don't tell me the band had been playing 'Because' and MacGonagal didn't like it."

"Ach, no." He made a contemptuous gesture, scattering loam broadcast. "They widnae hiv the gumption tae play onything that good. Naw, MacGonagal just startit makin' remarks, an' Ah wisnae havin' it—"

"McAuslan," I said patiently. "You were still a lance-corporal, weren't you? Yes, so if MacGonagal was insolent to you, the proper course was to book him, not belt him. Right?"

"Ye don't understand, sur. It wisnae me he was cheeky to. Ah couldnae book him." He clawed at his midriff in perplexity, and there was a sound of damp cotton tearing. "It was just that he startit makin' insultin' remarks, about the pictur'. Ye know, the big pictur' o' oor fellas haudin' ontae the cavalry's stirrups an' chargin' alang wi' them an' gettin' tore intae ra Frogs. Aye, ra Stirrup Charge. Here, it's a smashin' paintin', yon, so it is!" He beamed in admiration through his grime. "Ought tae be onna calendars an' whusky bottles, so it should."

I decided I wasn't hearing aright. McAuslan the music critic I had been prepared to accept – just. But McAuslan stirred to

131

violence because of aspersions cast on a Victorian painting . . . no. Where would it end? He'd be battering people over Henry Moore and Stravinsky before you knew it.

"What," I asked with bated breath, "did MacGonagal say about the painting, McAuslan?"

"He said it wis bluidy rubbish," replied McAuslan indignantly. "Ah didnae mind that, but. Fella's entitled tae his opinion, like ye said. But then he sez: 'Whit's it meant tae be aboot, onywye?' So Ah tellt him. Ah sez: 'That's oor fellas – oor regiment, no' the bluidy H.L.I. – haudin' ontae the cavalry's stirrups an' chargin' alang wi' them an' gettin' tore intae ra Frogs. Winnin' ra Battle o' Waterloo, MacGonagal,' Ah sez, 'pittin' the hems on Napoleon, see?' 'Zatafact?' sez he – ye know, sarcastic-like. 'Weel, Ah'll tell ye sumpn, McAuslan,' sez he. 'Ah don't think your bluidy regiment wis chargin' wi' the cavalry at a'. Ah think they were tryin' tae haud them back.'"

"Dammed cheek!" I exclaimed.

"That's whit Ah said!" cried McAuslan, vindicated. "Ah sez: 'Look, MacGonagal, no bluidy fugitive frae the Hairy-Legged Irish is gaun tae say that aboot *this* regiment! Ye bluidy leear, you tak' that back or Ah'm claimin' ye!' 'Ach, away an' shoot a few more cheeses,' sez he, an' gives me the V-sign. So that wis when Ah pit the heid on him."

So it hadn't been a case of wounded artistic sensibilities, but of regimental honour, which was rather different.

"An' he beltit me back, an' we got tore in." His voice took on a plaintive chant which was familiar. "An' then the Gestapo came, an' beltit the both o' us, and pit us in the cooler—"

"Yes, I understand," I said. "Well, he had provoked you, but you shouldn't have hit him, just the same." An intriguing thought struck me. "You came up before the Colonel this morning, I suppose – what did he say when he heard why you'd been fighting?"

"Och, he wis awfy decent, but. He's a great man, yon," said McAuslan affectionately. "When we wiz marched in, an' the R.S.M. cries: 'Here Lance-Corporal McAuslan an' Private MacGonagal been gettin' wired intae each ither' – or sumpn like that, onywye – ra Colonel tak's one look at me an' sez: 'Ah don't believe it.' Funny, him sayin' that, sur; Ah mean, Ah've been marched in before." He shook his matted head, puzzled, and I didn't like to tell him it was the lance-corporal's stripe the Colonel hadn't been able to believe.

"Aye, weel, he heard the evidence frae ra Gestapo, an' we didnae hiv nuthin' tae say, so he gives MacGonagal seven days and shoots him oot. Then he sez tae me: 'Ah sympathise wi' yer reaction, Corporal, but Ah'm afraid ye cannae continue as an N.C.O. Ah'll hiv tae reduce ye tae the ranks, an' gi' ye one day's C.B.' But he smiled, quite joco. An' that wis it."

Trust the Colonel to find a painless way of busting him. It had been bound to happen eventually, and it couldn't have been done more tactfully – mind you, the excuse had been made in heaven. I surveyed him, grubby and dishevelled but apparently content, and since we were conversing so amiably, for once, I ventured a sensitive question.

"Tell me, McAuslan . . . something that's been puzzling me. That tune, 'Because'. Where did you first hear it, d'you remember? And why do you like it so much? Does it just appeal to you, or is there some special reason?"

"Och, Ah can tell ye that, sur." He scratched happily. "First time Ah ever heard 'Because' wis in the auld Happy Days cabaret in Port Said, back in '42. Ye know the Happy Days, sur – in behind Simon Arts?* No? Aye, weel, that's where Ah heard it. Greatest tune that ever wis. So it is. Efter that, Ah used tae get ma mate Wullie Ferguson tae play it on his mooth-organ, when we wis inna desert, inna war."

"Fifty-first Div? Eighth Army?"

"That's right, sur. Wullie played it awfy bonny, but."

"What happened to him?"

"Wullie? He bought his lot just efter Alamein. Land-mine." He shook his head. "He wis a good mucker, just the same, Wullie."

So that was it. Only it wasn't, apparently, for he went on:

"But whit Ah like best aboot 'Because' is that it minds me o' the auld Happy Days. Aw, we had some rerr terrs in that place, Ah'm tellin' ye!" He scrubbed his noise with his sleeve, beaming with reminiscence. "Aye, wi' the wog band playin' 'Because'. See, there wis this big belly-dancer, an' it wis her signature tune,

* A famous department store on the Port Said waterfront, correctly spelled Simon Arzt but known to servicemen as "Simon Arts".

an' she did her stuff tae it. Goad, but Ah fancied that wumman! Never got near her, mind. None o' us did. But the tune stuck in ma heid. Fatima, her name wis." He gave a rasping sigh. "Ma Goad, see her an' her tambourine!"

Well, there are worse reasons for being a music-lover, I suppose. He sighed again and spat, surveying the guard-room rockery with sloth-like reluctance.

"Aye, weel, this'll no' pay the rent. Mind if Ah cairry on, sur? Ah've tae finish weedin' this lot or big McGarry'll kill me, swine that he is." He scooped up a pawful of mud. "It wid scunner ye, no kiddin'. Stoor an' muck an' wee crawly beasties! See them, Ah hate them! Ach!"

"Carry on, McAuslan," I said, and as I turned away I added, not quite insincerely: "Anyway, I'm sorry you lost your stripe."

"Ach, Ah'm no' bothered," said he, clawing at the soil. "It's better bein' back wi' the boys, Fletcher 'n' Forbes an' them. Ah didnae like havin' tae boss them aboot. Ye know sumpn, sur?" He paused, squatting, weighing a handful of ordure in a philosophic way. "Ye hiv tae be a right pig tae get promotion. Aye, an' it turns ye intae a worser pig, the higher up ye get, Ah'm sure o' that. Weel, ye ken that yersel'." Grunt, grunt, I thought. "So Ah'm no' carin' aboot getting bustit. Ah wisnae much o' a lance-jack onywye. Ah did everythin' wrang."

"Oh, I don't think you did too badly," I consoled him. "At least you never lost a guard-room."

"Loast a guard-room?" said McAuslan incredulously. "How the hell could Ah? Ah mean, Ah know Ah'm dumb, but it would tak' a right bluidy eejit tae dae that!"

"You're probably right," I said humbly. "Carry on, McAuslan."

The Gordon Women

There is a story they tell in Breadalbane:

Gordon of Achruach was at feud with Campbell of Kentallan, who hired certain Gregora, landless men, who took the Gordon unawares while he was hunting in the Mamore. And they cut off his head and put it in a bag to show the Campbell that the work was done. That was the way of it.

And as they fared for Kentallan the Gregora came by the Gordon's door at Achruach, and went in, and the Gordon's wife (little knowing she was a widow) bade them to table, as the custom is, and went out for the Athol brose. And while she was gone the Gregora winked at one another, and set the Gordon's head on a dish, with an apple in the mouth, to see what the good wife would make of it. That is the Gregora for you, hell mend the black pack of them.

And the good wife came in, and saw her man's head bloody on the board, but kept her countenance and said never a word, only smiled on the Gregora and bade them good cheer. The Gregora wondered at this. Has she not seen it? was in the mind of each of them. Still looked she never on the head, but said a word to her ghillie and sent him forth. And smiling on the Gregora, she told them a tale, never looking at the head, and held them spellbound, for she was great at the stories, and very fair besides. The Gregora wondered, has she not seen it yet? This is not canny, was in their minds, and they said they must be for the road, but she held them there by her tale and her presence, and so they bided whether they would or no. That was the way of it.

And still she spoke and looked not on the head, until the ghillie

135

returned with her men of Achruach, who came in swift and sudden and stood behind the Gregora seated, one to one, and each Gordon with his dirk at a dirty Gregora neck. And she told on till the tale was done – aye, she was great at the stories – and then said she: "I see my man is come home, and has but an apple to eat. Give him to drink also, wine red and warm." And at her word they slew the Gregora where they sat, and the red blood ran. That was the way of it.

And the ghillie said: "Oh, mistress, how did you keep your countenance this long while in the presence of yon fell thing, and beguile these stark men?" And she answered: "The day I cannot keep my countenance, and hold men in their place and work my will on them, that is a day you will never see."

That was the way of it. That was a woman of the Gordons for you.

Wade's House stands on the rocky side of a lovely little green cleft in the hills, with a deep brown burn gurgling under its white walls. In summer it is half-hidden among the rowans and silver birches and tall bracken, and you can pass by on the main highway two hundred yards below and never know it is there, which may be why General Wade made it his headquarters when he was building those roads which tamed the Scottish North two and a half centuries ago. It was the edge of beyond in his day, the last outpost before the hostile wilderness which Wade himself described as "a land as far away as Africa", the home of the last savages in Europe, the Highland clans. From his little valley he could look up at Ben Dorain, the first spur of the great Grampian range towering away north-east to the mists; only a few miles ahead of him was the mouth of the Killing Place, Glencoe, under the shadow of the most menacing mountain in Britain, the Buchaille Etive; how harsh and dangerous to his English ears must have sounded the names of those wild tracts beyond the hills – Rannoch, Badenoch, Lochaber, and they weren't the half of it.

But, good for Wade, he succeeded where the Romans had failed. He pushed his roads through the heart of the Highlands and along the chain of government outposts on the loch sides,

Fort William, Fort Augustus, and Fort George, letting in the law and the red soldiers who between them finally put the hems (and the breeks) on the wild men of the north. It all came to an end at Culloden – and a right mess that was, thanks to the MacDonalds and Lord George Murray and (to give the swine his due) the Duke of Cumberland, who had learned the vital lesson that if you can stop Scotland scoring in the first ten minutes, you stand an excellent chance, because they tend to lose interest. After that there was nothing for Ronald and Donald to do, once they had emerged cursing from the heather, but join the Highland regiments cunningly established by the government as a safety valve through which the clansmen could vent their exuberance on the enemies of the Crown for a change – which is how I came to return to Wade's House two centuries later.

I had known it from childhood, because after the general finished his roads and went home it had reverted to my uncle's family (a small, aggressive colony of Gordons who had come down from the north in the remote past to establish themselves among the local Stewarts, Camerons, Campbells, Black Mount MacDonalds, and those perpetual pests, the MacGregors), and when he married my aunt they farmed from Wade's House and kept the nearby hotel, an impressive tourist lodge catering for fishers, guns, and a strange new breed, the skiers, who in those pre-war days were just beginning to hurl themselves down the slopes of Ben Lawers. My uncle was a tall, courtly gentleman, a former county cricketer who dreamed that his nephew (with the advantage of English summers to practise in) would some day confound the Australians who were carrying all before them in that era of Bradman and O'Reilly. In my holidays he would have me out on the hotel tennis court, heaving up my juvenile leg-spinners until my wrist creaked, and once I twisted so hard that I achieved a googly and he lost it against the dark conifers and was trapped dead as mutton leg before.

He took me off in triumph to the still-room and filled me with orange juice, and showed me off to a vaguely-remembered group of large, tweedy, moustached men who spoke with the accents of Morningside and Kelvinside and the Home Counties; I think of them whenever I see a whisky advertisement in the *New Yorker*. They belonged to a world of which I was barely conscious then, of plus-fours and brass-capped shotgun shells, fishing flies and glossy magazines on low oak tables, stuttering motor cars with running-boards, and pipes smoking fragrantly; they had a sound and a smell and a presence that died in September, 1939.

There was another world outside the hotel, and its centre was Wade's House, from which my aunt used to send me out with the dinner-pails for the farm-men on the hill; I would trudge up through the heather and wait to take back the empty containers, watching the shy, silent men with their lean brown faces and wishing I could understand them. They were distant and wary of the small boy in his school jersey, and on the rare occasions when they spoke their voices were odd and high-pitched. I wondered if I seemed as strange to them; when one of them once asked me my name and I told him, he looked at me with a queer smile as though wondering: how did that happen? I was reminded of them years later, in Saskatchewan, when I saw Blackfeet straight off the reservation; they had the same quiet durability and strange shifting quality; you had an uncomfortable feeling that you had better watch them. When they came to the hotel in the evening, it was to the big public bar at the back, a thousand miles from the tweed and leather lounge of the motorists at the front, and I noticed with admiration the ease with which my uncle and aunt moved between the two worlds, at home in either.

To my childish mind, one world was safe and the other wild. In Wade's House I had discovered a book by a man called Neil Munro about these very hills; it was full of dangers and onfalls and swords in the night, and as I snuggled down in bed it was comforting to know that the walls were feet thick, for I could picture the edge of the rocky burn beneath my deep-embrasured window, and Col of the Tricks was standing there under the silent trees, with his bonnet drawn down, smiling to himself and turning his dirk in his hand, and his face was the face of the men on the hill.

It wasn't all imagination. Once I woke to the sound of stealthy footsteps and whispers under my window, and when I reported this sensation to my aunt in the morning she smiled in mock wonder and teased me by humming "Watch the wall, my darling, while the gentlemen go by", which I neither understood nor connected with the big salmon wrapped in ferns in the stone larder or the fact that Jeannie the maid was scrubbing scales from the back door step. On other occasions there would be a couple of hares or a brace of birds hanging under the rowans; in my infant innocence I assumed that a friend had left them – which was true, in a way. Once, in the season of the year, a great haunch of venison turned up mysteriously in the garage, and my uncle became as fretful as his genial, easygoing nature would allow.

"Oh, dear, I wish Jock wouldn't do it," he sighed. "Or Archie, or whoever it is this time. It's embarrassing."

"A switch for the laird from the laird's man," said my aunt cryptically. "It's probably the Dipper. Jock and Archie are busy on Lochnabee these days, according to Jeannie."

"Not again!" groaned my uncle. "Do they know how long they can get, if the gadgers catch them?"

"Probably, dear, but the gadgers never do. Don't worry about them."

"I don't worry about *them*. I worry about meeting the Admiral or old Buchanan and having them tell me that another stag's vanished without trace, or that there isn't a fish left in Loch Tulla, and who on earth can have done it? It puts me in a very difficult position."

"No, it doesn't," said my aunt. "The position's perfectly easy – you don't know."

"I can guess. If it isn't Jock, it's Archie, or the Dipper, or Roy Ban, or Wee Joe, or any one of a dozen. It wouldn't be so bad if I didn't employ half of them."

"What's a gadger, Aunt Alison?" I asked, and was told gently to run along and play with my ball, none the wiser.

Over the years I began to understand. Agriculture and legitimate field sports were the principal local industries, but poaching and illicit distilling ran them a close second, it being well known that a switch from the braeside, a fish from the burn, and a stag from the hill were the right of every Highlander, and that if he chose to manufacture his own drink it was nobody else's business. The surrounding estates, which catered for visiting sportsmen, employed armies of keepers and watchers who waged a constant war against the local poachers – this was before the big gangs from far afield came to despoil the glens systematically – and the Excisemen or "gadgers" (so called from the word gauger) combed the woods and corries in search of unlawful stills. Sometimes they even had to take to the water: my aunt had referred to Lochnabee, where the enterprising peasantry operated their little distillery in a small boat anchored in the middle of that gloomy tarn, the principle being that if the Law appeared on the shore, and capture was certain, you heaved the whole caboodle over the side, got out the rods to pose as innocent fishers, and defied the gadgers to prosecute when all the evidence was at the bottom of the loch. A shocking waste of equipment, but better than being nailed in some mountain hut or woodland fastness where hurried concealment of your Heath Robinson equipment was impossible.

My uncle was right: his position *was* difficult. He was by way of being what in England would be called the squire, because although his farm and hotel were small concerns compared to the great estates around, he and his had been there as long as Ben Lui, while the estates were new and commercial. He knew half his people were out with guns and nets and snares by night, lifting what wasn't theirs, and distilling the good news in secret, but what was he to do – clype on his own folk? He couldn't have proved anything, anyway. Tell them to stop it? Tell the fish to keep out of water. At the same time, he was on good terms with his neighbours, like the Admiral and other landlords, and being a gentleman and sensible of his conflicting loyalties, it troubled him. My Aunt Alison, not having been born with his social scruples, and having a wicked sense of humour, found it all rather funny, and suffered no pangs when goodwill offerings appeared mysteriously on the step. She knew they were not bribes, but tribute.

My uncle died early in the war, but where another childless widow might have sold up, Aunt Alison continued to run farm and hotel as though it were a matter of course for a woman past middle age, thereby confirming the suspicion that she had been the real manager all along; and she was accepted in that strong masculine world without question. She had been a great beauty, one of your tall northern blondes with eyes like sapphires, and even when she was white-haired she continued to flutter the hearts of such susceptible local bachelors as the Admiral and Robin Elphinstone, much to her amusement; she treated them as she treated everyone, with that frank easiness and direct good humour that you often find in northern women; it stops short of

140

being hard, but there is a tough streak of realism in it, and a touch of mischief – Stevenson caught it exactly with Miss Grant, the Lord Advocate's daughter, in *Catriona*. Aunt Alison had the same gift of tongues: educated Edinburgh in the drawing-room for her guests, pure Perthshire on the hillside when Dougal neglected the sheep-dipping, but with the same calm, pleasant delivery.

I had not seen her for three years when military duty took me north from Edinburgh not long after the battalion came home from North Africa. A truck-load of ammunition had to be taken from Redford Barracks to Fort William, and since an officer had to be in charge of that dangerous cargo I was told to take a 15-cwt, a driver, and two men as escort, and set off forthwith. The trip would take me past my aunt's door, so I got the Colonel's leave to stay over a couple of nights. As escort I chose Lance-Corporal Macrae and Private McAuslan – and if it strains belief that I should want to take McAuslan anywhere, I can plead good reason. He had just emerged, acquitted and crowing, from a court-martial for disobedience to a newly-promoted and offi-cious young corporal, and, knowing my men, I didn't want them falling foul of each other again in my absence. Macrae I took because he'd been a ghillie and stalker in that part of the country, and I thought he would enjoy it. Kind-hearted subaltern, you see; if I'd known what was brewing in Darkest Perthshire I'd have chosen more carefully.

Part of our load had to be dropped off at Dunkeld – why they needed land-mines there I can't imagine – so from Ballinluig we took the northern road which carries you along the Tummel and the Garry into the wilds of Badenoch by way of Killiecrankie Pass. We stopped at the marker stone where Bonnie Dundee was killed, and surveyed the grim heights from which his claymores had descended like a thunderbolt to drive Mackay's Government regiments into the river in five furious minutes.

> Like a tempest down the ridges
> Swept the hurricane of steel

in Aytoun's splendid onomatopoeic lines – or as McAuslan put it, scowling sternly round the battlefield: "That sortit the bug-gers! Here, izzat ra Bonnie Dundee in ra song, sur? He musta

141

been a helluva boy! Five minutes, no kiddin'? He wisnae messin' aboot, wis he?" He shook his unkempt head in admiration, and I hadn't the heart to tell him that, as a staunch Protestant, he'd probably have found himself being routed along with Mackay.

It was fine scenery as we went west to Fort William, and when we had shed the last of our cargo it was a pleasantly eerie journey down through the Weeping Glen of my tough grandmother's folk, where it's always raining and even the sheep wear their shawls over their heads. We halted short of King's House for a cigarette, and McAuslan waxed indignant at my description of the Glencoe Massacre; it had been, in his opinion, weel ower the score, even fur ra bluidy Campbells – mind you, knowin' that big swine Sarn't Campbell in A Company he wisnae a bit surprised. We drove on south, and it was a beautiful summer evening when we pulled up on the gravel drive before my aunt's hotel. They were doing heavy business, by the number of cars out in front, and the big entrance hall was full of tweeds and twin-sets having afternoon tea; I exchanged glad cries of greeting with several members of the hotel staff and was informed that herself was in the office with the Admiral.

"He's still about, is he?"

"As ever, the wee pest!" said Jimmy the Porter. "Still the lord o' creation, five foot o' wind wi' a hanky in his cuff! She's far too soft with him, and I don't give a dam if he *has* got a party of twelve for dinner! Away you in, Dand, and maybe he'll have the grace to make himself scarce."

I escaped the mountainous hug of Bridie the linen-mistress, dried myself off, and entered the long passage to my aunt's office–sitting-room, whence came the sound of an Admiral in full voice, minatory and plaintive:

". . . I just don't understand you, Alison, I really don't! You're a landowner yourself, but you take it far too lightly, in my opinion. Far too lightly. I'm sorry, but . . ."

"Well, we don't all strut about the place as though we had dominion over palm and pine." She sounded more amused than impatient. "Since when has the Excise been your business, anyway?"

"It's the business of all right-thinking people," snapped the Admiral. "Of whom I had always thought you were one, Alison—"

'Ach, don't be so damned pompous, Jacky!" She was laughing at him. "You're just being officious. And vindictive, let me tell you. I don't know which is worse."

"I happen," said the Admiral, "to be a magistrate . . ." and at that point I coughed loudly, knocked, and went in. The Admiral, who resembled an ocean-going tug in a R.Y.S. blazer, was planted indignantly before the fireplace; my aunt, seated in silver-haired elegance behind her desk and looking as usual like an elderly but mischievous Norse goddess, whooped at the sight of me. "My, will you look at the bonny sojer!" After exclamations and embraces she demanded if the Admiral remembered me, and he shook hands, beaming, crying of course, of course, the young spin-bowler, eh? I had known him from my infancy, and liked him, for he was a decent, hearty wee man, if given to self-importance. We exchanged pleasantries while my aunt watched, smiling, and then he said, well, he must be pushing along, frowned pleadingly at her and said *do* give serious thought to what I've been saying, won't you, my dear, and stumped off.

"Trouble?" I wondered. She gave her sharp, pleasant laugh, shaking her head.

"Just an attack of responsibility. Poor Jacky, he has hopes of being Lord-Lieutenant, and can't sleep for the glorious prospect. He can be a right wee pest, at that."

"Jimmy the Porter's very word. How pestilential?"

"Och, he's heard that the Dipper has an illicit still going, so he's worked himself into a fine indignation. As if it mattered. Heavens, the Dipper's being making malt since grouse grew feathers, and who's the worse for it?" She laughed again, and frowned. "Aye, the trouble is, I hear they're on to him – two Excisemen are up from Glasgow, and that's a sure sign. So Admiral Jacky gets all blown up with civic duty and bustles about saying it's a scandal and the law must be upheld. The wee twirp," she added warmly. "The truth is he has a grudge because the Dipper and the other McLarens poach him blind, and he can't catch them at it."

"He's got a point," I said.

"Devil a bit he has! They poach *me*, and do I ken the difference? What's a bird or a fish more or less – or a beast, either? The man's just chawed at the Dipper, and wants his own back."

I could have pointed out that they didn't poach her more than enough to keep the game alert, no doubt because the Dipper was her faithful slave, having been in my uncle's outfit (and lost an eye) in Flanders. He was the oldest and idlest of the ne'er-do-well McLarens, and performed odd jobs about the district to supplement his income from poaching and moonshining. A long grey man of deep guile and so little scruple that he lured game birds with whisky-sodden grain and shot them while they were reeling drunk. I asked if she knew where his illicit still was.

"I take good care not to. It's no business of mine. Jacky had the cheek to ask me that very question, so I advised him to look between Cruachan and Crianlarich" – a distance of over twenty miles – "and he flew up into the trees. Well, good luck to him and the gadgers if they take the hill after the Dipper." But she looked anxious all the same; then she was smiling again. "So I'm to put you and your ruffians up for two nights? Well, there's no room at the inn, so you can have the house to yourselves, and see they keep their tackety boots off the furniture. They'll be teetotal – I don't think. Cook'll give them their meals here. As for you, my lad, you'll dine in state with your old aunt and try not to disgrace her. Robin Elphinstone's coming." She winked and patted her coiffure. "That's sure to infuriate Jacky."

She came out with me to the truck, and won my three Jocks with the obvious pleasure she took in meeting them; it was interesting to watch their different reactions to her smiling handshake. From Brooks, the driver, an Englishman, it was a hesitant: "Pleased to meet you, mum"; Macrae the hillman drew himself up to his lean dark height and inclined his head formally, saying: "Mem"; McAuslan, beaming expansively, greeted her with "Aw, hullaw rerr, missus! Hoo's it gaun?" As usual he looked as though he'd just been exhumed by Burke and Hare, but Aunt Alison didn't seem to notice; she laughed and talked for a few minutes, reminded me not to be late, and then we drove the quarter mile up the road to Wade's House in its little tree-lined valley.

It was good to be back, under the low beamed ceilings, to look round at the massive white walls hung with brasses and old prints, smell the faint drift of fir-wood, and hear the burn chuckling by. We settled in, McAuslan observing that it wis fair champion, and my aunt was an awfy nice wumman; he hoped we werenae pittin' her tae bother. I reassured him, and presently we strolled back to the hotel in the warm August dusk. I turned the three of them over to the cook and the kind of dinner soldiers dream about, and walked through to the dining-room, which was filled with hotel guests and local worthies. Those were the days of rationing and the five-shilling maximum charge, which in a Highland hotel with resources denied the city was just an invitation to gluttony. To my surprise there were a number of dinner jackets and evening dresses making a gallant protest against post-war austerity; the little Admiral, presiding (as foretold by Jimmy the Porter) over a table of twelve, even had miniature decorations on his mess jacket. He kept frowning in the direction of my aunt's private table in an alcove near the door, the object of his dark glances being Robin Elphinstone, a burly gentleman farmer of the district; if my aunt noticed she gave no sign, but surveyed the long crowded room contentedly, remarking that at her age the greatest pleasure in life was just gaping at folk. Elphinstone, no hand at the social graces, said: "Oh, come off it, Alison, you're not that old!" with such evident sincerity that she went into fits of laughter, which attracted another indignant glare from the jealous Admiral.

"Can't stand that chap Elphinstone," he told me later, when I ran into him in the hall and was commanded peremptorily to join him for a drink. "He's uncouth. And we see far too much of him hereabouts." He gestured impatiently, spilling gin. "Your aunt is so generous, of course – wonderful woman! Gracious, delightful – couldn't say an unkind word if she wanted to." That's all you know, Nelson, I thought. "I do wish, though, that she'd take a firmer line with people like that. Ought to be put in his place. Not the right type at all. Do you know," he fixed me with his glittering poached eye, "a few years ago he lost some stock to a golden eagle up on the Conanish, and – you'll hardly credit it – there was a rumour that the bounder actually shot it! A golden eagle, my God! Imagine it!" He leaned heavily on his gin for support. "That shows you the kind of bounder he is. Well, I ask you, is a brute like that a fit dinner companion for . . . for . . . well, for anyone, I mean to say? Have another. No, I insist . . ."

He went on to say that if the ghastly Elphinstone were so rash as to repeat the offence, and it could be brought home to him,

145

he, the Admiral, would have no hesitation in bringing a prosecution. "And it wouldn't be the only one, either," he added with grim satisfaction. "Did your aunt tell you? That old scoundrel McLaren is at his tricks again – yes, an illicit still! Would you credit it?" I said it boggled the imagination. "It isn't enough that he and his cronies strip the country bare of game, they have to try to poison it, too, with their vile potheen, or whatever it is. Well, it's not good enough. He's going to be laid by the heels this time. Stamp it out. Someone's got to take a stand."

He was having difficulty doing that very thing by the time his chauffeur helped him into his limousine, and I walked round to the back of the hotel where the public bar was getting out. My three Jocks were emerging with the crowd of farm-workers and ghillies, Brooks and Macrae gratifyingly sober and McAuslan happy but not obnoxious. I knew this because he was still wearing both boots; in a more advanced stage of inebriation he would have removed them and tied them round his neck (why, I never discovered); when he discarded them altogether it was a sure sign that he was approaching the paralytic. As I waited for them I caught sight of the Dipper, in his battered tweed hat and long shabby overcoat, slipping away by himself. He saw me, and gave me his slow smile and a lift of the hand before disappearing into the quiet night.

I found myself wondering about him as I lay in bed in Wade's House, listening to the burn and the sigh of the night wind in the leaves. He would know, of course, that the forces of law and order were mustering to close in, but it would not occur to him to lie low. They never had, his kind; if anything, he would go his unlawful ways harder than ever, out of pure devilment and defiance, and when the grip came he would meet it with all the craft and cunning that was in him. It would be on ground of his choosing, too, rock and heather and brown water – good luck to the Admiral and his gadgers, as my aunt had said. Yet he was no longer young, the same Dipper – he must be near seventy by now, and the legs and lungs would be failing. If it came to trouble on the hill, well . . . it would be a far cry from Loch Awe, as the saying is.

I slept sound, and half-woke only once, sometime near dawn, fancying I had heard a step on the gravel and a door closing softly. For a moment I wondered if I'd been dreaming a memory

146

from childhood, and then I remembered that my three stalwarts were bunking down on the ground floor, and that the hotel maids were more than average pretty.

It was after nine when we got up, and to save the kitchen staff the trouble of finding a late breakfast we caught a few trout from the burn (something I hadn't done since boyhood), grilled them on hot stones, and had them in the open with tea and digestive biscuits – there are some meals so far beyond Escoffier that they belong in another world. Elphinstone had invited me to play golf at Dalmally, and since Brooks was a golfer I took him along down to the hotel; the other two were content to spend the day loafing. McAuslan had already fallen in the burn twice, and been prevented in the nick of time from eating rowan berries – like many city-dwellers discovering countryside for the first time, he was going around open-mouthed, exclaiming at the size of the heather spiders and generally communing with nature. I told Macrae to keep an eye on him, and left them at the house, with the truck parked under the trees.

It was one of those beautiful tranquil days, until we got to the hotel, where the peace had been shattered at breakfast-time by the arrival of an Admiral with blood in his eye, to quote Jimmy the Porter. For some days, apparently, a troop of stags had been observed on the lower slopes of Ben Vornach, on his land; this morning they were nowhere to be seen, having evidently been scared into the high forest, but the Admiral's head keeper had heard a shot in the night, and on venturing forth at dawn had discovered blood on the rocks, and signs of tracks carefully covered. In a word, poachers, and the Admiral's land was now being beaten, under the supervision of its owner gone berserk, in search of the carcase and clues to the miscreants.

"It's now or never, of course," said Elphinstone, from whom I had the details in the hall. "They wouldn't get a beast that size off the hill before first light, so it'll be snug under a ledge until they can bring it near a road and pick it up with a car. Jacky's boys will have to find it today or tomorrow at latest." He shook his head. "Sooner them than me, on Ben Vornach."

"Do they know who did it?" I asked, and he looked at me slantendicular.

"Jacky thinks he does. If he heard someone had shot an elephant when there was an 'r' in the month he'd put it down to

147

the McLarens. He's probably right, but he'll have to catch them with it. There'll be no sleep for any man of his this fine night, I'll wager."

The Admiral's troubles didn't come singly; first it was the Dipper's illicit still, and now poachers on his own domain.

"Aye, there's a coincidence for you," said Elphinstone. "And don't think he hasn't noticed."

"And why should he come bawling aboot it here, to the hotel, will you tell me?" demanded Jimmy the Porter indignantly. "Spoiling herself's breakfast on her, as if his dam' beasts were any concern of hers! Did I not hear him at it? 'This is what comes of apathy among those who should ken better,' cries he, and her at her boiled eggs and the *Oban Times*. 'A fine thing, when the lower orders take advantage of indifference and slack management by their betters. It's a positive encouragement to crime!' Lower orders, and be damned to him! And heckling at her, as though his bluidy stag was in her larder!'

"What did she say to him?" I asked.

"Offered him a cup o' coffee and warned him aboot apoplexy," said Jimmy. "She's far too easy on him. I've told her. Aye, and I told him, too. 'Have ye no manners, that ye'll break in on a lady at her meat, stopping her ears wi' your drivel?' says I. 'How dare you, my man?' says he. 'I'll report you to your mistress!' 'Ye can report me to MacCallum More and his great-grandmither,' says I, 'but you'll leave herself alone in her own hoose. I'm the porter,' says I, 'and I'll have no disturbance in this hotel, not if it was the Duke himsel'!' He went off, grindin' his teeth, vowin' vengeance on half the country." Jimmy snorted, straightening his uniform coat. "The impudence of the man!"

"What's apathy, Mr Robertson?" asked the junior porter.

"A disease of the spirit, boy. Apathy, says he! He'll find enough of it among his own folk by the time they've finished beatin' the bracken for his precious deer. And then he'll be off colloguin' wi' the gadgers aboot the Dipper's still. Oh, there'll be a fine crying of 'Cruachan' hereabouts today!"

I asked Elphinstone if there was anything we could do, and Jimmy the Porter exclaimed in outrage.

"Do for the Admiral, d'you mean? You'll be off to your gowf, young Dand, and let the silly sailor take care of himself!"

148

It seemed reasonable, so Brooks and I piled into Elphinstone's ancient Argyle and were driven the few miles to Dalmally, which is one of the great undiscovered golf courses of the world. We played a leisurely threesome with one set of clubs, driving with care, for golf balls were like gold dust in those days and Dalmally's rough was like Assam after the monsoon. It was late afternoon before we set off for home, and nightfall by the time Elphinstone left us at the foot of the gravel drive winding up to Wade's House. The house, when we reached it, was in darkness, but there was light enough to reveal one disturbing absence. Our 15-cwt truck was missing.

"What the blazes?" I said. "Macrae knows better than to take it without permission." But Macrae wasn't there, nor McAuslan, and there was no message or explanation in the house. I was demanding of the empty night where they and the truck had got to when Brooks reminded me of something even more startling: neither of them knew how to drive.

I left him at the house in case they turned up, and set off in some alarm for the hotel – whoever had taken the truck had removed Army property for which I was responsible, and a right damfool I was going to look if it wasn't recovered forthwith. I had a half-hope it might be on the gravel sweep before the hotel, but it wasn't; the Admiral's limousine was, though, and a couple of farm lorries, which was unprecedented in a spot reserved for visitors' cars; there was also a plain black saloon with a man in a diced cap at the wheel – police. Plainly great things were happening, and I sought enlightenment from Jimmy the Porter, who was at the reception desk with the local police sergeant.

"Who else would it be but the Admiral?" snapped Jimmy. "He's ben in herself's office wi' the gadgers and Inspector MacKendrick, planning his bluidy campaign, like Napoleon he is. No, they haven't found the stag, so he's turning his fury on the Dipper, wi' the bile spilling out of him." He dropped his voice. "The gadgers think they have their eye on the still, is that not the case, Rory?" He glanced at the portly Sergeant, who was looking stern and official and trying to pretend he wasn't taking sidelong keeks through the open door of the drawing-room, where the dinner guests were having coffee – it probably wasn't often that he got this close to the High Life.

"The gadgers' information is aaltogether confidential," he said importantly. "Classified, and canna' be divulged."

"Classified your erse and parsley," said Jimmy vulgarly. "Who d'ye think ye are, the Flyin' Squad? If it's all that confidential, why are you turnin' my hotel into a damned circus? We havnae got the Dipper's still – or maybe you think Bridie the linen-mistress is his confederate, aye, his gangster's moll! Polis!"

"I've got something else for you, Rory," I said, and told him about the missing 15-cwt. Jimmy whistled and muttered "Dalmighty!" and the Sergeant produced his notebook and said this was very serious and the Inspector must be informed instanter. He set off majestically for my aunt's office, and I learned from Jimmy that neither McAuslan nor Macrae had been seen since the public bar closed in the afternoon. I asked him to send out scouts, discreetly, and followed the Sergeant.

The office was like an ops room on D-Day; Operation Dipper was in full swing. The Admiral, duffel-coated and binoculared, had an Ordnance Survey map spread out on the desk, and was poring over it making little barking noises; with him were the Inspector and two solid-looking men in dark coats who must be the gadgers from Glasgow, and the Admiral's stalker and a uniformed constable stood uncomfortably in the background. Unconcerned at all this official activity, Aunt Alison was seated in stately calm in her armchair; she was in evening dress, smoking a cigarette in a long holder, and knitting – a triple combination I have not seen elsewhere. She winked imperceptibly at me and grimaced towards the desk, where the Admiral was issuing his signals to the fleet, and loving it.

". . . and your party will take position on the north shore of the loch, Inspector, is that clear?" So the Dipper's still was afloat this time. "My party will be to the south. That should make it airtight. Lights on at my whistle, but not a moment before. Got that? You have the warrant, and will effect the arrest – and you gentlemen will make the confiscation! Capital! Right!" You could see he hadn't enjoyed himself so much since Jutland, rubbing his hands and looking like a triumphant toy bulldog. "Well, Sergeant, what is it, what is it? Come along, come along, man!"

The Sergeant told him, and the Admiral glared, bewildered.

"What? A truck? What truck, man? Whose truck? Your truck? Is this true, Dand? Stolen?"

"Takken awaay wi'oot the consent o' the owner," the Sergeant corrected him. "By pairson or pairsons unknown . . ."

"Yes, yes, yes! An Army truck? What has that . . ." He gave a sudden cry of "Ha!" and leaped vertically. "A truck! My God – the deer! That's it – those infernal poachers have stolen it, to move the stag!" He thumped the desk with his fist, something I thought they did only in novels. "That's it, Inspector! Look here!" He pounced on the map. "There are only two ways to Ben Vornach for a vehicle . . . the Kildurn road, there . . . and the dead-end from the lodge, d'you see? They must be blocked at once!"

He wasn't slow, I'll say that for him – but then you can't afford to be, if your job has been warping aircraft carriers through the Magellan Strait. I hadn't linked the truck's disappearance with the poachers, but it made sense: every local vehicle must be known and accounted for, and here was the perfect one dropped in their lap. Thank God the non-driving Macrae and McAuslan were in the clear . . . I wouldn't be, if the Colonel got to hear about it.

My aunt counted her stitches, put down her knitting, and rose. "I think all this excitement calls for a little refreshment," she said, smiling at the Sergeant and gadgers. They looked hopeful, and with a glance at the Admiral and Inspector, deep in their map, she went out.

Meanwhile dissension seemed to be breaking out in the High Command. The Inspector, a young, slow-spoken man with a fledgling moustache, was plainly doubtful about undertaking two separate operations with limited resources; one or the other should be postponed, or "I can chust see us faalin' between two stools, sir. Aye, I can that." The Admiral wouldn't hear of it: didn't the Inspector realise, for heaven's sake, that the stag would be halfway to Glasgow by morning? As for delaying the Dipper raid, it was unthinkable; give the scoundrel another twenty-four hours and he'd have his still dismantled or moved or presented to a museum, dammit! The Inspector, sweating visibly, spoke of "a waant of personnel", and was told not to be so damned defeatist, it was simply a matter of intelligent planning. They argued back and forth, the Admiral's voice and temperature rising with each objection, until he pointed out

151

sternly that *he* was chairman of the Watch Committee, and before that majestic title the Inspector finally gave way, red and resentful.

"We must divide our forces!" snapped the Admiral, bursting with initiative. "Inspector, I leave it to you to post men on those two roads to intercept the thieves. I shall proceed to Lochnabee, as planned. Certainly I shall need additional men. Sergeant, you will see to it." That took care of that, apparently. "If communication is necessary we shall send messengers here, to the hotel, which is our base . . . with Mrs Gordon's permission, of course," he added with a placatory smirk to Aunt Alison, who was ushering in two maids bearing loaded trays.

"How exciting," she said. "Are we being commandeered?"

Good heavens, no, cried the Admiral, simply a matter of convenience, central point, lines of communication. "And I'm sure, gentlemen," he added impressively, "that I speak for us all when I say how grateful we are to Mrs Gordon for . . . ah, for so kindly allowing us to use her premises, and so graciously—"

"Och, stop behaving like Rommel, Jacky," said my aunt. "I didn't allow anything. You just breenged in as usual. Tea or coffee, Inspector? Or a little of the creature? And don't tell me you're on duty . . . I won't have that." She patted his arm conspiratorially. "Help yourselves, gentlemen. There are the sausage rolls, Rory . . . Janet, a glass for the Admiral, and those sandwiches . . ."

"I say, this is awfully kind of you, Alison," protested the Admiral, "but I'm afraid we really don't have time—"

"You wouldn't send men out on the hill at night without something in them?" Aunt Alison reproved him. "Not from this house! No water for the Admiral, Janet . . . Those are smoked salmon, Jacky – your favourite. Now, are our friends from Glasgow being attended to? That's a grouse pâté – you won't get that in Craigs or the Ca'doro. Sit you down, constable, and put your feet under the table . . . Rory, is that the single malt? Good lad, don't let the sausage rolls defeat you . . ."

She moved about the room, recommending and directing, seeing that plates and glasses were refilled, and even the Admiral had to admit it was a sound basis for the labours ahead. The police and gadgers obviously agreed, from the way they were engulfing the delicacies; I noticed that Janet removed an empty Glenlivet bottle when she went out for a fresh tray of sandwiches, and the Admiral allowed my aunt to prevail on him to try the pâté, and then really, Alison, we must be moving . . . well, just a spot of the ten-year-old, then . . . capital . . . not too much . . .

"It's a lot better for you than gin," smiled Aunt Alison, pouring. "There, we'll make a Highlandman of you yet. Not that we haven't tried . . . how many years has it been?"

"Lord, I hate to think! Let's see . . . I bought Achnafroich in '32 . . . or was it '31 . . . yes, March, '31, but I'd been coming up for years before that, you remember . . ." He sipped and reminisced, with my aunt smiling encouragement, and when he looked at his watch she remarked that he seemed to be in a most ungallant hurry to be off, which kept him protesting through another glass of the ten-year-old.

All told I'd say that collation occupied half an hour, by which time the troops were pink and contented. Finally the Admiral called a halt, thanked Aunt Alison on behalf of them all, and dispatched them to the vehicles. As they trooped out he turned to her, looking contrite.

"I say, Alison, I do apologise again. We've put you to enormous trouble – shocking imposition, I mean, intruding on you like this . . . but I'm sure you understand that I . . . well, I mean . . ."

"You wanted to give me a chance to line up with the landed gentry, didn't you?" she teased him. "Well, it was nice of you, and I'm touched. Now, off you go, and I hope you kill a lot of Germans."

"Oh, really, Alison! I do wish you'd be serious! It's no laughing matter – and I'm sorry, but I must ask again . . . we're going to be short-handed, so will you please allow me to take your people along? We need every—"

"I've told you, you're at liberty to approach any employee of mine, and if he wants to go, well and good." She sat down and picked up her knitting. "But it's up to them; I can't order them."

"My dear, if you'll forgive me, that's nonsense. One word from you—"

"Well, I won't say it, and that's flat." She gave him her gentlest blue-eyed smile, like the Rock of Gibraltar, and he let

153

out a whoof of despair and impatience, said he *did* wish she'd be reasonable for once, it would make things so much easier, and stumped reproachfully out, returning immediately to thank her again for the drinks and canapés, and finally departing. Even with the door closed we could hear him trumpeting orders in the hall.

"Now you ken how the French Revolution started," said Aunt Alison. "Confound those McLarens!" She threw down her knitting and said something ugly in Gaelic. "And confound Jacky for a meddling wee ass! Could he not let the Dipper alone?" She lit a cigarette and got up, tapping her foot. "That boy Macrae of yours. Where did you say he was from?"

"Macrae?" I was startled. "Aberfeldy. He used to be ghillie thereabouts."

"Macrae! God save us." She gave her sharp laugh. "There's a name for a Highland midnight. And you're sure he's not about?"

"Not since this afternoon. Auntie dear," I said, "what's happening?"

"That remains to be seen," she said. "Dand, I want you to go to Lochnabee with Jacky."

"What? I can't get mixed up in that sort of thing! I'm a soldier! Besides, I'm shot if I'll help nab the Dipper—"

"I'm not asking you to. Just do as you're told." Immediately I was six years old again. "Stay with Jacky and see what happens. Off you go, double quick. Now."

When Aunt Alison says "now" in that quiet way, she means yesterday. I went, and found the Admiral marshalling his squadrons in line ahead on the gravel. The police car and farm lorries were roaring off in pursuit of poachers, leaving the Admiral's limousine, the gadgers' car, and an antediluvian shooting-brake packed with the Admiral's shock-troops, three or four ghillies from his own estate. He hailed me with enthusiasm. "Ha! In for the kill, eh? Good show! Off we go, Cameron!" We sped into the night, the Sergeant breathing heavily beside me in the back seat, the car redolent of the hotel's malt, and all the way to Lochnabee the Admiral, up front, told me what a wonderful woman Aunt Alison was, but headstrong, did I know what he meant? Pity, because she had such brains and character, and could have been such a helpful influence on the restless jacquerie if only she would take her responsibilities more seriously . . . charming, though. Pity she hadn't been out in Wei-hai-wei when he was a young lieutenant . . . yes, wonderful . . . I looked at the back of his reddened neck, the ageing pocket Dreadnought suffused with gin, and thought of my late uncle, tall, dark, handsome Alastair of the lazy smile . . . it would have made you weep, it really would.

Lochnabee is a hill loch on the high tops, cold and black as a witch's breath, and lonely, with not a tree or a bush for miles. The last place you would choose for making funny whisky unless you were a crazy old brock like the Dipper. It was a bare two hundred yards wide, and the only road was a rough track up which we bumped and rattled in the dark – if the Dipper didn't know we were coming he must be stone deaf. We stopped a half-mile from the loch in surroundings straight from Macbeth, Act One, and the stalker scouted ahead and presently came back with the word: there was a boat on the loch.

"That's him!" cried the Admiral. "Right! Pay attention! Right! Sergeant, Dand, stay with me! Cameron, keep the engine running! The rest of you know your positions! Move quietly" – this with his car back-firing like a Bofors – "spread out, and wait until I bring up the car! Then I shall give the signal, and on with the lights! Got that? Remember, our man will make for the shore, so be on the look-out! He may put up a fight! Right . . .!"

It was a farce from start to finish. We waited by the car, the Admiral stumping up and down muttering "Right!" and striking matches to look at his watch; when he shouted "Right!" for the last time we drove the final half-mile at top speed on side-lights which is no joke halfway up a Scottish mountain, and came to a shuddering halt with the loch glinting palely in front of our bonnet. The Admiral leaped out, blowing a whistle, the headlights were switched on full, and the powerful torches of the gadgers blinked on from the other shore. Sure enough, there was a boat in the middle of the loch, with three men in it, and one of them was shouting:

"What the hell d'you think you're doing, scaring the fush? Get away, you with your pluidy motor car, and put out those pluidy lights!"

"He's bluffing!" roared the Admiral. "Sergeant, do your duty!"

The Sergeant lumbered forward and fell in the loch. The Admiral swore on a high note, the sounds of altercation between the boat and the watchers on the far shore floated across to us, and the Sergeant emerged like some great sea-beast and shouted: "In the King's name!" It may have been an oath or an announcement of majesty, but it got a great horse-laugh from the boat, and at that moment the car's headlights went out.

"Switch them on again, Cameron, godammit!" cried the Admiral. "Sergeant! Where are you?" Drowning, by the sound of it, for in that sudden blackness he had evidently taken the wrong direction, and was wallowing in the shallows. "Come out of that, you fool! Cameron, will you put on those blasted lights?" I could hear the driver cursing as he scrabbled at the dashboard, and for no apparent reason the Admiral blew his whistle again. He was stumping about in the dark, and presently there was a sharp musical sound as of metal meeting bone. "God damn the thing! Sergeant, what the hell are you doing? Where are you, man?"

"I'm here, sir, and I'm drookit!" cried the Sergeant, but they're made of fine stuff, these Perthshire policemen, for after a few hippo-like squelches in the gloom he bawled:

"McLaren, do you hear me? The jig is up! You are sur-roonded on aall sides! Chust you bring in your boat this minute and surrender! We have a warrant! Do you hear me, McLaren?"

"Away you, Rory, and polish your pluidy handcuffs!" came the answer. "Have you nothing petter to do than spoil sport, you and that merchant skipper wi' the pot belly?"

"Damn him!" cried the Admiral, enraged. "Damn his insolence! Give yourselves up, you scoundrels, or it will the worse for you!"

"Ach, go and torpedo yourself!" laughed the voice. "You should be in your bed, you silly sailor!"

"Now, you listen to me, McLaren!" shouted the Sergeant. "You chust give up this nonsense like a good laad, and maybe when it comes to the charges we'll be going easy on you—"

"We'll do nothing of the dam' sort!" bellowed the Admiral. It struck me that perhaps he and the Sergeant had worked out the routine of Hard Man and Soft Man used by clever interrogators, but if they had it was wasted effort. The response from the boat was an indelicate noise, and in his fury the Admiral shouted, most unreasonably: "Sergeant! Arrest that man!"

Knowing Rory's devotion to duty I half-expected him to strike out for the middle of the loch with his handcuffs in his teeth, but at that moment the headlights came on again, and in their glare the boating trio were seen to be on their feet, manhandling a large contraption which looked like an oil drum with metal curlicues and other interesting attachments. The Admiral let out a neighing scream.

"It's the still! Don't let them jettison it! Get a boat, Sergeant! It's no use, you villains, we've seen it! Sergeant, you're a witness! Oh, my God, it's gone!"

There was an almighty splash, the boat rocked, and a small wave rippled across the face of the loch. The Admiral actually shook his fist, the Sergeant strode into the shallows and cried: "I arrest you, Aeneas McLaren, alias the Dipper, for illicit distillin', you godless hound of hell, you!" The headlights blinked, dimmed, and went out again, and I climbed into the back of the car for a quiet cigarette. These big co-ordinated police operations are too much for mere civilian nerves.

What they would have done if the Dipper and his companions had chosen to stay where they were, I can't imagine. Stood around the loch until they grew moss, probably. But the Dipper was considerate; he and his friends rowed slowly in, singing some Gaelic boat song, and when Rory laid hands on him and said that anything you say will be taken doon and may be used in evidence against you, and haud your tongue, Dipper McLaren, and the Admiral announced triumphantly that he could expect a jail sentence without the option, the Dipper smiled on them tolerantly and asked: "And what for, skipper? Fushin'?"

"You know damned well what for!" cried the Admiral. "For illicit distilling! What was that you threw over the side, hey?"

"Bait," said the Dipper, and laughed softly with the whole length of his lean body. The Admiral laughed, too, on an unpleasant note, and said he would sing a different tune when they'd dragged the loch, but I noticed the gadgers weren't smiling as they surveyed that black surface, and Rory was oddly hesitant about clapping the darbies on the prisoners, as the Admiral demanded.

"We know where to put our hands on them, sir, when required," he said, scowling on the Dipper, and although the

157

Admiral got quite purple about it, he couldn't get Rory to go beyond charging the trio, and finally letting them go – for, as the Sergeant fairly pointed out, we simply didn't have room in the vehicles to carry them back. The Dipper listened with amiable attention, touched his hat to the Admiral, flung his old coat about his shoulders like a musketeer, and with his two friends simply wandered off into the darkness.

It seemed a bit of an anti-climax, but although the Admiral was baulked of the satisfaction of bringing back his captives in chains behind his chariot, so to speak, he was grimly cheerful on the way home. They knew where the still was, and when it had been dredged up it would be a case of Barlinnie for three, and no nonsense. And if the Inspector had done his part with comparable efficiency, the Admiral added, that would be one gang of poachers less to trouble the countryside. Not a bad night's work, young Dand; we've earned our nightcap, what?

Any thought of nightcaps vanished from my mind as we drove over the gravel to the hotel. For there, parked outside, was my 15-cwt truck, with the Inspector and a constable standing guard.

The Admiral was out of the car like a salmon going up the Falls of Falloch, demanding information, and the Inspector gave it with disgruntled satisfaction. No, they hadn't found the deer; no, they hadn't caught the poachers. Of course, had he been given aa-dequate perr-sonnel—

"Then where the devil did you find the truck?" blared the Admiral. "And how the devil did you get in that condition?" For both officers were plastered with mud to the waist, as though they had strayed into a peat-cutting – which, it transpired, they had: obviously it wasn't the Perthshire constabulary's night for keeping dry. The Inspector explained with what dignity he could.

He had established road-blocks as instructed, and was driving back towards the hotel with the constable when they had spotted the truck coming towards them along the Tyndrum road – the one we had taken en route to Lochnabee. "You hadnae seen it – no, you would be busy up at the loch, no doubt." The Inspector's sniff was eloquent. The truck had pulled up sharply at sight of the police car, and four men had taken to the heather, but although the officers had pursued them vigorously they had escaped in the darkness.

"Blast!" exploded the Admiral. "But didn't you get a look at them, dammit? Can you identify them, man? You must have—"

"I haff said it wass dark, and we wass undermanned!" retorted the Inspector. "Mind you, wan o' them sounded like a Glasgow man, for we heard him roaring in the night, and he had an accent." He glanced at me. "He micht have been wearing a sojer's tunic."

"Half the demobilised men in the country wear soldiers' tunics!" snapped the Admiral. "What a shambles! The whole thing has been bungled to the hilt!" He glared at the unfortunate Inspector. "Well, you haven't covered yourself with glory, have you? I send you out, with precise instructions. . . ."

I was no longer listening. I knew only one man in the neighbourhood who wore khaki and roared in a Glasgow accent when pursued – but it couldn't be him, surely? McAuslan, stag-poacher? Impossible; he wouldn't have known how, for one thing . . . and then I remembered Aunt Alison's words: "Macrae! There's a name for a Highland midnight . . ." Macrae the stalker; he would know how. But that wasn't credible, either . . . we'd only been in the district twenty-four hours; they couldn't have taken to crime (and highly technical crime, too) in that time. Not McAuslan, anyway – and yet every instinct told me that, however bizarre the explanation, he was out there in the heather somewhere, doing his disorderly impression of Rob Roy, and unless immediate steps were taken he would undoubt-edly blunder into the arms of the Law, and . . . It didn't bear thinking about – McAuslan, court-martialled for killing the King's deer (well, the Admiral's, anyway). What could I do?

Fortunately the Admiral and Inspector were too busy upbraiding and making excuses to notice me, and when the Admiral finally made for the hotel, muttering savagely about incompetent bumpkins and the decay of discipline, I followed, a prey to nameless fears. He surged up the steps like an ice-breaker, and was heading for my aunt's office when Robin Elphinstone came out of the passage, started violently at the sight of us, and half-retreated into the passage again, looking furtive.

"Elphinstone!" cried the Admiral, scoring a bull for identifi-cation. "What the blazes are you doing here?"

The aggressive tone seemed to strike fire in Elphinstone. He

159

was normally a bluff, confident character, but emerging from the passage he had reacted like Peter Lorre caught in the act, twitching and glancing sideways. Now he recovered, drew himself up, eyed the Admiral with loathing, and demanded:

"Why shouldn't I be here? This hotel isn't your flagship, is it? Who the dickens d'you think you are – Captain Bligh?" He snorted and shot his cuffs rather defensively, I thought. "If you must know, I've been having coffee with Mrs Gordon," he added, and the Admiral ground his teeth.

"Your trousers are wet!" he said accusingly.

"So are yours," retorted Elphinstone. "What would you like to do – form a club?" He gave a pleased snort, wished me goodnight, and went off, but not without another wary glance back as he reached the door.

"Damned impertinence!" fumed the Admiral. "Mark my words, that fellow wants watching. Did you see him just now – looked as though he'd had his hand in the till? What's he been up to, eh? Outsider!"

Aunt Alison was knitting placidly and listening to the wireless in the warm comfort of her room. "Home from the wars!" she said, smiling, exclaimed at the wet state of our feet, rang for coffee and sandwiches, placed us before the fire, dispensed whisky, and listened with soothing attention while the Admiral poured out his troubles from the hearthrug, starting with the insolence and evil cunning of the Dipper ("which won't save him, I'm glad to say, once the evidence is recovered") and ending with a scathing denunciation of the luckless Inspector. He didn't refer to our encounter with Elphinstone, but I noticed his glance strayed to the muddy tracks on the carpet, as though he were trying to deduce how long his detested rival had spent on the premises.

"My, it's the exciting night you've had of it!" said Aunt Alison admiringly, and sighed. "And the poor old Dipper's nabbed at last. Well, I won't pretend I'm not sorry for the old devil."

"Old devil is right. But your sympathy, my dear, is far too precious to be wasted on him," chided the Admiral. "The fellow's been a menace for years. Well, now he's going to pay for it – and so," he concluded grimly, "are those infernal poachers."

160

"Didn't you tell me they'd got away?"

"Thanks to that yokel policeman, yes. But the truck didn't," said the Admiral triumphantly. "And if the fingerprints on its steering-wheel belong to anyone named McLaren . . . well, I'd say that was conclusive, wouldn't you?"

I'd been listening with one ear, preoccupied as I was with visions of McAuslan roaming the Highland night while I sat powerless to rescue or prevent him, but at the suggestion that my truck would be Exhibit A in a poaching trial I was all attention. So was my aunt, only she seemed amused.

"Conclusive of what? Only about who was driving the truck, and took it away. But that," she reminded him, "is Dand's concern, Jacky. Not yours."

"Not mine?" The Admiral went into his halibut impersonation. "But . . . but, goodgoddlemighty, they were using it to poach my stag! They were—"

"Were they? What stag? You haven't even found it yet." She rose, holding the decanter. "And until you do, you'll be ill-advised to cry 'Poacher!' just because you've got a bee in your bonnet about the McLarens. More toddy?"

The Admiral gargled, going puce. "A bee? In my bonnet? You know as well as I do they've got my stag cached out there—"

"You're blethering," she said pleasantly, filling his glass. "I know no such thing, and neither do you. Fingerprints, indeed! You've been seeing too many Thin Man pictures. Well, nobody's been murdered—"

"Alison!"

"—and all that's happened is that Dand's truck has been taken without his permission – and now he's got it back . . ."

"Alison, I—"

". . . And the last thing he wants is a lot of handless bobbies crawling over it with magnifying glasses. Even if every McLaren in Scotland had his pug-marks on it, what could they be charged with except taking it away without the owner's consent? And I don't suppose you've considered the trouble and embarrass-ment that would cause my nephew with his superiors? Well . . ." She gave him her level, blue-eyed look. ". . . I wouldn't think much of that, I can tell you."

She wasn't alone there: I could think of one Colonel who

would hit the roof. And the Admiral, to do him justice, took the point, although it was nothing to him compared to the prospect of incurring her displeasure. That was what took him amidships, and his indignation vanished like May mist; he blinked at her in a distraught, devoted way, and admitted he hadn't thought about that side of it . . . last thing he'd want to do . . . and no doubt she was right, there was no positive proof . . . yet. But what could he say to the police? If they had reason to believe the truck had been used for criminal purposes, he didn't quite see how he. . . .

"Och, use your wits, Jacky! Tell them Dand's satisfied, and doesn't wish to press matters. Bully them, man, if you have to! Goodness me, the Inspector wants to be a superintendent some day – he's not going to cross the leading man in the district, is he?"

The leading man looked doubtful. "Well, I suppose . . . if you say so . . . it'll look a bit odd, though, after all the fuss . . ."

"Havers!" laughed Aunt Alison. "I can just see McKendrick raising objections. A word from you and he'll be jumping through hoops and saluting." She smiled warmly on him and sweetened the pill still further. "You can come and tell me about it at dinner, and we'll talk it all over, the two of us."

The Admiral cheered up considerably at this, and when he took his leave after a final toddy it was with expressions of good will all round. As the door closed Aunt Alison gave a long, delicate sigh and subsided into her chair, reaching for a cigarette.

"My God, and they talk about Sarah Bernhardt! If I'd had to be ladylike a minute longer I'd have burst!" She inhaled deeply, raising a hand to still my clamour. "Not now, Dand. I know you're full of desperate news, but it can wait. Now . . . stiffen your drink, because I have a wee surprise for you, and I want you to sit there, keep calm, and hold your peace till it's over."

She rose, and opened the door to the little box-room off the study. "Come out of that," she said, and before my disbelieving eyes Lance-Corporal Macrae sidled warily into the room, and behind him, like an anxious tomb-robber emerging from a pyramid, shambled Private McAuslan.

I don't know what I'd have said if I hadn't been bidden to silence; nothing, probably. Unexpectedness apart, they were a sight to numb the senses: Macrae was wild and dishevelled, but

McAuslan looked as though he had been in the ground for centuries. Filthy I had seen him, but never like this; he had broken all previous records. Mud and slime of every shade and texture seemed to cover him, his hair was matted with it, through the beauty-pack on his face he was regarding me in terror, and then he quivered to attention as my aunt addressed them.

"You two men," and she looked and sounded like a Valkyrie at the end of her tether, "will haud your wheesht, now and hereafter. Do you see? Mr MacNeill will have something to say to you later, but just now you'll go out by the back way, like mice, and up to the house without being seen. Is that clear?" She raised a finger. "And Macrae – if ever you put your neb into West Perthshire again I'll have you hung by the heels. *Aighe-va.*"

I counted five when they had gone and, restraining myself with difficulty, asked for an explanation. Aunt Alison gave me a look.

"Are you sure you want to know?"

I pointed out that since *they* obviously knew, I ought to, if only for discipline's sake, and she sat, resting her brow on her finger-tips, and finally said: "I could greet. Dand, next time you come to see me, just bring a couple of nice wee city criminals, will you? Not reivers like Macrae. Mind you . . . if he's looking for a job when he leaves the Army . . . ach, never mind. Well, bide and listen, if your nerves can stand it."

It seemed that on the first evening Macrae and McAuslan, refreshing themselves in the public bar, had made friends with the lads of the village, including the notorious McLarens, the Dipper's crew. They and Macrae had discovered mutual interests, and in no time he was abreast of local affairs, such as the pressing danger to the Dipper's illicit still from the Admiral and the gadgers. A raid was imminent, and what was needed, said the Dipper, was some diversion to keep the Admiral busy while the still was moved to a new hideaway – shooting a stag, for example. A task for a skilled night hunter . . . aye, but it would be worth his while. Oh, Macrae was a bit of a stalker, was he? And then they would be needing transport for the carcase the next night . . . what, Macrae knew where a truck was to be had? Here, Erchie, come you and listen to this. . . .

I could contain myself no longer. "Aunt Alison, are you telling me Macrae was bribed to poach a stag before he'd been here five minutes? I can't believe it! How do you know this, anyway?" I regarded her in sudden terror. "Have you known all along?"

"Will you hold your peace? And don't jump to unflattering conclusions," she said with some asperity. "I've been telling you that since you could toddle. I knew nothing at all until this evening. But I'm not a gommeril, and like everyone else I knew the McLarens would try *some* ploy to set Jacky running in circles. And when he came yelping to me this morning that a stag had been shot, I thought, aye, that's their red herring. There was no point saying anything to Jacky, with the steam rising from him; besides, it was no business of mine. But when you came to the hotel in the evening, and said your truck was missing, and two of your lads nowhere to be found – then, it was my business."

"When the Admiral was here, planning his raid? You never said anything. You went to arrange a snack for his men."

She gave me a pitying look. "Aye, didn't I just? I also went to get Rab, my grieve, because he's one that knows every mortal thing that goes on hereabouts. I don't pry as a rule, but I knew this was an emergency, and I grilled the whole black tale out of him, with the promise that if he held back he'd be on the dole tomorrow. Now, may I continue?"

Rab, under pressure, had described what my aunt had just told me – how Macrae had conspired with the McLarens, contributing some refinements of his own to their diversionary plan. The upshot was that he had gone out that first night with Erchie McLaren's rifle and a flask of rabbit's blood which he had smeared artistically on a rock on Ben Vornach; he had faked signs that a stag had been carried off through the heather, fired a shot, and so home to bed. (And I'd thought he was out wenching.)

"You mean there wasn't any dead stag? But then . . . why did they take the truck tonight, if there was no carcase to shift?"

"I guessed that before Rab got the length of telling me," said Aunt Alison complacently. "They needed it to shift the Dipper's still. That was the whole point – to make Jacky think the truck was being used to carry off a carcase that didn't exist, when in fact they were getting the still away from Lochnabee."

"But they *didn't* get it away! The Dipper had to jettison it! I saw him!"

Aunt Alison shrugged. "Aye, well, the best-laid schemes . . . Jacky took their bait – but he went to Lochnabee as well, and no doubt got there ahead of them, and spoiled their plan. But that's by the way. All I knew, and cared about, when Rab had told his tale, was that *your* truck was about to be used for bootlegging or moonshining or whatever you call it. With one of your men, Macrae, red-hand in the mischief – and yon other poor bedraggled idiot as well, probably. What's his name? McAuslan? He hasnae the look of a gangster."

"He's not. I shouldn't think he knew what the hell was happening. I don't think I do."

"Well, thank your stars I did. It was plain that with Jacky bound for Lochnabee they were in great danger of getting caught, and I had to prevent that, for your sake – I don't ken what the Army does to officers whose men are lifted for moving illicit stills (or for trying to) but I'm sure it's something embarrassing. So," she continued serenely, "I phoned Robin Elphinstone and told him to take his car and scour the road about Lochnabee, and find those clowns of yours before the police did, and get them safe away. And to give him time to do that, I kept Jacky and his minions busy here with grouse pâté and Glenlivet. I thought it went down rather well," said this amazing woman complacently, "and I wasn't bad myself."

It's remarkable, about family. You think you know them, but you don't. Here was this good, respected widow lady of advancing years, who had guided my infant steps, heard my prayers at night, and read to me from the *Billy and Bunny Book*, sitting there looking like the matriarch of some soap-opera family of Texas tycoons, and apparently concealing the combined talents of the Scarlet Pimpernel and a Mafia godmother. I didn't know where to begin.

"You could try saying thank you, and bring me a glass of sherry," she reproved me. "Well, Robin didn't like it, much, but he's biddable. He took his car and waited in a quarry near the Lochnabee turn-off until your truck came by, going like fury. He saw the police car head them off, and your two boys and the McLarens taking to the heather, and being a good man on the hill himself he waited until the police had given up, and then went after your lads, leaving the McLarens to take care of themselves." She took a wistful sip of sherry. "It's a fact, men have all the fun. Well, he found them: the poor McAuslan cratur was up to his neck in a myrtle bog, bawling like a bull, but he got them to his car and brought them here – which wasn't so clever, but Robin has his limitations. He sneaked them in by the back, and they had barely been in here long enough to foul the carpet when we heard Jacky waking the echoes at the front door. I whipped them straight into the box-room and told Robin to make himself scarce."

"No wonder he looked panic-stricken! Aunt Alison, he could have got the jail! So could you, I dare say . . . don't ask me for what – obstructing justice or something—"

"Ach, stop blethering, boy. What did I do but telephone a friend asking him to give two soldiers a lift?"

Legally, she may have been right: I doubt if there are laws against obtaining information from an employee with threats of dismissal, dragooning a neighbour into rescuing stray soldiers from bogs, playing Lady Bountiful to keep Excisemen from their duty, or beguiling choleric naval men with fair words and malt whisky while their mud-spattered quarry lies hidden in the next room. But they do call for an unusual ability to think on your feet, to say nothing of imperturbability, man management, and sheer cold nerve. And as I watched her now, taking a vanity mirror from her bag, turning her head critically, and adjusting a silver curl, I said as much. She was amused.

"Dear me," she said, "have you forgotten, when you were wee, I told you about the woman of Achruach and the Gregora? Well," she gave a last glance at her mirror, smoothing an eyebrow, "I may use reading glasses and gasp a bit on the stairs, but the day I cannot keep my countenance, and work my will on the likes of Robin Elphinstone and Admiral Jacky – that, nephew, is a day you will never see."

They were feigning sleep when I got back to Wade's House, Macrae in silence, McAuslan with irregular staccato grunts which he probably imagined sounded like rhythmic breathing. I didn't rouse them, partly because I was too tired to listen to the lies of one and the pathetic excuses of the other, but chiefly because my sadistic streak was showing and I was only too

166

pleased to let them stew in their guilty fear until morning. Even then I ignored them, telling Brooks that we would do without breakfast and get on the road at once; I had no wish to linger in a locality whose inhabitants had proved themselves about as safe as damp gun-cotton.

When we were safely south of Balquhidder I told Brooks to pull over on a quiet stretch, and went round to order the criminal element out of the back for a man-to-man chat by the roadside. Macrae, haggard but presentable, stared stolidly to his front; McAuslan was in his normal parade order, filthy, abject, crouched to attention with animal fear in every ragged line of him, and sneezing fit to rattle the windows in Crieff. Forcing myself to look more closely, I saw that he had shed most of the muck he had been wearing last night, and that he was wringing wet; a small pool was forming around his sodden boots.

"What the devil have you been doing?" I demanded.

"Please, sur," he croaked, and sneezed again, thunderously. "Oh, name o' Goad! Please, sur," he repeated, through hideous snuffles, "Corporal Macrae threw me inna burn, sur. Las' night, sur, when we wis comin' hame."

I fought down an impulse to deal leniently with Macrae. "Why did you do that, Corporal?"

"Tae get him clean, sir. He was manky. Ye saw him at the hotel, sir, covered wi' glaur. I wisnae lettin' him in your auntie's hoose in that state."

"Well, that was very thoughtful of you. And by the looks of you, McAuslan, you slept in your wet uniform. Why?"

"Becos . . . aarraashaw! Aw, jeez, beg pard'n, sur! Jist a wee tickle in ma nose. Aye, weel, ye see, Ah kept ma claes on fur tae keep me warm."

"Ah, of course. Well, we don't want them to get creased, do we, so why don't you get back in the truck – and strip the disgusting things off, you blithering clot, you! Dry your horrible self, if you know how, and wrap your useless carcase in a blanket before you get pneumonia, although why I should worry about that I'm shot if I know! Move!"

A normal enough preliminary to a meeting of minds with McAuslan. When he had vanished, sneezing and hawking, over the tailboard, I turned back to Macrae.

"Right, Corporal. Tell me about last night."

He licked his lips, looking past me. "Did your auntie . . . Mrs Gordon, I mean . . . not tell you?"

"She told me. Now you tell me."

It was like getting blood from a stone. After some evasion, he admitted faking the stag-shooting. Why had he done it? Och, well, the McLarens were good lads, and it was a bit o' sport. No, he'd had no money from them. (I believed this.) Yes, he had let them take the truck in my absence, and gone with them; aye, he knew it was a grave offence, but he was deep in the business by then, and couldnae let them down; they were good lads. Forbye, he didnae think I would ever know. Yes, he knew that conspiring with illicit distillers was a criminal matter, and that he and McAuslan might have landed in jail. Didn't he realise what a dirty trick it was to involve a meat-brain like McAuslan in the first place? At this he looked uncomfortable, and shrugged, with a sheepish little laugh – and that was when I caught the smell on his breath.

"Half a sec," I said. "Where did you get a drink at this time of day?"

"Drink, sir? Me, sir?"

I went straight to the truck and climbed in, ignoring the débutante squeal of McAuslan caught en déshabille. Sure enough, in the well of the truck beneath the floor, safe from the prying eyes of policemen, were a dozen bottles – no labels, of course, but all filled with the water of life, clear as glass. I wetted my palm and tasted, and it was the good material, smooth and strong and full of wonder. Not more than a hundred proof, probably. I knew old soldiers who would have killed for it.

"Well, well . . . so the Dipper paid you in advance, did he?" I said. "Generously, too – twelve bottles for nothing."

Macrae, at the tailboard, was silent, presumably resigned to confiscation, but McAuslan, clutching his blanket about him like the oldest squaw on the reservation, was startled into contradiction.

"Wisnae fur nuthin', sure'n it wisnae." He sounded quite indignant. "Sure'n we shiftit his bluidy still for him."

Like my aunt, I too can sometimes keep my countenance.

"Och, sure," I said, "but that's no great work."

"Wis it no', but?" said McAuslan, and emitted another

crashing sneeze. When he had finished towelling his nose with his blanket he resumed: "See that still, sur? It wis bluidy heavy, Ah'm tellin' ye. We'd a helluva job gettin' it oot o' the boat an' into ra truck, an'—"

"What time was this?"

"Jist efter dark. Is that no' right, Macrae? Aye, soon's it wis dark, that Erchie McLaren an' anither yin came up tae the hoose, an' we a' got inna truck, an' drove up tae that loch where the Dipper has his boat . . ." He paused, apprehension clouding his primitive features as it dawned on him that he was Telling All. He gulped, gasped, closed his eyes, shuddered, was convulsed by another monumental sneeze, muttered "Mither o' Goad, Ah've jist aboot had it!", shot an appealing look at the saturnine Macrae, and then gave me a furtive, fawning grin which I think on the whole was the most repulsive expression I've ever seen on a human face.

"Eh . . . eh . . . Ah'm awfy sorry, sur," he said. "Ah've forgot the rest."

"No, you haven't, McAuslan. But you don't have to worry," I reassured him. "It's all right. You can tell me. Because if you don't, I'll kill you."

He digested this, stricken, and decided there was nothing else for it. "Aye, weel, like Ah wis sayin'. We got up tae the loch, an' the Dipper an' his boys, an' the fower of us, we got his bluidy contraption oot the boat – here, it was a right plumber's nightmare, sur, so it wis! An' that's whit they mak' ra whisky in! Ye widnae credit it. Onywye," he went on, wiping his face with his blanket in an oratorical gesture, "we wis staggerin' aboot wi' the thing in the watter, an' no' kiddin', sur, Ah wis aboot ruptured, an' the Dipper wis next tae me, an' he lets oot a helluva roar. 'Whit's up?' sez Ah. 'It's ma ee!' sez he, 'it's fell oot. It's in ra watter!' Ah couldnae figure 'im oot. 'Yer ee?' sez Ah. 'Whit ye talkin' aboot, Dipper!' 'Ma gless ee!' cries he, an' starts floonderin' in ra watter, an' efter a bit he cam' up wi' it, and slipped it back in. Tell ye the truth," said McAuslan, "Ah wis a bit disgustit. But we got the still on the truck, an' Ah sez tae the Dipper, 'Hoo did ye lose yer ee, auld yin?' 'Got it shot oot in France in sixteen', sez he. 'Away!' sez Ah. 'Wis you in the Airmy?' 'Wis Ah no',' sez he. 'See your man MacNeill, his uncle wis ma officer. Brung me back in aff the wire efter ma ee got shot oot. Ah widnae be makin' malt the day, if it hadnae been for him.' "

Actually, that was news to me. McAuslan paused to beam on me. "He musta been a'right, your uncle, eh?"

"Yes, he was," I said. "Go on."

"Aye, weel, we'd jist got the tailboard up when here's a caur comin' up the hill road tae the loch – we couldnae see it, but we heard the engine. 'Claymore!' bawls the Dipper. 'Here the King's Navy an' the bluidy gadgers! Oot o' this, Erchie, or we're lost men!' An' him an' his two fellas tumbled in the boat an' starts rowin', an' we got inna truck, but we couldnae tak' the road, wi' the caur comin', so Erchie jist went straight doon the side o' the hill. Inna dark, helpmaGoad! Whit a helluva ride it wis! We wis bashin' ower rocks an' breengin' through bracken, an' ma innards comin' oot ma ears, an' Erchie McLaren's roarin': 'Thy will be done, oh Lord! Keep a grip o' the still, lads!' Hoo we got ontae the main road, guid kens, an' then we drove for miles—"

"Where to? Where did you take the still?" He looked blank. "Do you know, Macrae?"

He shook his head. "Nae idea, sir – honest. It was as black as the Earl o' Hell's breeks. Somewhere off the Tyndrum road, in a dry cave in a corrie."

"So what was it the Dipper dropped in the loch in front of the gadgers?"

He tried in vain to keep a straight face. "An old stove and a lot o' bed springs."

The classic selling of the dummy, in fact. Well, good luck, Admiral, I thought. You'll drag the loch for that still, and never find it – but you'll always believe it's there, somewhere at the bottom of Lochnabee. While the Dipper sits in his dry cave, distilling away to his heart's content and quietly enjoying what, to the Highlander, is the perfect victory: the one the enemy doesn't know about.

It occurred to me that Aunt Alison's delaying tactic on behalf of my errant soldiery had also given the Dipper time to get his still safely away. Not that she could have foreseen that, of course. Interesting, though . . .

"Aye, but here, sur, ye hivnae heard the hauf o' it!" McAuslan, girding his sodden blanket about him, was eager to resume his role as saga-man. "See efter that, but? Onna way hame we ran intae ra durty polis, an' had tae scram oot o' ra truck an' run fur it, an' Ah near drooned in a bog, an' got a' covered in—"

"Thank you, McAuslan, I know all about that."

"—an' that man Elphinstone dragged me oot by the hair o' the heid – an' where the hell were you, Macrae?" he demanded at a sudden tangent, glaring balefully at his superior. "Fat lot o' help you wis, an' chance it! Lookin' efter Number Wan ye wis, an' me uptae ma neck in the—"

"All right, McAuslan, that'll do . . ."

"Aye, weel, sur, Ah'm jist sayin'. Nae thanks tae Macrae Ah got oot . . . an' then the man Elphinstone got us tae his caur, an' took us tae yer auntie at ra hotel, an'—"

"McAuslan!"

"—beg pard'n sur, Missus Gordon, Ah shoulda said. Awfy sorry. An' she sez: 'Jeez, will ye look at the state o' ye!', or sumpn like that, an' then the man Elphinstone cries: 'Here somebuddy comin'!', an' she had us through yon door afore ye could say knife – sure'n she did, Macrae? Here, sur, wis it yon wee nyaff o' an Admiral? See the bluidy Navy, Ah hate them, so Ah do—"

"Shut up!" I shouted, and he fell silent, with the pained surprise of a Cicero cut off in full peroration by the Consuls, although I doubt if the great orator ever scrubbed his nose with his toga, or asked can Ah pit ma soaks on noo, sur, ma feet's fair freezin'?

"Wait till they're dry, idiot!" I snarled. "Socks, forsooth! Hasn't it sunk into your concrete skull yet that you committed a crime last night? That you could have wound up in Barlinnie?"

He blinked, scratching himself while he digested this, and made a deep guttural noise of concern. "Zattafac', sur? Here, aye, Ah s'pose that's right. Ah'm awfy sorry, sur, Ah didnae think aboot that." He towelled his matted head in a contrite way, and then brightened. "Aye, but it wis a'right, ye see. Your auntie – beg par'n, Missus Gordon, Ah should say – she took care o' us, nae bother. Organised, so she wis. Had us through that door sae fast wir feet didnae touch." His gargoyle face creased in complacent approval. "Ah think she's smashin', Ah do. Awfy nice. Awfy clever . . ."

I gave up – not for the first time. As I climbed out of the truck I

171

realised that Macrae was regarding me warily; I knew what was going on in that practical mind, but I'd already weighed this against that and decided, reluctantly, that there was only one thing for it.

"Right, Macrae," I said. "In you get."

He hesitated with his hand on the tailboard. "Eh . . . what aboot the whisky, sir?"

"What whisky?" I said. "Get in, and be quiet. And think yourself lucky."

". . . never panicked. Kept the heid. Just says, 'In there, the pair o' ye, an' no' a cheep oot o' ye'." McAuslan was still extolling Aunt Alison's presence of mind. "Ah think she's marvellous, so Ah do. She's a great buddy . . . Ah mean, wumman . . . Ah mean, leddy." He regarded me over the tailboard, shaking his grimy head in solemn respect, and bestowed the Glaswegian's ultimate accolade. "She's a'right, but."

Or as they say in Breadalbane: that is a woman of the Gordons for you.

Ye mind Jie Dee, Fletcher?

Ten years ago Scotland's footballers were in the World Cup finals in Argentina. That bald statement gives not the remotest idea of the emotional convulsion which the event produced north of the Tweed; whenever Scottish prestige is at stake in any major international contest (war and soccer especially) the population tends to go into an inner frenzy of apprehension and wild hope, and those stern Caledonian virtues of sound judgment and common sense have to struggle for survival. Whatever the odds, however unlikely victory may be, the fever takes hold: dreams of glory and memories of past heroes and triumphs mingle with anxious speculation, and if outward opinion of the country's chances is often muted and even disparaging, don't let that fool you – under the surface all the old passions are on the boil again, the savage joy of impending conflict, the charging up of confidence, the growing, shining conviction that this time – this time, at long last! – it is all going to come true. Now and then it does, as witness Bannockburn 1314, Wembley 1928, Lisbon 1967, and Muirfield Village 1987. (The fact that other nations were also on the winning side on that last occasion is, to Scots, irrelevant. Whose game is it, anyway?)

But few things rouse Scottish emotions so much as football – another game which they regard as their personal property. England, the mother of sport, laid down with typical Anglo-Saxon tidiness the laws which imposed form and order on the old wild celebration in which two sides battled over a ball; they invented the game, but the Scots gave it the style which made it the most popular team sport on earth. More than a century ago they cast a calculating eye on football as it was played south of the Border, saw its possibilities, and transformed the charging, kick-and-rush recreation into a thing of science and even beauty; not for them to chase pell-mell after the ball with the reckless exuberance of the hunting field; they actually *passed* it to each other, ran into open space for the return, moved in ever-changing formations, perfected control with foot and head, and turned to advantage the short, wiry stature and lightning nimbleness which three generations of slum-dwelling had bred into a people who had once been the biggest in Europe. Like Pygmalion, they fell hopelessly in love with their creation, and have been faithful ever since.

For sixty years it was a blissful honeymoon, up to the Second World War. The Scottish professionals held undisputed mastery, and only England, with its tenfold superiority in sporting manpower, could hope to match if not to overtake them; Ireland and Wales provided interesting practice, and the rest of the world didn't count. Soccer was only spreading then; young enthusiasts like Nikita Khrushchev were learning the art of the sliding tackle in the Donbass, and a goalkeeper named Albert Camus was cherishing the dream (later realised) of playing for his country, but it was still a British game, and its high priests served their novitiates at Ibrox, Tynecastle, and Parkhead.

It all changed after 1945. England began to beat Scotland more often than not. Moscow Dynamo came to Glasgow and held the mighty Rangers to a draw, Austria became the first foreign side to win on Scottish soil, quicksilver South Americans dazzled the traditionalists with a style of play that ignored the old sacred forms, and when Hungary took England apart at Wembley with clinical efficiency, Britain was no longer football's Olympus, and Scotland was a second-rate power. But the Scottish temperament being what it is, the dream remained, kept alive by national sides who were occasionally brilliant, more frequently awful to the point of embarrassment, and chronically inconsistent.

This is a characteristic which has bedevilled the Scots (and not only in sport) since Macbeth was a boy. At their best they are matchless; at their worst they defy description, and you never know which extreme you are going to see. Given pygmies for opponents, they are liable to get slaughtered; faced by giants, they will run rings round them – and then snatch defeat from the jaws of victory by some last-minute folly. England, on the other hand, are steady and predictable; only they could have restored British prestige by winning the World Cup in 1966 with sound if uninspired football and bulldog determination. Scotland, who hadn't even been able to qualify, promptly suffered a rush of blood to the head and thumped them next time out, and the nation lived in a tartan euphoria – until the next disaster.

To supporters as proud and passionate as the Scots this is frustrating to the point of trauma. They bear their burden of tradition with a fierce nostalgia, knowing that their players are still the equal of any, but sensing too, in their heart of hearts, that Scotland will never win the World Cup (except in imagination every four years). But irrational hope springs eternal, fuelled by occasional wins against England, and such heady triumphs as that of 1967, when a Celtic team who were arguably the best club side ever to come out of Britain, brought back the European Cup from Portugal, and for six weeks afterwards the British Embassy staff in Lisbon were terrified to open cupboards in case little drunk men in tartan scarves fell out, demanding the fare back to Glasgow.

That victory, and an appearance in the World Cup finals of 1974 from which, by a quirk of the system, they were eliminated without actually losing a game, sustained Scotland until 1978, when they qualified for the finals yet again. And that was when the madness took hold, and a conviction arose as never before that this would be Scotland's year at last. A new manager, Alistair Macleod, somehow convinced his eager countrymen that the Scottish team, a workmanlike enough collection, were world-beaters; Scottish fans, describing themselves as "Ally's Army", sang excruciating victory songs beforehand and gloated that England had failed to qualify for Argentina; the presence of two insignificant sides, Peru and Iran, in Scotland's preliminary group seemed to augur a triumphal progress to the final stages, and even the fact that the fourth team in the group, Holland, were probably the best side in the world at that time, could not damp Caledonian ardour. It was in the bag, the World Cup was as good as back in Glasgow, here's tae us, wha's like us, we're the wee boys, etc., etc. . . . Never were the Fates so tempted.

Well, Scotland were clobbered 1–3 by the despised Peruvians, scrambled a draw with Iran (Iran!), and to crown all, had a player sent home for taking "an innocuous but illegal stimulant". There had been nothing like it since Flodden, and the anguished cries of rage and grief from the faithful were heartbreaking. Scots exultant are unbearable, but when disappointed and betrayed their recriminations are worthy of the Old Testament. I didn't see or hear it, for I was far from Scotland at the time, but I could imagine all too well what was being said – and by one voice in particular, a voice I had not heard in thirty years, but which I didn't doubt would be upraised in denunciation and wild lament, just as I remembered it from the parade grounds and barrack-rooms of North Africa. I just had to close my eyes and there it was, drifting raucously across the ether, the plainsong of ex-Private McAuslan, J., reviewing the World Cup scene and reflecting on what might have been, but was not . . .

See ra Sco'ish team in ra Argenteena? Jeez an' name o' Goad! Ah never seen such a bunch o' bums since ra chorus at ra Metropole done ra can-can. No kiddin', they couldnae beat *me*! See the state they were in? Whaur were yer inside forwards feedin' ra centre, whaur were yer wing-hauves haudin' doon ra midfield, whaur were yer wingers crossin' ra ba', whaur were yer Tommy Walkers an' Jimmy Delaneys bangin' it in? It's a goal! Aw-haw-hey! Come away ra wee boys! Scotland furrever! HA! Fat chance onybody got tae shout *that* in ra Argenteena, but. Play fitba'? Them? They couldnae play a bluidy barrel organ if Ally Macleod was tae wind it up for them. Mind you, Ah'm no' sayin' he would make a helluva good job o' that, either. Dearie me! Come home, Macleod, yer fan club's waitin'. Pathetic, so it is.

Hey, see me, but. Ah'm staun'in' in ra Mull o' Kintyre Vaults on ra Garscube Road wi' Fletcher, watchin' it onna telly. Ah couldnae believe it, so Ah couldnae. They're playin' ra wogs – ye know, Irran. It was efter they got beat aff the dagoes – aye, Perroo, tae rhyme wi' burroo, an' that's whit the hauf o' them should be on, aye, includin' that yin that got sent hame wi' his bladder full o' diabolic aspirin or whitever it was. But whit a shambles, Ah ask ye! The Irran wogs is gaun through them like they wisnae there, an' Hartford an' wee Erchie Gemmell an' Macari an' a' the rest o' them's rinnin' aboot like chickens wi' nae heids, an' Ah says, "Fletcher, Ah don't believe whit Ah'm seein' – it's no' happenin', it cannae be happenin', sure'n it cannae, Fletcher?"

"Can it no'?" says he. "Ah'm no' watchin'. Ony time Ah

want tae look at a tragedy Ah can go an' see 'Macbeth'."

"Macbeth?" says Ah. "Wis he yon big fella used tae play centre hauf fur Airdrie? Ach, he wisnae worth a tosser, him, great big feet clumphin' a' ower ra penalty box. Aw, jeez, will ye look at Rough? That's a' we needit, a goalkeeper frae ra Partick Thistle! Mind you, the boy's no' a bad goalie – that's the thing aboot ra Thistle, a'ways had a good goalie, ye mind Ledgerwood, Fletcher? That wis a goalie an' a hauf – GET RID OF IT, BUCHAN! IT'S NO' YOUR BA', YOU DIDNAE PEY FOR IT!! Oh, so helpma Goad! Aw, jeez! Aw, dearie me! If auld Jimmy Delaney, auld Jie Dee, could just be oot on that park fur five minutes! Or Walker, or Last-minute Reilly, or wee Billy Steel, or McGrory, or onybuddy that hisnae two left feet! Goad, if Ah could jist be oot there masel'!"

"You!" says Fletcher. "You couldnae get oot yer own way. Mind that own goal against A Company?"

"Aw, fur Pete's sake, Fletcher, come affit!" Ah says. "Ye still gaun oan aboot that? Ah nivver even seen ra ba' comin', hoo wis Ah tae know McGuffie wis gaun tae dae a back pass – the eejit! – it wisnae ma fault, Ah wis markin' the winger, Ah wis—"

"It's that gommeril Macleod!" says Fletcher, glowerin' at ra telly. "He'll haftae go! The man's no' up tae it. Trust the Esseffay tae pick a teuchter as Scotland's manager. A Macleod, no kiddin'. The Macleods is a' away wi' the fairies, everybuddy kens that. Ye know they've even got a fairy banner?"

"Zattafac'?"

"Aye, they fly it on their castle at clan gatherin's, an' Ally Macleod mustae been wearin' it draped ower his heid a' the way tae Argenteena frae Gartnavel, or he'd have seen whit a pile o' rubbish his team wis. Shootin's too good fur him—"

"Haud oan," Ah says. "Jist haud oan, Fletcher. Keep the heid. Cool it. Tak' it easy. DON'T PANIC!! Macleod, ye say? Weel, Ah'll tell ye sumpn, Fletcher. Ah've been watchin' while thae bums has been gettin' crucified by Perroo, an' noo by the bluidy Assyrians or whitever they are – GAUN YERSEL, JORDAN! BREENGE AT HIM! IT'S WIDE OPEN! HIT THE THING, FUR GOAD'S SAKE! Aw, ye widnae credit it! Jie Dee widda had that past ra keeper in his sleep! Honest tae Goad, they want tae wrap the ba' up in a parcel an' post it tae ra wog goalie, it'll get there sooner! Onyway, Fletcher, whit Ah'm sayin' – Ah've been watchin', an' ye know, Ah hivnae seen *Macleod* make a single bad pass, or miss a single tackle, or balloon ra ba' ower the bar, or fa' on his erse, or dae ony o' the things thae wandered bums in blue jersies has been daein'. It's no' Macleod that's oot there playin' like he'd been ten year in the Eastern Necropolis. Leave Macleod alone, the man's daein' his best. Sich as it is. Goad preserve us frae his worst. He'll be keepin' that fur ra game against Holland.

"Whit's that ye say? Ach, whiddy ye mean, he should have watched Perroo beforehand, an' he didnae get dossiers on a' their players, an' he didnae show oor boys fillums o' the Perroovians? So whit! Naebuddy showed us fillums o' A Company, did they? Awright, awright, we got beat aff A Company! Ah know, Ah wis there, wisn't Ah? That's no' the point at a'. D'ye hear whit Ah'm sayin', Fletcher? Will ye listen? The point Ah'm makin', if Ah can get a word in edgewise – the point Ah'm makin's this: naebuddy done me a dossier on that dirty big animal that A Company had playin' at ootside right, an' kicked me stupit afore hauf-time. Ah didnae *need* a dossier, or fillums o' the beast, did Ah? No' bluidy likely. Ah just went oot there an' kicked *him* stupit in the second hauf. So the point Ah'm makin' – will ye sharrup? The point Ah'm makin', is that if ye cannae come up against a side, an' tak' them as ye find them, an' beat them at their own game, then you're no' much o' a fitba' team. Ye neednae blame it on the manager, even if he isnae fit tae be a lollipop man at the Gobi Desert Secondary School. Whaur's the Gobi Desert? Hoo the hell dae Ah know? Whitsat gottae dae wi it, that's a red herrin', Fletcher – COME OOT, ROUGH, FUR THE LOVE O' GOAD!! THE WOG'S GAUNAE SCORE! AW, LOVELY, ALAN! Aw, did ye see that? Whit a save! Oh, jeez, Ah thought fur a horrible minute. . . . Ye're awright, Alan! Even if ye do take fits. Oh, gie's anither pint, Ah'm needin' it! An' a wee hauf, miss – KICK IT UP RA PARK, YE GREAT MARYHILL MUG, YE!! Aw, Goad, aw, dearie me . . .

"Awright, they're rubbish. Awright, they're hellish. Awright, they're no' fit tae play for the Normal School Reserves. So whit? They've been rubbish afore, an' they'll be rubbish again. But Ah've seen them when they wis good. Ah mind them at Wembley an' Hampden an' Lisbon an' a' sorts o' places when they made the park seem like it wis a magic carpet,

178

and John White wi' the ba' like it wis tied tae his boots, an' Tommy Gemmell bangin' them in frae thirty yards, an' big George Young guardin' ra box like a polis, an' Denis Law flickin' it in wi' the back o' his heid, an' Slim Jim Baxter sittin' on the ba' – *sittin'* oan it, but, inside his own eighteen-yard line, waitin' fur the English tae try tae tak' it aff him! The cheek o' the man! Goad, they could dae wi' Baxter oot there the night. Jist fur five minutes. Or auld Jie Dee. Ye mind Jie Dee, Fletcher, wi' his baldy heid?

"Weel, they're daein' their best, Ah suppose. Okay, so it's no' much o' a best. They're no' very good – the noo. Ah've seen them good. Awright, awright, they're bluidy terrible the night. But – CENTRE IT, GEMMELL!! CROSS IT, YE BAMPOT, THEY'RE LINED UP WAITIN' LIKE IT WIS A BUS STOP! Aw, wid ye believe it? AFFSIDE? Hoo the hell could yon be affside? There's mair wogs in that goal area than there is in Egypt! Who's that referee, Fletcher? Whaur's he from? Does he speak English, even? He'll be a Yugoslavakian, by the looks o' him. Or a cannibal. AWAY TAE LIZARS AN' GET YER EYES TESTED, YA BIG POULTICE! Referees? Aw, Ah've had it . . .

"Whit wis Ah sayin'? Aye! Ah wis sayin' they're terrible. Aye, but, see you, Fletcher. Mind when Jordan hit ra post, an' Dalgleish pit one jist past, an' Masson scraped ra cross-bar? Suppose they'd gone in – suppose they'd been six inches the ither way – suppose they'd been three goals instead o' three misses – you'd no' hiv been bawlin'; 'Bring back hangin'! Macleod's got tae die!' Aw, no! Ye'd hiv been takin' the width o' the Maryhill Road, gassed tae hellangone, singin' 'Ally is ra greatest, Ally fur king, Ally fur Pope!', an' ye widnae hiv bothered yer backside if the ootfield play wis rubbish, an' the defence lookin' like a Sunday School treat in the rain, an' big Jordan performin' like he wis between the shafts o' a coal-cairt. No fears. As long as the ba' went in the wog net, or the dago net, ye widnae care hoo it got there! There's a' you ken aboot fitba', you . . ."

"Look, McAuslan," says he. "It didnae go in the wog net! Did it? It didnae go in the dago net! Did it? No, it didnae! *That*'s whit Ah'm complainin' aboot!"

". . . an' ye widnae hiv cared if the whole Scots team wis

mainlinin' on sulphuric acid or sherbet, ye'd hiv been screechin':
'Scotland can beat ra world an' ooter space! Aw-haw-hey!
We're the wee boys! We're the champs!' "

"Look, McAuslan!" cries he. "They got *beat*! B-E-E-T! An'
Ah'm scunnered! Disgustit! Ye hear me?"

"Aye, Ah hear ye. Ah know. Pathetic, so it is. But whit's the
point o' belly-achin' at the boys? Ah've nae time fur that. See
yon yahoos, ca' themselves supporters, mobbin' the team bus,
bawlin': 'Macleod is rubbish! Awa' hame, Forsyth, yer tea's
oot! We want wur money back! Scotland are rubbish!' See
them? Ah widnae gi'e them the time o' day. Did *they* qualify fur
ra World Cup finals? No' on yer nellie! Did *they* beat ra Czechs
an' ra Welsh? They did not! Did they ever dae onything but
staun on ra terracin' makin' pigs o' themselves when Scotland
wis winnin', and yellin' dog's abuse when they got beat? So whit
entitles them . . . SEE THE WINGER, MACARI! HE'S OOT
THERE LIKE RA UNKNOWN SOJER, NAEBUDDY
KENS HE'S THERE! Aw, jeez, aw Goad – ye bampot, Macari,
ye pudden, are ye related tae that Irranian sweeper, ye're aye
gi'in' the ba' tae him! As Ah wis sayin' . . . Ach, whit the hell,
itsa waste o' time. Ah've had it. Up tae here. Switch that
damned telly aff, barman, or let's hiv Bill an' Ben the Floorpot
Men, at least they've got mair intelligence than whit we've been
watchin' . . . Ah jist wish . . . Ah jist wish. . . . Ach, whit's the
use? Jie Dee disnae play here any more. Neither does Toamy
Walker. Hughie Gallacher's deid, an' Ma Ba' Peter isnae
aroond (thank Goad, he wis a' they needed in Cordova, anither
Partick Thistle comedian – but he wis magic on his day, mind).
Aye, they're a' gone. Jimmy Logie's sellin' papers oan Piccadilly, Erchie Macaulay's a traffic warden, an' Baxter's got a
pub in ra Govan Road. It's no' the same . . .

"Here, but . . . that boy Souness isnae bad. An' there must be
ither young fellas comin' on. When's the next World Cup,
Fletcher? 1982? Dear Goad, we goat tae go through a' this
again? Ah cannae stand it, so Ah cannae. But Ah'll hiftae. It's
like politics an' dry rot; ye cannae get away frae them, an'
there's nae cure. An' noo we're gaun tae hiv tae sit through the
game against Holland – can ye picture it, Fletcher? We'll get
murdered! Murdered! It'll be aboot six-nil, Ah'll no' be able tae
watch . . . Mind you, Ah know the Dutch are good, but they're

180

just eleven men, efter a'. Ye nivver know, fitba's a funny game. Aye, no' that funny. Still, Scotland cannae be worse than they were tonight . . . weel, no' much worse. Ah hope. Tell ye whit, though. Ah'll tak' them tae beat England at Wembley next year. Mebbe.

"Ye mind Jie Dee? Aw, Goad . . ."

[It seems only just to record that Scotland, unpredictable as ever, played like champions against Holland and beat them convincingly – but not by a big enough margin to qualify for the final stages. Still, I have no doubt that the memory of that victory was enough to sustain McAuslan through the next World Cup, and the next, and so on for ever after.]

Extraduction

> The Highland battalion in this book never existed,
> inasmuch as the people in the stories are fictitious . . .
> and the incidents have been made up from a wide
> variety of sources, including my imagination . . .

I wrote those words in 1970 as part of the preface to the first collection of stories about Private McAuslan and Lieutenant MacNeill, entitled *The General Danced at Dawn*. They seemed true at the time, and again four years later when I repeated them in the sequel, *McAuslan in the Rough*. Now, reading them over so long after, I'm not so sure. This closing chapter may explain why.

For thirty years after leaving the Army I had no contact with my old regiment. Of course I followed their fortunes, at first in newspapers and cinema newsreels, and later on television; just the sight of that stag's head badge or the sound of a certain pipe tune, and I would be on the edge of my seat with the hairs rising on the nape of my neck. I rejoiced when they escaped amalgamation (a wicked and unnecessary exercise which effectively put an end to so many great regiments), and felt that strange mixture of exultation and anxiety whenever I heard of them on active service in some corner of the world – Malaya, Korea, Africa, Cyprus, and, now that the frontiers have dwindled, in Ulster (which looks like an even nastier version of Palestine from where I'm sitting. Flak-jackets and camouflage blouses instead of kilt and K.D., and a most unwieldy-looking rifle in place of the lovely Lee Enfield – but I notice they still persist in wearing their bonnets pulled down like coal-heavers' caps, and the faces underneath might have come straight from my old platoon. I watch them on T.V., doing that dirty, thankless job on the graffitied streets of Belfast, and just pray that they're as quick and hard and canny as the men I knew. I needn't worry, of course. They are. But I worry, just the same.)

That was as close as I came to the regiment in three decades, although very occasionally I might run into a former comrade, now civilian – and that was a disturbing experience, because they had got so ridiculously old; why, the youngest of them was bald and middle-aged and overweight. Extraordinary, when I had hardly changed at all. Well, perhaps an inch or two on the waist and a few grey hairs . . . and then I would glance in the mirror, and compare the reflection of the dyspeptic old man glowering out at me with the fading photo of that jaunty, innocent, child-like subaltern who was here just the other day, surely? What really put the tin hat on it was when I read not long ago that the regiment's commanding officer was retiring – and recognised his name as that of a young second-lieutenant who had reported his arrival to me when I was a company second-in-command. That's when you realise that those clear bright memories, of faces you knew and voices you heard only a moment ago . . . are history. It wasn't a moment ago; it's as far away in time as the Second World War was from the Boer War. And that's when you begin to wonder how well your memory has served you.

It was almost exactly thirty years to the day after I left the Army that I found myself in London en route for Yugoslavia, where I was to work on a film. Thirty years away from the regiment, in which time I had married, had children, emigrated, come back, worked my way from junior reporter to (briefly) the editor's chair of a great newspaper, retired from journalism, and written several books. The latest one had just come out, and before catching my plane I was to attend a signing session at Hatchards of Piccadilly.

Signing sessions are ordeals. In theory, you stand in the bookshop, and the eager public, advised beforehand that you will be there in person (wow!), flock in to buy autographed copies. In practice, you can stand all day grinning inanely behind a pile of your latest brainchild, and the only approach you get is from an old lady who thinks you're a shop assistant and wants to buy *The Beverly Hills Diet*. (This happens to all authors except the real blockbusters, and celebrities of sport and show business.)

Hatchards, fortunately, is different; being at the heart of the most literate metropolis on earth it is heaven-made for signing sessions – if you can't sell your book there, it's time to climb back on your truck. So it was with some relief that I arrived to find a modest queue forming to have their copies signed, and I was inscribing away gratefully and only wishing that my name was a more manageable length, like Ben Jonson or Nat Gould, when I became aware that the next customer in line was presenting for signature not my new novel but two battered copies of *The General Danced at Dawn* and *McAuslan in the Rough*. He was a tall, erect, very elderly gentleman in immaculate tweeds and cap, leaning on a ram's horn walking-stick and looking at me like a grimly amused Aubrey Smith. I must have gaped at him for a good five seconds before I recognised him as the Colonel whom I had described in those two books (and have described again in this one). I hadn't even heard of him since 1947, and suddenly there he was, large as life, looking nothing like the 80 that he must have been.

"Stick your John Hancock on those, will you?" he growled amiably. "No, carry on – we'll say hullo later, when you've dealt with the rest of your public. You've put on weight," he added as I scribbled obediently – and I won't swear I wasn't doing it with my heels together, muttering "Yes, sir, of course, sir," for he was every bit as imposing and formidable, even in mufti and long retirement, as he'd been in North Africa. Now he was taking up the books with a drawled "Obliged t'you", and limping stiffly away to seat himself at the side of the shop, filling his pipe and watching me from under shaggy eyebrows with what looked like sardonic satisfaction.

I went on signing like a man in an anxious dream. It's strange – when you write a book and put a real person into it, you don't seriously consider the possibility that he'll actually *read* it – at least, I hadn't, idiot that I'd been. And now he was sitting not ten feet away, the same leathery grizzled ramrod with the piercing eye and aquiline profile, and obviously he'd read the damned things, and couldn't have failed to recognise himself . . . oh, my God, what had I said about him? With dismay I recalled that I'd described him as "tall and bald and moustached and looking like a vulture". Feeling sick, I shot a sidelong glance at him – well, it was true. He still did, and a fat consolation that was. Wait, though, I'd been pretty fair about his character,

184

hadn't I? Let's see . . . I'd said he was wise, and just, and experienced and tough (but considerate), and respected . . . oh, lord, had I said "wise" or "crafty"? In growing panic I scribbled on, and realised that the lady whose book I'd just signed was looking at it, and then at me, with a glassy expression.

"Thank you so much. I do hope you enjoy it," I said, beaming professionally. She gave an uneasy smile and held out the book.

"I think there's some mistake, isn't there?" she faltered.

I couldn't see one. "With all good wishes, George Mac-Donald Vulture", was what I'd written, and then sanity returned and I wrenched it from her, babbling apologies, and signed a fresh copy. She hurried away, glancing back nervously, and I went on signing, trying to take a grip and telling myself that he couldn't have taken offence, or he wouldn't be here, would he?

Well, of course he hadn't. I knew that – I'd always known it, or I'd never have set typewriter to paper in the first place about him and the regiment and McAuslan and the Adjutant and Wee Wullie and the Dancing General and all the rest of them. I had done it out of affection and pride, and to preserve memories that I loved. Not strict fact, of course, but by no means fiction, either – many true incidents and characters, as well as adaptations and shapings and amalgams and inventions and disguises, but always doing my best to keep the background detail as accurate as I could, and to be faithful to the spirit of that time and those people. And because newspaper training teaches you that truth is either the whole truth or nothing, it had had to be described as fiction. Hence that preface.

Once or twice, over the years, I had regretted the blanket quality of that disclaimer – as, for example, when readers and reviewers obviously regarded as complete invention some story in the books which was 90 per cent stark truth. But there was nothing to be done about it – until that day, after the signing session, when the Colonel and I finally got together, with effusion on my side and paternal tolerance on his, and repaired to the deserted bar of a West End hotel, where we hit the Glenfiddich together, and as we talked it gradually came to me that the disclaiming preface I had written for the first two books wouldn't do for a third one, if I ever wrote it – which I have now done. I can't reword it, because there is no satisfactory way of defining the misty margins where truth and fiction mingle. The best thing is to report as accurately as I can what he said that afternoon.

We talked and laughed and reminisced, and to my boundless delight he leafed through the books, commenting and quoting with that ironic little grin that I remembered so well; he seemed genuinely pleased with them, and what with happiness and the single malt I forgot all about the plane I was supposed to be catching, and just sat there content, studying the lined brown face and hooded bright eyes, and listening to the clipped Edwardian drawl of three generations ago. At last he said:

"I've only one bone to pick with you, young fella." He flipped open *The General Danced at Dawn* and nailed the preface with a gnarled forefinger. "Yes, there it is. What the devil d'you mean by saying 'The Highland battalion in this book never existed'?" He sat back, pipe clamped between his teeth, and fixed me with a frosty grey eye. "You know perfectly well it existed. You were in it, weren't you? I commanded the dam' thing, I ought to know—"

"Yes, sir, I know – but I can't pretend that *all* the things in the stories actually happened . . . not in our battalion, anyway—"

"And here again," he went on, ignoring me. "This next phrase, or clause, or whatever you call it: 'inasmuch as the people in the stories are fictitious'. That's rot. In fact, I'm not sure it isn't libellous rot. Am I a fiction?" He sat upright, regarding me sternly over his pipe, looking extremely factual. "Are you? Can you look me in the eye and tell me that McAuslan never existed? I'm dam' sure you can't – because he did."

"Yes, but that wasn't his real name—"

"Of course it wasn't. His real name was Mac—." He grinned triumphantly. "Wasn't it?"

"Oh, my God," I said. "Yes, it was. D'you know, sir, you're the only person who's ever identified him—"

"You surprise me. I'd have thought that anyone who'd ever seen the brute closer than half a mile would have recognised him in the book at once."

"Mind you," I said, "he's slightly composite. I mean, the character in the book is 90 per cent Mac—, but there's a bit of another chap in him as well."

186

"Quite so. Private J—, of C Company. Sandy-haired chap, with a slight squint, shirt-tail kept coming out."

I stared at the man in disbelief. "How on earth did you know that?"

"Your trouble," said the Colonel patiently, "is that you think no one else in the battalion ever noticed anything. It was perfectly obvious – whenever you had McAuslan doing something that wasn't characteristic of Mac—, I thought: 'He's got that wrong. That's not like Mac— at all. Who is it?' And then I remembered J—, and realised that you'd tacked a little of him into the character. Sometimes you changed people over altogether. Take the second-in-command . . . the man you've made the second-in-command was actually in our first battalion, and you never met him till we got back to Edinburgh, isn't that so?" He smiled at me knowingly, and took a smug sip of Glenfiddich. "Yes, his real name was R—. That's the fellow. You're an unscrupulous young devil, aren't you?" He leafed over a few pages. "Ah, yes, Wee Wullie – why did you call him that? You couldn't hope to disguise the real man. Not from anyone who knew him."

"Law of libel – and a bit of delicacy," I explained. "After all, he's a pretty rough diamond, as I've described him."

"Well, so he was, wasn't he? And he comes out pretty well, in your story." He studied his glass for a long moment. "No more heroic than he really was in fact, though. You'll have to tell the true story some day, you know."

"I know," I said. "I will."

"See that you do." He picked up the book again, chuckled, frowned, and laid it down. "Anyway, you shouldn't have said the battalion didn't exist, or that the people were fictitious, or given the impression that the stories were made up—"

"Well, they're a mixture – a lot of fact and a bit of fiction. The trouble is, the bits people think are fictitious—"

"Are usually the truest bits of the lot. I know. The Palestine train, and the football team in Malta, eh? And the haunted fort, and the one-hundred-and-twenty-eightsome reel?"

"Well, there's a bit of exaggeration here and there – and I *have* said that I've used my imagination—"

"As if you ever had any! Mark you – you've certainly used it in one direction." He made a performance of filling his pipe, grumbling to himself and looking across the room. "You've been far too dam' kind to that old Colonel," he said gruffly.

It was my turn to study my glass. "Not half as kind as he was to me," I said.

We finished the bottle, and in an alcoholic haze I glanced at my watch and realised I had a bare forty minutes to get to Heathrow for my flight to Zagreb.

"Yugoslavia?" said the Colonel. "What the devil are you going there for? Ghastly place – nothing but mountains and Bolshevik bandits."

I explained that I was going out to write a film script – or part of a script. Another writer had done the original, but there had been cast changes and various alterations were wanted, including a new ending.

"Most films are tripe," said the Colonel firmly. "*Bambi* wasn't bad, though. What's this one about?"

"Our special service people in the war . . . blowing up a bridge to stop a German advance. Partisans and all that."

"Sounds all right," admitted the Colonel. "Who's making it – our people or the Yanks?"

"They're American producers, I believe."

"Well, for God's sake don't let them have our chaps going about shouting '*On* the double!' and 'Left face!' and saluting with their hats off. Damned nonsense!"

I dropped him off near his home in Chelsea, and the last I ever saw of him was the tall spare figure in tweeds leaning on his stick and throwing me a salute which I returned (without a hat on) as the taxi sped away. For the next year or two we exchanged Christmas cards, and now and then I heard odd scraps of gossip about him. He'd been on holiday in the Middle East, in a country where some crisis had blown up all of a sudden, and British nationals had had to be evacuated quickly – he'd taken charge, quite unofficially, of the evacuation, and everyone had got out safely. Another time, he'd visited our battalion in Northern Ireland, going out with a street patrol at night, just to get the feel of things, an octogenarian in a flak-jacket.

And then one morning I got a phone call to say that he had died, in Erskine Hospital above the Clyde, where old Scottish soldiers go. And because he was, as fairly as I could depict him, the Colonel of these stories, I inscribe this book to his memory,

188

with gratitude and affection, and no qualms whatever about identification:

Lieutenant-Colonel R. G. (Reggie) Lees
2nd Battalion, Gordon Highlanders

"Ninety-twa, no' deid yet"